Snowize & Snitch

Highly Effective Defective Detectives

KAREN BRINER

Holiday House / New York

For my mother, who read to me;
For my father, whose word inventions inspired me;
And Jim, this is for you.

Text Copyright © 2016 by Karen Briner
All Rights Reserved
Illustrations Copyright © 2016 by Holiday House, Inc.
Illustrations by Victor Rivas

HOLIDAY HOUSE is registered in the U.S. Patent and Trademark Office.
Printed and Bound in March 2016 at Maple Press, York, PA, USA.
www.holidayhouse.com
First Edition
1 3 5 7 9 10 8 6 4 2

Library of Congress Cataloging-in-Publication Data
Names: Briner, K. H. (Karen Hilarye), 1969-
Title: Snowize & Snitch : highly effective defective
detectives / by Karen Briner.
Other titles: Snowize and Snitch
Description: First edition. | New York : Holiday House, [2016] |
Summary: A once-intrepid spy, a dignified rodent, and a girl with a
perplexing past team up to find out who is draining the minds of great
scientists of their knowledge.
Identifiers: LCCN 2015027759 | ISBN 9780823435678 (hardcover)
Subjects: | CYAC: Mystery and detective stories. | Scientists—
Fiction. | Foundlings—Fiction.
Classification: LCC PZ7.B777 Sn 2016 | DDC [Fic]—dc23
LC record available at http://lccn.loc.gov/2015027759

Contents

1

A Message from the Future

The voice came from a wobbly branch at the very top of a eucalyptus tree. It floated down on the summer breeze and said things to Ever that she would rather not have heard on an afternoon like this, when her thoughts had been drifting happily toward the invisible ice cream and freshly picked strawberries that awaited her at home.

"A mind is a terrible thing to lose." This was the first thing the voice said, and while it was an odd thing to say, it was perfectly true. But even though Ever could not agree more, she didn't say so. She was too astonished to say anything because the voice, it turned out, belonged to a big, black crow who glided down from the eucalyptus tree and sidled up to her.

"Ever Indigo Nikita Stein, I presume?" the bird asked, quite formally.

Ever was used to being teased about her name. It was always the first point of attack, so she waited for the punch line, for the bird to say something mean and then laugh.

"Are you, or are you not, Ever Indigo Nikita Stein?" asked the crow, sounding a little bit impatient.

"What does it matter?" said Ever, half under her breath and crossing her arms tightly across her chest.

"Is that a rhetorical question?" asked the bird, tilting his head to one side and observing her with his deep black eyes. "Because if it's not, then permit me to say that you matter to far more people than you can imagine."

Clearly, this was no ordinary crow. Ever felt unsettled by its penetrating gaze. She had seen plenty of unusual things in her life, and it took a lot to surprise her; but this was absurd. As far as she knew, crows didn't talk—at least, not like this. According to *The Encyclopedia Brittanicus*, which Ever had once read from cover to cover, crows, of the genus *Corvus*, are curious by nature and skilled at imitating a few words here and there. *Individuals in captivity have been taught to count up to seven, with some able to recite in excess of forty sentences*, she recalled. Even so, this bird was off the charts for linguistic skills. It struck her that this talking animal might be a trick, something dreamed up by her clever classmates at the School for Gifted Children of Genius Parents. As she contemplated this possibility, she tugged on the end of a braid and whistled through the slight gap between her teeth. If she fell for it and was spotted talking to a large bird, there'd be no end to the teasing. She stepped up her pace and concentrated on outdistancing the inquisitive creature who was, she noted, slightly clumsy for a bird. He hobbled along with a strange gait, tilting slightly to the right in the most peculiar, lopsided way.

"Wait!" called the crow, trying desperately to keep up with her. "What if I told you that your mother and father are alive and well?" At this, Ever paused. But as much as she wanted to believe the crow's words, they couldn't possibly be true.

"I don't talk to birds," she retorted. "Especially not to ones that lie. My parents are missing and presumed dead, and I don't care to hear anything else you have to say." As she resumed walking, she kicked an empty can into the gutter, trying to hide how deeply shaken she was by the crow's suggestion.

The whereabouts of her parents was a painful topic, one that she thought about constantly. In fact, she had promised herself she'd quit obsessing about them as soon as she turned thirteen, which would be in ten months, eleven days and twelve hours. She was sure that by then she'd no longer need to wonder what had really happened to them. She'd be able to get on with her life and not dwell on the idea that she was all alone in the world.

"Well," said the crow, finally catching up to Ever, "you *should* care about what I have to say. Especially concerning your parents."

Ever came to an abrupt halt. Her green eyes filled with the sadness she'd carried within her for so long—sadness she often covered up with anger. "Why?" she demanded furiously. "Why should I care? What did they ever do for me but saddle me with a humiliating name and then abandon me to the care of a lunatic genius?"

"He's not a lunatic," insisted the crow, fixing Ever with a beady black eye.

She gave the bird a sidelong glance. He was a particularly large crow with an intimidating, sharp beak and an even sharper intelligence glittering in his dark, watchful eyes. His sleek feathers shimmered a deep blue-black in the sunlight.

"At least," added the crow after a moment, "he's not a *total* lunatic."

Ever managed a half smile, but it flickered for only a moment and then died.

"Besides, there's nothing wrong with your name," the crow said. "It's a perfectly lovely name."

"It's a hard name to live up to," said Ever.

The crow tilted his head once more. "Let's see. Ever Indigo Nikita Stein. Miss E.I.N. Stein." Ever lowered her head in embarrassment as the crow made the connection. "Ah. I see. Miss Einstein. Yes. That could be problematic, being named after such a famous and brilliant scientist. Your parents obviously had high hopes for you."

"Well, if they saw me now, I'm sure they'd be disappointed," said Ever. "All I am is a magnet for bad luck."

Ever suspected the only reason she'd been accepted to the elite School for Gifted Children of Genius Parents was because of the Doc, her guardian. He was the genius—a little crazy perhaps, but still a genius—and she was certainly not his child. It was clear to Ever and all of her teachers that she didn't belong there. The school accepted only the most brilliant children from around the world who then relocated to its exclusive address in the city of Cape Town, South Africa, at the very bottom of the very tip of Africa. Ever felt she couldn't compete with so much brilliance. Her classmates all scored a hundred and ten percent on their tests—they never even missed bonus questions—while she lagged way behind in the eighties.

She was certain it was only a matter of time before the school threw her out, but the Doc always assured her that they would never have the gall to do that. "They'd have to get past me," he'd say with a wink and a smile, "and no one gets past the legendary Doctor Professor David Ezratty."

Ever used to find those words comforting, but lately she'd started to cringe when he said them. This was because she'd recently discovered that the Doc was considered more of a joke than a legend at the school. Both teachers and classmates called him "Scatty Batty Ezratty" behind her back.

The crow interrupted her thoughts. "Take it from me," he said, seeming to read her mind. "Your Batty Ezratty is actually a remarkable genius and inventor."

"Well, everyone else thinks he's a weirdo and a loser, and I'm tired of defending him," said Ever. "I'm tired of being stuck with him." She immediately felt bad for saying that. After all, if she didn't have the kindly inventor to look after her, she really *would* be quite alone in the world. The Doc had taken her in without hesitation when he'd found her, at age three, abandoned on his doorstep with a note saying "Help!" pinned to her coat.

"Wait a minute!" said Ever, suddenly aware that against her best intentions she'd struck up a conversation with the odd bird. "Why am I having this conversation with a complete stranger?" She stared hard at the crow.

"I'm not so complete," said the crow sheepishly. "If you look carefully, you'll see that I have a toe missing." Ever noticed that this was true. The crow's middle toe on his right foot was indeed missing. Regardless, Ever was growing impatient.

"Shouldn't you be collecting shiny objects or picking at something dead on the side of the road?" she asked.

The bird looked slightly insulted. "Well!" he huffed. "It seems I ought to get straight to the point. I've come from the future to bring you a message."

Ever laughed in disbelief. "A message? From the future? That's a good one." Now she couldn't stop smiling. It was suddenly obvious that the Doc had sent the bird as a joke. Her smile broadened, and she automatically raised her hand to her mouth to hide the gap between her teeth. The Doc had tried everything in his power to convince her that her smile was charming and gave her character, but the kids at Ever's school weren't so kind.

"Mind the gap, Einstein," they'd say whenever she grinned. Ever wished they'd never taken that school trip to London, where her classmates mimicked the underground train system's famous refrain until she vowed to never show her teeth again.

The crow stretched his wings behind his back and cracked his neck, and Ever suddenly grew uneasy. "Listen up and listen well, Ever," the crow said. "When you get home, things will have changed. The Doc will not be there, and it's imperative that you do not panic."

"Something's happened?" asked Ever, her unease turning into dread. The crow nodded solemnly. "What?" she asked cautiously.

"Things," replied the crow. "I cannot say exactly what things have happened. But one thing is for certain: For all intents and purposes, the Doc has disappeared, and you are essentially on your own. That is the first part of the message that I was sent to deliver forthwith."

Now Ever was genuinely alarmed. The Doc was always using the word *forthwith*. His sentences were generously sprinkled with it and Ever often found the word popping out of her own mouth when she least expected it. Like now.

"You will tell me what you have done to Doctor Professor *forthwith*!" Ever cried.

The crow looked confused. "But I don't know any Doctor Professor Forthwith."

"Don't twist my words or play games!" Ever shouted, surprised by her rising anger and the deep concern she felt at the thought of her guardian in danger.

"Easy now," said the crow. "I'm on your side. It's my task to provide you with information that will enable you to make the right choices. Already it's too late for some poor souls, but you might be able to save the rest. Like the detectives, for instance. You need their help, but ultimately you have to save them."

A stream of questions tumbled out of Ever's mouth, colliding with each other. "But I don't know any detectives. And what must I save them from? How am I supposed to—"

The crow shook his head, silencing her. "Sorry, no questions. I'm running out of time."

It was then that she noticed the bird appeared to be sweating. Great beads of moisture were slowly rolling off his back and wings. It was all too much for Ever to absorb. Her head started to hurt.

"I know it's confusing. I would be confused, too, if I were you," said the crow, "but I'm afraid I have to go before I perish." He flapped his wings once and a shower of droplets fell to the ground, collecting in a puddle.

"Wait," said Ever, still staring at the drops on the ground. "Are you sweating?" Curiosity always got the better of her, often landing her in trouble. "I didn't know that birds sweat."

The crow shook his head. "I can't stay to explain. It's a side effect of traveling through time. I have to leave. Before I fall apart."

Ever felt butterflies in her stomach, and her heart began to race.

"There's more," said the crow, starting to look a little panicky himself as he tried to recall the rest of the message. "Now that the Doc has disappeared, the only three humans you can trust are Harry Snowize, Deodora Miffingpin and . . . yourself."

Besides herself, Ever had never heard of these people.

The crow added gravely, "And I almost forgot: the

growling box. Remember the box won't bite you. It will save your life. Guard it with your soul. Protect it with your heart. Do not, I repeat, do not, not let it fall into the wrong hands."

"A box?" asked Ever. "What box? What growl? What wrong hands?"

"Sorry," said the crow with a voice that sounded like he was speaking underwater. "Gotta go."

Ever gasped as the crow disappeared in a melting sort of way, until all that remained was a puddle of clear liquid.

Then she started running.

2

The Scientist Vanishes

Ever pumped her arms and legs harder and sprinted faster and faster. The crow's words echoed and bumped around inside her head, making her feel sick and dizzy, until the inevitable happened and her sandal caught itself on the uneven paving. She came crashing down with a sickening smack.

Both her knees were scraped and bruised. Despite the burning pain, she pulled herself up. When she tried to sprint again, her legs felt like jelly and buckled beneath her. Still, she persevered, fueled by a desire to protect the Doc from an unnamed danger.

As she ran, her head spun with the confusing words she'd just heard: Her parents might be alive; her guardian had disappeared; something about a growling box and saving detectives. Could she trust a highly articulate bird with a message from the future who had melted before her eyes? Could she even trust her own eyes?

By the time she arrived home, she was wondering whether she'd imagined the whole thing. Completely out of breath and close to tears, she pushed the front door open and stumbled inside.

"Doc? Doctor Professor!" she called, trying to catch her breath as she scanned the entrance hall. "Doc? Are you here?"

There was no response. The house was unusually silent. Ever fought back the tears that had started to well up in her eyes. She never cried, that was her rule. Tears were a sign of weakness, and signs of weakness could give your enemy the upper hand. Usually, her enemies were a group of spiteful classmates who enjoyed making her life miserable. But right now she wasn't sure whom or what she was up against.

She tried to recall the bird's message, but it had been so jumbled she could hardly remember it. It felt like exam time at school when, as soon as the questions were handed out, she froze. Her mind went blank and even though she'd studied hard, she couldn't remember a thing. All she could do was watch as her genius classmates scribbled down perfect answers in record time and took home evidence of their brilliance to their delighted parents.

Ever had only two memories of her parents. One was a warm and fuzzy memory of the three of them laughing together at something she'd done. She couldn't remember their faces. There was just a sense of a man with a delightful smile and a woman who smelled of cinnamon and roses, both of whom loved her very much.

The other memory she tried to push from her mind whenever it crept up on her. It was one of fear and panic: her parents speaking in hushed tones as she was bundled into a coat and then kissed good-bye. Her mother fighting tears as she hastily pinned a note on Ever's coat. Then her mother and father embracing as if they might never see each other again.

"Go," her mother had whispered. "Go before we change our minds. Go now, so at least she'll be spared."

Tears were still streaming down her mother's face and her father moved away reluctantly, his eyes deeply troubled. He buckled Ever into their old-fashioned car, a blue VW beetle painted with daisies, and after a rushed journey through the night, they stopped outside a peculiar house. Her father hugged her tightly and promised that they would come back for her when it was safe. She was left standing on a doorstep.

That was all Ever remembered, and now her only remaining guardian might be gone, too.

"Doctor Professor?" Ever called out again, and her voice started to tremble. He was nowhere to be seen.

A dull, monotonous voice interrupted her panicked thoughts. "Good afternoon, Einstein," said Melschman, sounding incredibly bored. "Would you care for a three-day-old sandwich? Or perhaps a bowl of invisible ice cream of indeterminate flavor?"

Melschman was one of the Doc's more unfortunate inventions, a computerized fridge with robotic arms and legs, and a severe attitude problem.

"Oh, Melschman," said Ever. "Not now. I don't have time for you. I need to find the Doc."

"Perhaps," droned Melschman, "I could interest you in some pickled fish that has been in my freezer section for over a year and has turned a lovely shade of malachite." Melschman swung his freezer door open, reached inside with his robot arm and pulled out the fish in question.

"No thanks. Not hungry," said Ever, ducking just in time as the greenish fish flew over her head and hit the wall with a loud crack.

Ever sighed as she crawled under the table for cover. This was not the first time Melschman had reacted violently when she'd refused one of his offerings. Ducking and diving out of his way was something she now did quite reflexively. She often complained to the Doc that Melschman was dangerous and might, accidentally-on-purpose, fatally injure them one day. But the Doc had a soft spot for Melschman and always defended his wayward invention.

Moving ever so slowly, she reached up to pull a white napkin from the table and waved it in surrender.

"Okay, Einstein," said Melschman in a sulky voice. "You can come out now."

"I need to know where the Doc is. I think he's in danger. Have you seen him, Melschman?" She cautiously emerged from her hiding place.

"The Doc was last seen in his laboratory working on Project VOV, his ingenious plan for world peace, where I served him a plate of frozen boiled cabbage, which he ate with surprising gusto. . . ." She didn't stay to hear the rest.

The laboratory was where the Doc went to think and invent. It was fifty feet underground, accessible by either a wobbly spiral staircase or an elevator. Ever preferred the staircase. She was down three dizzying twists of it when Melschman called after her.

"And then the Doc disappeared. Just like that. In the middle of a mouthful of frozen cabbage." Ever stopped dead in her tracks. Melschman was a big pain in the aorta, as the Doc liked to say, but he never lied. With increasing dread she made her way downstairs.

The laboratory door was sealed, so she placed her thumb on the fingerprint recognition pad and waited as several locks automatically unlatched themselves. The heavy wooden door swung open with an eerie creak. Her heart danced wildly. The crow was wrong!

There sat the Doc, as plain as day, behind his desk. He was staring down at a small silver box. His shock of wild, white hair stuck out in numerous directions, making him look a lot like Albert Einstein, the scientist he so admired. The Doc had Einstein's unruly eyebrows, and he ran a hand over his forehead to smooth them out.

"Doctor Professor!" shouted Ever with delight.

The Doc turned toward her and smiled sadly. "I'm so sorry, Ever," he said. "Sorry that things had to happen this way. I was trying to protect *you*. Now it's I who needs your help. They're after me. They want what is most precious to me." At this he nervously tapped his temple with his fingertip. Ever raced up to her guardian and flung her arms around him, only to discover that her hands went right through him.

"This is just a prerecorded holographic message," said the hologram of the Doc. "If you are watching this, then you have already received a message from a big, black crow. There is one more piece of information you need, one that the crow couldn't tell you because I knew you would never believe it unless you heard it from my lips."

"What is it?" asked Ever, forgetting that the hologram could neither hear nor see her. It was as if the Doc had anticipated this question, for his hologram paused and took in a deep breath.

"You have to go, Ever. You must depart forthwith! Remember the tunnel? You have to go through it! You *must* go through it. It's up to you entirely to save the detectives. And listen to everything the crow told you. It's important. Especially the bit about the growling box. You'll need it. It will save you. It may save us all."

Ever vaguely noted that he was pointing to a small silver object on his desk. "But you told me never to go near the tunnel door. You made me promise!" cried Ever, feeling that familiar sense of panic rising.

The hologram didn't respond. The image of the professor flickered for an instant and then was gone. Never had Ever felt more lost or alone in her life.

3

The Fear of Fear Itself

DANGER!
NEVER, NEVER, NEVER, NEVER
TOUCH OR OPEN THIS DOOR!
(EVER!)

Ever stared at the big red letters engraved on the door to the Doc's secret escape tunnel. He'd warned her repeatedly not to go near it. Ever, who was generally frightened of the unknown, had obeyed without question. Now as she reached out to touch it, every bone in her body told her not to open the door.

"What do I do, what do I do, what do I do?" she wondered out loud, pulling her hand back as if she'd touched a searing hot plate.

"Take me with you," came the reply. Ever whirled around, startled to see Melschman standing behind her. He'd unplugged himself from his wall socket and had taken the elevator down.

"I can't," said Ever. "You're a fridge. You can only last a few hours on your battery. And you're big and bulky, and I never know when you're going to attack me next."

"I could feed you," said Melschman in a plaintive tone.

"You'd have a great supply of invisible ice cream. Besides, I'm the only family you've got left now."

Ever paused for a moment. She'd never thought of it like that before. She'd always been so fixated on her missing parents that she never considered that she, the Doc, and Melschman were, in the strangest of ways, a family. Even if Melschman regularly threw food at her and was a great big pain in the aorta, she knew that she would miss him if he weren't around.

"Please, take me with you," Melschman begged. A drop of water dripped from his water dispenser and splashed to the floor.

"You're . . . crying," said Ever, surprised. This had happened only once before, when the Doc had threatened to dismantle Melschman and reprogram him with a better attitude.

"No, I'm not," Melschman replied, a little too quickly. "It's just a leak. I've sprung a leak." And more drops of water began to fall. "I don't want to be left alone," he added.

"Don't worry," said Ever. "I'll come back for you. I promise." As soon as the words were out of her mouth, she regretted them. Those were the last words she'd heard her father say. And he'd never come back for her.

Every year, on her birthday, she would pack a small suitcase and sit outside on the pavement, convinced this was the year her parents would return. She would wait until the sun sank behind the great oak tree and the moon rose above the small hill. Then the Doc, who had been keeping an eye on her all day, would come out, take her by the hand and gently lead her back inside.

On the table, there would be a birthday cake with candles and her name on it. There were also numerous wrapped presents. But Ever didn't want cake or presents. She wanted her parents. The Doc seemed to know this, so he, Melschman and Ever would sit in silence, staring at the cake.

"It's unnatural," Melschman would eventually say. "No child should be able to resist cake."

On her ninth birthday, while they all sat there, staring once again at the cake, the Doc cleared his throat and spoke solemnly. "Ever, they're not coming back."

"Never ever, Ever," added Melschman.

"They are!" she insisted. The Doc shook his head. He pulled at his unruly eyebrows. This was difficult news he had to share.

"I've had word. They were . . . their sailboat was—was sucked down by a whirlpool off the coast of Sicily. Your parents are officially missing, presumed dead."

Ever could not move. She found it hard to breathe. It was as if all her energy had been drained right out of her, all in one go.

"According to my built-in dictionary, a whirlpool is like a tornado in water," said Melschman in his robotic monotone, trying to be helpful.

Ever and the Doc ignored him as a horrible silence filled the room. Melschman cleared his throat. He didn't like awkward silences, so he filled them by making ice cubes as noisily as he could. Ever barely noticed. It was as if her world had just been split in two. There was her life before hearing this terrible news, and there would be her life after it. It was a defining moment, one that would haunt her forever.

"Your father would have wanted you to have this," the Doc said, once her silence became too hard to bear. "He gave it to me in case things didn't work out. It belonged to your mother."

In his palm the Doc held a small locket on a silver chain. He handed it to Ever and she carefully opened it. On one side was a grainy black-and-white picture of her parents on their wedding day; on the other was a picture of Ever, age two. She wordlessly allowed the Doc to place the locket around her neck. Then he picked her up and hugged her for the longest time, while she cried until she could cry no more and finally fell asleep in his arms.

That was the last time she had allowed herself to cry. She had worn the locket ever since that day and reached for it whenever she felt nervous. It offered her comfort, to be able to touch something that had once been close to her mother's skin. When she pressed it against her cheek, she could smell just the slightest hint of cinnamon and roses.

Ever clutched the locket now as she stared from the escape-tunnel door to Melschman, and back again. "The Doc needs my help." she said. "I have to do this. And I have to do it alone."

"So, this is the thanks I get," snapped Melschman, folding his arms and stomping his feet in a clunking way befitting an indignant robot fridge.

Ever took a deep breath and held the silver locket briefly against her cheek, hoping it might give her courage. Then she took an even deeper breath, but still she couldn't do it. She could not open the door. Her legs trembled with fear, and a sense of terrible foreboding paralyzed her entire body.

Just then a packet of moldy carrots whizzed past her ear and slammed against the forbidden door, followed by an eggplant and a prickly pineapple at extremely high speed.

"I knew you couldn't do it," said Melschman. "You don't have it in you, Ever. They should have called you 'Never.' Because there are so many things you'll never have the guts to do."

"That's not true," said Ever, knowing deep down inside how painfully true it was. She was afraid of a growing list of things, from heights and depths to small, dark

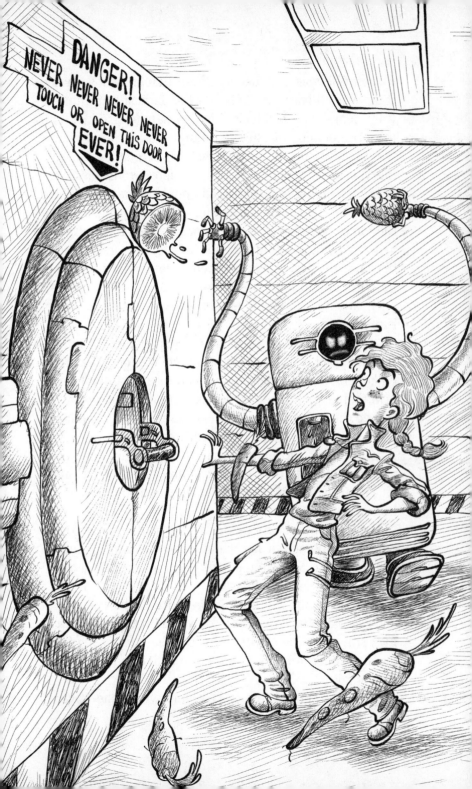

spaces. She was also deeply afraid that somehow everything was all her fault. This was her darkest fear, that she was a magnet for bad luck. First her parents had met with misfortune, and now, her guardian.

"Luckily for the Doc," said Melschman, "I'm giving you no choice in this matter. Here's your passport," he said, flinging a pocket-sized booklet toward her like a Frisbee so that Ever could catch it. "I was storing it next to the Limburger cheese. Hope it doesn't smell too bad."

"Why would I need a passport?" asked Ever, wrinkling her nose in disgust as the smell of fetid socks filled her nostrils. Limburger cheese was the Doc's favorite. He'd once explained how it's fermented with the same bacterium that causes foot odor.

"What if you land up in Ouagadougou? Or on the moon? Travel these days is prohibitive without the correct documents, Ever," Melschman said loftily. "I don't know how that magic wormhole works, but I never once saw the Doc go through that door without his passport. He told me it takes you there, but it cannot bring you back."

This new information made Ever queasy and even more reluctant to turn the door handle. But Melschman, true to his word, was not going to let her disobey the Doc's instructions.

In each of his robot hands he held up four eggs, one between each of his metal fingers. When it came to egg throwing, Melschman could turn an egg into a lethal weapon, and he never missed.

The first one hit her on the back of her head and leaked cold, slimy egg white down the back of her neck. Ever shivered. Then, without further hesitation, she flung open the door to the forbidden tunnel and took a terrified leap of faith.

She was sucked into a dark void where she hovered

in the air, as if suspended in a strong magnetic field. Her body felt both weightless and heavy at the same time.

"Force field initiating," said a computerized voice. "Prepare for hurtling."

The last thing she heard, before her body was propelled headlong at incredible velocity, was the sound of eggs smashing against the closed door. Thwack. Thwack. Thwack. By the time the rest hit, she was already several miles away, traveling at a dizzying speed.

4

Hurtling Through Darkness

While Ever was hurtling through a tunnel of darkness, wondering if the words *hurt* and *hurtle* were connected in any meaningful sort of way, two other events of great significance were taking place.

The first incident was taking place in Japan and therefore in Japanese. Yoshinobu Azayaka, scientist, inventor and genius, stood on the slopes of snowcapped Mount Fuji, talking to himself. Anyone observing might have guessed that he was either on his cell phone or out of his mind. They would have been wrong with both guesses. Instead, Yoshinobu was completely *without* his mind. He was without his mind simply because his mind had been stolen. And while a mind may be a terrible thing to lose or waste, it is far, far worse to have it stolen.

What Yoshinobu was saying to himself, over and over again, were the following words: *Midori desu. Pinkuga-katta shiro desu.*

While these words once made perfect sense to Yoshinobu, they now were devoid of meaning. As if in a trance, he withdrew his family's ancient sword from its lacquered sheath and held it aloft. The blade was polished to

24

perfection, and the metal glinted brilliantly in the bright sunlight. The sword had a name, a beautiful, lyrical name that spoke of an eternal fire, but Yoshinobu Azayaka could not recall it. The name had been ripped out of his brain, stolen along with almost every thought and memory he'd ever had.

Pinned to Yoshinobu's lapel was a single white rose. The rose had the same icy sparkle as the dazzling snow on Mount Fuji.

Yoshinobu repeated the words he'd been saying to himself one final time. Translated into English they did not make much sense, either. "It's green. It's a pinkish white," he said. Then, without blinking and without thinking (for it's difficult to think without a mind), he raised the mighty sword and turned the blade toward himself. It was not something he would ever have chosen to do. But the great scientist was as helpless as a puppet on a string. Only the imposing mountain stood as silent witness to this terrible crime: a cruel and perfect murder.

The second incident taking place while Ever whooshed through the tunnel was happening somewhere in Spain and mostly in Spanish. Professor Gustav Cadiz, another brilliant scientist, stood before the door to his laboratory. He was about to unlock it when he had the vaguest sense that something was wrong. He stopped his cheerful humming and listened carefully, thoughtfully twirling and untwirling the ends of his magnificent mustache.

He glanced down and realized what was wrong: He was wearing a pair of mismatched shoes. The shoes were not only different colors, but one was a boot and the other, a dancing shoe; one had a thick heel while the other was completely flat. This inconsistency explained why he had developed a limp and had been hobbling around all day.

Gustav was quick to laugh at his own foolishness. He had been so concerned about this sudden limp that he'd made an appointment with his doctor, thinking he might need a hip replacement or some other unpleasant surgical procedure. Now he broke into a lengthy chortle.

"Ah. My dear Octavia will have something to say about this. She'll say that at my advanced age, I'm finally losing my mind." Little did he know how prophetic these words would turn out to be. He chuckled again to himself as he turned the key in the lock and stepped into his private laboratory.

When the lights flickered on, he was met with a sight that made his heart stand still for several seconds. A terrible sense of despair washed over him. Every item in the room had been smashed into the tiniest of fragments; every piece of equipment had been crushed. Worst of all, his three beloved rabbits, Europa, Ganymede and Jupiter, were lying facedown on a pile of dust that used to be his desk. He could tell by the awkward angles of their limbs that they were not alive.

Gustav's hands started to tremble, and his eyes filled with tears. Who would be so cruel? And for what reason?

"Why?" he asked as the tears began to spill. "Why? Why? *Why?*"

From a gloomy corner of the room, shrouded in darkness, a gravelly voice answered, "Simple. Compound 37d. That's why."

"Compound 37d?" Gustav was astonished. In fact, he was so startled by this answer that he forgot to be afraid. In the moment when he should have tried to escape, he was wondering how anyone else could possibly know about his secret discovery, one he'd made quite by accident. Before he could articulate the question, a hand clamped itself over his nose and mouth. A whiff of ether assaulted his nostrils, and darkness washed over him.

At precisely the same moment that Professor Cadiz lost consciousness, Ever glimpsed a light at the end of the tunnel. It was a tiny, dull glimmer of yellow light, and she was heading straight for it.

5

Highly Effective Defective Detectives

Ever tried to scream, but her voice stuck in her throat. She was speeding headfirst toward a small, perfectly round wooden door, and there was nothing she could do to stop herself. Light seeped into the tunnel around the edges of the door like a mystical halo. Just when she feared it was too late, the computerized voice returned with an announcement.

"Hurtling complete. Distance traveled in the Superloop: 1,536 miles. Time elapsed: two hours. Time zones crossed: zero. Injury to body and soul: undetermined."

Ever came to an abrupt halt and found herself floating once more in midair, in near darkness.

"Force field deactivating," said the voice and there was an audible click. "You have arrived at your destination. Good-bye and good luck."

Ever felt gravity return with a rude bump as the force that held her in suspension suddenly disappeared. She found herself sliding in a narrow tunnel that smelled of damp earth. Roots and dirt brushed against her skin, and then she slowed to an unexpected stop. Much as she didn't want to admit it, she was now stuck upside down underground, with darkness closing in around her. Her heart started to beat at a rapid pace, and she could almost taste the raw, clammy earth that pressed against her.

"Don't panic. Don't panic. Don't panic," she told herself as terror filled her stomach. She squeezed her eyes shut. She was stuck for what felt like an eternity, but it was actually closer to a minute. Then, just as Ever was about to give in to despair, she started sliding once more, heading for the glimmer of light at the end of the tunnel.

To her relief, the round door swung open gently, and she slipped right through the threshold into a brightly lit room. She landed ever so gracefully on an oversized red silk cushion that seemed to be waiting just for her.

Ever sat quite still, catching her breath, as she took in her new surroundings. At one end of the room was an old wooden-frame door with black letters stenciled onto a pane of frosted glass.

The sign on the door read:

SNOWIZE & SNITCH
HIGHLY EFFECTIVE DEFECTIVE DETECTIVES
PARTNERS IN CRIME

Ever thought it odd that the sign was on the inside of the door, where no one but those in the office could see it. Then the Doc's words came back to her: *It's entirely up to you to save the detectives.* There had been no mention about them being defective.

At the other end of the room was a large table covered in antique chessboards, and sitting there in deep concentration was a man with dark, clever eyes, playing eight games of chess at the same time. He was perfectly still except for his knee, which bounced restlessly beneath the table. Ever noted that he was dashingly handsome in a careless sort of way; he looked like he'd just gotten out of bed and had forgotten to brush his hair. There was a shadow of stubble on his face that gave him the air of one who ought to be out hiking in the wilderness, surviving by his wits, rather than sitting in an office wearing a slightly rumpled suit and a pair of incongruous, red-canvas sneakers.

Ever guessed from the flecks of silver in his black hair that he was about the age her father would be, if he were alive and not missing and presumed dead.

The man's opponent in this epic chess game was a large, well-groomed rat, about the size of a cat, who ran his front paws nervously through his whiskers as he studied each of the queens on the eight boards.

The rat had a gleaming, brown coat, white fur on his underbelly, a long tail and kind, brown eyes. The fur on his four paws was also white, giving Ever the impression that he was wearing socks. Ever had an unconditional love for animals and an encyclopedic knowledge of them. She felt especially connected to animals that are misunderstood and loathed for the wrong reasons. The creature in front of her she instantly identified as an African giant pouched rat or *Cricetomys gambianus* of the family Nesomyidae, order Rodentia. She remembered this from a research paper she'd written on rodents, for which she'd received eighty-five percent. This score was considered so poor at the School for Gifted Children of Genius Parents that the teacher had called the Doc in to discuss it. The teacher suggested that Ever might be infinitely better off at a school for less intelligent children. Needless to say, the Doc didn't take kindly to that suggestion.

"Two things are infinite: the universe and human stupidity," he had responded, quoting Einstein's famous

words. "This girl has a photographic memory with an ability to recall word for word things that she's read. She also has a knack for problem solving and has come to my aid many times without her even knowing it. Just because she doesn't perform well in exams or research papers doesn't mean she isn't a shining star in her own right."

Ever didn't know what else he might have added, but after that the teacher never mentioned her grades again. She was convinced the Doc was exaggerating her skills to make her look good so they'd keep her at the school. It was true she had a photographic memory, but she never thought much of this talent, because, quite frankly, what use was it if it failed you when you needed it most?

She pushed these thoughts aside as she stared at the creature before her and recalled that African giant pouched rats get their name from their hamsterlike cheek pouches in which they store food. They are very endearing creatures best known for their remarkable sense of smell, which makes up for their terribly poor eyesight. Perhaps poor eyesight might explain why neither the rat, nor the man, appeared to notice Ever at all. They continued playing their games of chess as if nothing out of the ordinary had happened.

The man had particularly expressive eyebrows, which could move independently of each other; he now raised one as he contemplated his next chess move with a growing sense of delight.

Ever gave a small cough. The man glanced briefly in her direction, and she thought she detected a subtle darkening of his eyes. He quickly returned his focus to the chessboards, as if he hadn't seen her. Ever was perplexed. The rat didn't turn to look, either; he merely stood up on his hind legs, sniffed the air searchingly with his nostrils and then turned back to the game. With lightning speed, the rat moved a piece on each of the eight boards, his whiskers twitching as he did so.

The man furrowed his brow for a moment and then smiled. It was a charming smile. A winning smile. *A smile you didn't need to be ashamed of,* thought Ever, thinking of the gap between her own front teeth. It lit up his whole face and crinkled the corners of his eyes, which sparkled with a mischievous gleam.

"Checkmate. Checkmate. And," he said as he jumped up with boyish enthusiasm to move another six pieces in quick succession, "checkmate."

The rat bowed his head in defeat.

"It took me long enough," said the man, reaching out gallantly to gently shake the rat's paw with his smooth, strong hand. Then he leaned over the table and spoke in hushed, worried tones.

"Snitch, tell me, is there . . . er, say, a little girl sitting in the corner of the room?"

The rat nodded and motioned with his paws.

"Did she just slide in here through a secret hatch in the wall?" asked the man, who Ever assumed, from the writing on the door, must be Snowize.

Again the rat nodded and signaled, moving his paws quite eloquently.

"Good," said Snowize, still whispering loudly, "because for a moment there I thought I was seeing things."

Ever was relieved that she'd finally been noticed. It also surprised her to find that she understood the sign language the rat was using. The Doc had taught it to one of the guinea pigs he'd consulted for advice on his invisible ice cream. At age four, Ever had watched while the guinea pig tasted ice cream all day and reported back on the different flavors in sign language. Ever had picked up the signs in no time.

"So," signed Snitch, nodding in Ever's direction, "what are we going to do about her?"

"I was rather hoping," said Snowize, scratching the back of his head, "that if we ignored her, she might go away." He said this loudly, as if he were hoping she might take a hint.

"I don't think it works that way," said Snitch in sign. Now the rat was looking myopically in her direction.

"Well, she's a breach of security, if you hadn't noticed. She just appeared in our secret underground office through a hatch in the wall that, I'm quite positive, was not there yesterday. I don't like it, Snitch," Snowize added. "I don't like it one bit."

Ever was taken aback by how they continued to speak about her in the third person, as if she wasn't there. She let out a slightly louder cough in protest, but to her dismay neither of them paid her the slightest attention.

"All I'm saying," signed Snitch, with a wave of his paw, "is that we can't just hope she'll crawl back into the wall. Perhaps we should ask her what she's doing here, make her feel a little bit welcome."

"Bidding her welcome," said Snowize, "would be dishonest because she is most certainly not. And I don't trust her. If you hadn't noticed, she's now observing us with those big, green eyes, no doubt making copious mental notes to take back with her."

It wasn't true. Ever was merely wondering how it was possible for a rodent to have human intelligence.

"Look, maybe we should be decent hosts. Perhaps offer her something to eat?" signed Snitch.

"Well, if you want to feed her, then she's your problem, and you'll have to clean up after her. And if that's your priority, then you'll never make it to partner in this detective agency." Snowize leaned back in his chair, put his feet up on the desk and clasped his hands behind his head.

"But," exclaimed Snitch, pointing to the sign on the door, "we're Snowize & Snitch! Snowize *ampersand* Snitch. Snowize *and* Snitch. Don't you remember you promoted me to partner? After we solved the mysterious case of Mrs. Winterbottom, the rabid squirrel, and the mild-mannered hot-chutney salesman?"

Snitch appeared anxious for his partner to remember. He ran his white paws nervously through his whiskers.

"Frankly, Snitch," said Snowize, "I'm disappointed that you've resorted to making up absurd tales. We both know *I* solved that case."

"But only after I delivered the missing piece of the puzzle. Namely, the diagnosis that the squirrel was rabid. And that's when you promoted me," countered Snitch.

"You may have sniffed out some important facts," said Snowize. "And your genetically engineered intelligence may have helped you make a deduction or two. But I would have remembered such a significant event as promoting you to partner. Unless you're implying that I for—" Here, Ever observed, the detective's twinkly eyes darkened once more as he cleared his throat and shifted uneasily in his seat. For a moment, he seemed to lose his unshakable confidence, and he couldn't bring himself to finish his sentence.

"It's simply impossible that I misremembered the whole event. That I for—"

"I think *forgot* is the word you're looking for," signed Snitch.

"Don't be ridiculous," said Snowize. "I never, ever for—I never have problems remembering."

Ever noticed the shadow of fear that crossed the detective's face and wondered why he was so afraid of the word *forget*.

The truth, one that Ever would only later discover, was that Harry Snowize was afraid for reasons that he himself could not quite fathom. He had always had a diamond mind that was razor sharp with a memory that was nothing short of photographic. His ability to remember the tiniest detail was what made him one of the world's finest detectives. Forgetting was not an option.

Snitch sighed. "I'm sorry. When I was assigned to you they warned me . . ." The rat quickly hid his paws behind his back, as if to stop himself from saying too much.

"Warned you of what?" asked Snowize, with one eyebrow raised. Ever leaned in closer.

Snitch groomed his whiskers nervously. "Well, that certain words might upset you. Words like *forgot*, *forgotten* and *forget*. As well as similar-sounding words and phrases like *forgo*, *forgone*, and, *for pity's sake*, even the number *four*. Forgive me, as your partner I should have known better."

"The only reason it says partners on that sign," said Snowize, leaping up from his chair and striding over to tap the door, "is that the painters we hired couldn't see what they were doing or hear our instructions."

"And whose brilliant idea was it to insist that they wear earplugs and blindfolds in the first place?" signed Snitch.

"I had no choice," said Snowize. "It was the only way to keep our location secret. Besides, they're brilliant artists. They did a bang-up job, didn't they? Look at that lovely lettering."

The rat made a squeaking sound that Ever thought expressed his growing indignation.

"And just how much longer are we going to remain in hiding deep underground beneath a giant baobab tree in Zimbabwe?" he signed, exasperated.

"As long as it takes," said Snowize, quite solemnly. "As long as is necessary."

Ever was stunned. She was beneath a baobab tree in Zimbabwe with two quarreling detectives who were blaming each other for a badly inscribed sign that was not even visible to the outside world. As the argument turned to how effective a defective detective agency could possibly be, she felt increasingly hopeless. All she knew was that the Doc was in danger. This was no time for insane arguments about an inane sign. Clearly, the only thing these detectives needed saving from was themselves.

"Excuse me," said Ever in her loudest, boldest voice. She was naturally shy and didn't like to draw attention to herself, but these were exceptional circumstances. "I don't mean to interrupt—"

"Then please don't," said Snowize.

"But I must," insisted Ever. "I need your help. The Doc is in trouble. His life is in danger. Someone is after what is most precious to him!"

Snowize squinted at her. "Do you have an appointment?" he asked, casually opening up a large, heavy ledger and flipping through it.

"No," said Ever in a small voice.

"Well, unfortunately we are fully booked today."

"I can wait," said Ever, remembering to cross her arms and lift her chin. She'd read countless descriptions of chins being lifted defiantly in the many novels that lined her bookshelf. She hoped angling hers just so would make her a force to be reckoned with.

Snowize ignored her raised chin and perused the big appointment book once more. "Regrettably, we are busy for both the foreseeable and unforeseeable future." He allowed the ledger to fall shut with a dull thud that sent up a small puff of dust.

"Foreseeable!" Snitch signed to Snowize. "That was another word I was told might upset you." The rat quickly bit his paw, as if regretting his outburst.

The detectives resumed their arguing, and Ever started to tremble. Her heart did a strange lurch as she remembered the look of sad desperation on the Doc's face in his hologram message. Clearly, she was wasting her time here.

With an air of determination, Ever stood up and walked over to the door. She had no idea where she would go, but she could not let any more precious time slip by. As she twisted the doorknob, she suddenly realized she'd forgotten the most important thing of all. The box that growled.

It will save your life. Guard it with your soul. Protect it with your heart, the crow had said. And hadn't the hologram of the Doc pointed to a small silver box on his desk? A fact she'd overlooked because she was so worried about the forbidden tunnel. Without the box, she was doomed, the Doc had said so himself. *It will save you. It may save us all.* Judging from the stinging in her eyes, Ever knew it was only a matter of seconds before she broke her own rule and burst into tears. And she would have done so if a peculiar machine in the corner of the office hadn't burst into flame first.

6

The Treacherous Telegram

The machine in the corner of the office didn't simply spontaneously combust or blow up. First, it emitted a series of clicks and beeps and some rather embarrassing burps. While Ever found this very disturbing, the quarreling detectives paid it no heed. They didn't even blink when the spluttering machine coughed so wretchedly that it sent a strange rattling through its rusty parts. Then it spat out a single piece of paper before promptly exploding in a plume of bright electric sparks.

The paper floated up above the burning machine and wafted down in front of Ever, who caught it and blew out the tiny flames still licking at its edges.

"Look," she said, quite amazed. "I think . . . it's a telegram."

Snowize and Snitch had fallen into a stunned silence. They stared at the burning machine.

"Yes, it is," said Snowize, after a while. "I had no idea that old telegraph machine still worked." With that he sprang up, smashed a glass panel, extracted a fire extinguisher and put out the fire, all in one perfectly fluid movement. Ever was impressed.

"I'll take that," said the detective as he reappeared through a cloud of smoke and removed the telegram from Ever's hands. "It's top secret information and certainly not for the eyes of an intruder."

"I'm sorry. It's too late," said Ever. "I've already seen it."

"You barely glanced at it," said Snowize as he dusted charred bits from the edges of the telegram.

"I have a photographic memory," said Ever apologetically.

"Really?" said the detective, raising a single eyebrow. "Prove it then. Tell us what it says." He held the telegram behind his back.

Ever closed her eyes and pictured the singed piece of paper. She could see the words clearly. "Scientist Yoshinobu Azayaka dead STOP By his own sword STOP Gustav Cadiz missing STOP Presumed kidnapped QUESTION MARK Check your t-mail for once STOP Regards Deodora Miffingpin END."

There was a long, awkward silence. Ever opened her eyes to find both Snowize and Snitch staring at her. If they were impressed with her total recall, they didn't show it. Instead, Snowize placed his hand over his eyes as if he was in sudden and terrible pain. Ever recognized that pain, the pain of unbearable loss that strikes with such a blow it weakens your entire body. For a moment, the detective's shoulders slumped, and Ever caught sight of what she thought might be a tear that he quickly wiped away.

"I'm sorry," said Ever as the terrible meaning of the telegram struck home. She worried that the detectives would somehow blame her for the bad news she'd just delivered, as if they'd instantly realize that bad luck and misfortune followed wherever she went. She decided now was not the time to ask about t-mail or the significance of the name at the end of the telegram. Miffingpin. The crow's words whispered themselves back to her: *The only humans you can trust are Harry Snowize, Deodora Miffingpin and . . . yourself.*

"Yoshinobu would never take his own life," Snowize declared, still in shock from the horrible news. "It's unthinkable." He crumpled and uncrumpled the telegram as if hoping the words would rearrange themselves into anything other than the grim message they carried.

"You knew him?" asked Ever, curiosity once again getting the better of her.

"If it weren't for Yoshinobu Azayaka, I wouldn't be here today," said Snowize.

"He's the one who saved your life?" signed Snitch. "The one who used electro-thermo-magnetic-something-or-other to get you into the strangest of all hiding places?"

Snowize nodded. "Yes. Yes. He did the impossible and hid me in a human tooth. Several times, I might add. And while it was not a comfortable place to hide in for years at a time, it is the only reason I am alive today. It's the only reason the Brothers Weiss failed to hunt me down and have my liver for breakfast. For this reason, I am forever in Yoshinobu's debt. And now my dear friend is gone."

Snitch placed both his paws over his heart and bowed his head. This was the sign for deepest sympathies. It was far more powerful than words.

Ever knew this was not the time for questions, but the words tumbled out before she could stop them. "Are you serious? You really hid in a tooth?"

Snitch raised a cool, questioning eyebrow at Snowize, who studied Ever as if weighing whether or not he could trust her.

"It's a long story," he said, "and we don't have time

for stories right now. But perhaps we could start afresh. Tell us who you are, why you appear to understand rodent-specific sign language and how you came to be troubling us with your presence at this very troubling time."

Ever introduced herself in a few short sentences.

"Ever," mused Snowize, unimpressed. "Ever so interesting. Ever so ridiculous. One has to wonder what kind of parents give their child an adverb of frequency for a name. It's preposterous."

"They're missing and most likely dead," said Ever, "so I guess I'll never know what made them do it." She carefully opened her locket and held it up for the detectives to see.

"Interesting," said Snowize, sharing another unspoken exchange with Snitch. "Although I can't really see the resemblance."

He ran a hand anxiously through his tousled hair as Snitch shot him a look, warning him to be kind. "You're lucky they removed themselves from your life when they did, before they could cause you any further grief," he said. "I mean, that is quite a name they saddled you with, so who knows what other outrageous things they would have done, if they'd stuck around."

These words stung, but Ever didn't let it show. She was still hoping that the crow was right, that however impossible it might seem, her parents were alive. That tiny bit of hope had settled in her heart, and she felt protective of it. She quickly changed the subject and went on to tell them about the crow's message and how she came to be there. Once she'd finished, Snowize and Snitch shared another look.

"A message from the future. That is interesting. But this is all unlikely . . . especially the idea that you have to save us. That's entirely ridiculous, considering that you're a young girl with a developing brain and limited knowledge, while we're experts in our fields. And quite frankly, you're more of a hindrance to us than anything. We need you about as much as Eskimos need more snow in winter."

"I'm just repeating what I was told," said Ever, slightly hurt. "Besides, when you consider climate change, it's possible that in the future, Eskimos might need more snow in winter."

"Okay," said Snowize, "let's not get caught up with semantics and wordplay. What else did the crow say?"

"He told me I could trust Snowize and Miffingpin, and that I must protect a box that growls with my life. And then the crow just vanished in a puddle as if he had melted."

Snowize held her gaze and drummed his fingers on the desk a few times, searching for the right words.

"Children are known to have very active imaginations," he said. "We all know crows don't melt, hold intelligent conversations or bring prophetic messages from the past, present or future."

"Yet you expect me to believe you hid in a human tooth?" retorted Ever.

Snowize held up a hand to silence her. "We'll have to discuss this later," he said. "Because right now we have a murder and a kidnapping on our hands."

"And my guardian's disappearance," added Ever, but Snowize ignored her.

He passed the telegram to Snitch and proceeded to pace up and down with his hands clasped behind his back. As he spoke, his dark eyes grew distant, and his voice was grim. "When a top scientist is found dead and another great scientist is kidnapped, you might think it mere coincidence," he said. "But I predict that we will find a connection between Yoshinobu Azayaka's death and Gustav Cadiz's kidnapping."

He stopped to look at Ever before continuing. "It's not a good day for scientists," he said, shaking his head. "If this is what I think it is, then we could be up against the worst kind of evil."

"Don't you see?" asked Ever. "The Doc's disappearance is linked to what's happened to these other scientists. I can feel it in my heart and in my bones, and I've never felt more sure of anything."

"It's called a hunch," said Snowize, "this feeling that you describe. I have them frequently, and unlike yours, mine are never wrong. Leave the deductions to the experts. You popped out of a hole in a wall. You are abandoned and orphaned and clearly desperate to see connections where none exist at all."

Ever was distracted by a strange clanging noise in the distance, but Snowize was too preoccupied to notice. He continued in his solemn tone. "My hunch tells me those evil brothers are behind this," he said gravely, as if announcing the end of the world.

The distant clanging sound had now become a screeching noise of metal scraping against metal and then metal scraping against roots and earth.

"I hear something," said Ever.

"I smell something," signed Snitch.

"Indeed," said Snowize, still lost in his own thoughts, "there can be no doubt that Trouble with a capital T is on its way."

And trouble it certainly was, because at that very moment there was a tremendous clunking noise, and something came crashing through the secret tunnel and into their office. It knocked Snowize to the ground and narrowly missed Snitch's tail, which the rodent whisked out of the way just in time.

Snowize recovered instantly and assumed a ninjalike stance, ready to destroy the intruder. "Prepare to be dismantled and discombobulated at once!" said Snowize, sizing up his attacker.

"Don't!" said Ever, jumping in between the new arrival and the detective.

"This had better be ever so good, Ever," said Snowize, not moving from his position of attack. "Give me one good reason why I shouldn't destroy this strange robotic fridge-like thing."

"Anyone care for some invisible ice cream?" asked Melschman, as if his arrival were the most natural thing in the world. "Or perhaps you'd prefer some pickled frogs' legs that may have turned a little slimy but would still go well with this Dijon mustard I've been keeping chilled for a special occasion?"

"Not for me," said Snowize, momentarily letting down his guard. "I'm a strict vegetarian. I avoid eating the legs of any creature."

Melschman, stung as always by rejection, swung open his lower door and reached in for the jar of frogs' legs. As the robot fridge aimed the jar at the detective, Ever knew that she was going to have a lot of explaining to do.

7

Venom

If Melschman's offer of slimy frogs' legs was unappetizing, it was about a million times better than what poor Professor Gustav Cadiz was about to face. Halfway across the globe, the old scientist was just beginning to regain consciousness. He'd been out cold since the kidnapping, and he now found himself sitting in a darkened room, strapped to something not unlike a dentist's chair. A dull, throbbing pain wrapped itself around his head and his tongue seemed glued to his palate. Even his twirly mustache ached.

Beside him, he noticed a giant fish tank. Floating ominously in the tank were thousands of octopi, their luminous rings giving off an eerie blue glow. For the longest time, the only sound in the room was the soft hum of the tank's filter as it sent tiny bubbles through the water. Gustav was almost lulled back to sleep when a gravelly voice cut through the darkness.

"There is no antidote for the venom of the blue-ringed octopus," said the voice. "The creature's bite is painless, but the poison kills within three minutes, paralyzing the victim and rendering him completely helpless."

Gustav remembered the voice from earlier. It brought

back a flood of terrible memories. He saw his vandalized laboratory and his beloved rabbits, Europa, Ganymede and Jupiter, lying dead on the ground.

"You want Compound 37d, and you're prepared to kill for it," he said. At least, that's what he meant to say, but his tongue was so sluggish and numb that his words came out sounding like, "Dshou wan kamplind shirshty shendee andshou pshepshed tokkeel foheet."

This was met with cold laughter. "I'm afraid the ether I used to knock you out may have some side effects. You might find it difficult to talk."

Gustav wondered how anyone could hope to get the formula for Compound 37d if he couldn't speak. The secret formula was not written down anywhere. It was stored safely in his head. For a moment, he wished he'd never stumbled across the magical compound; it had already caused too much trouble in his life.

Once again, the owner of the gravelly voice answered his unspoken question. "We know you have the formula in your head, Professor Cadiz. That's precisely why we're going to extract it directly from your mind."

It was then that the old man felt the cold metal probes attached to his temples.

Oh, my word, thought Gustav, *they're reading my mind. They have some sort of device that can read my every—*

"—Your every thought. That is correct," interrupted his captor. "So, you won't be able to hide anything from us. Remember, your pain is our pleasure. Any resistance and you'll be swimming in that tank full of delightful sea creatures. "

Gustav tried to be brave and look on the bright side, but no matter which way he looked at it, there was no bright side.

"You're going to steal my invention?" asked Gustav.

"We don't like to call it stealing," his tormentor answered. "My Master prefers to call it borrowing without returning. It has a much nicer ring, don't you think?"

Gustav's heart sank.

"Now," said his captor quite cheerfully, "we can remove your mind the easy way, or we can remove it the not-so-easy way. Either way, once your mind is taken, you won't really miss it much at all." The owner of the voice stepped into view, and Gustav found himself looking into the very face of cruelty: a pale, smooth face devoid of any expression. No laughter lines. No smile creases. Not even the hint of a frown. Yet it was the eyes that made this merciless face even creepier—electric blue eyes that shone with a strange neon glow.

"Take a good look at my face," said his captor, "because soon you will not remember it. In fact, you will not remember much of anything at all." His captor wore a neat blue suit with a silver pin stuck to the lapel.

Gustav realized there was no pleading with this man. He was completely without any human emotions.

"I was programmed that way," answered the man. "Genetically engineered to have no warm, fuzzy feelings. It makes life much less complicated. It also makes us more efficient. Especially since we only have the capacity for hate, anger, malice, spite and, when appropriate, shame."

Us, wondered Gustav, hoping it didn't mean that there were more of his kind out there. A sudden whirring, clicking noise caught Gustav's attention as a metallic orb was lowered in front of his face. The orb shimmered and then opened like a flower with glittering metal petals. In the center was a needlelike probe.

"Say good-bye to everything you ever knew," whispered the clone. "But don't be afraid. This is only going to hurt a teeny tiny little bit."

8

Dances with Lions

Back inside the detective agency, Ever was trying desperately to apologize to Detective Snowize, who was covered from head to toe in slimy frogs' legs. The strange thing was that instead of being angry, tears of laughter streamed down his face. He was laughing so much he was bent double. His behavior seemed to worry Snitch, who kept grooming his whiskers nervously. As the laughter continued, the rat surreptitiously signaled to Ever that he was concerned about his partner's mental health.

"Ever since he emerged from hiding in a tooth, he has not been one hundred percent himself. Something's missing . . . here," he added, pointing to his head.

Snowize finally straightened up and wiped his eyes, still chuckling.

"I'm so sorry," said Ever, unable to stop smiling as a frog's leg slid from the detective's forehead to his nose.

"Mind the gap, Einstein," Melschman intoned, and Ever instinctively covered her mouth to hide the gap between her teeth. She regretted her moment of weakness when she'd confided in Melschman about her classmates' hurtful taunt.

"Melschman is also sorry, aren't you, Melschman?" Ever asked crossly. The robot fridge remained silent. "You see, he can't help himself. He was badly programmed and sometimes attacks people when they refuse his offerings. He really doesn't mean it, though. At least, not in a bad way."

"Oh, but I do," interrupted Melschman. "I mean it in the worst way possible."

Ever felt like kicking Melschman, but since a robot has no pain receptors, there was no point. "In fact," explained Ever, through her teeth, "the Doc was supposed to dismantle Melschman and reprogram him because of his bad attitude."

"No need to explain any further," said Snowize, giving her a warm smile. "This has Batty Ezratty's signature all over it. Only a fool like the Doc could have invented a robot fridge with a personality disorder. It's hilarious."

Ever felt a flush of anger rise to her cheeks. "It's almost as funny as the man who hid in a tooth like a coward and thought that was clever."

Snitch quickly stepped in to smooth things over. "How can you call someone who holds the title of 'doctor' and 'professor' a fool?" the kindly rat signed. "Obviously the Doc must be a brilliant man."

"I'm afraid not," said Snowize. The bounce was back in his step, and the mischievous gleam had returned to his eyes. "You see, Doctor Professor David Ezratty is neither a doctor, nor a professor. He doesn't have a PhD in anything, nor does he qualify as a medical doctor. The truth is, he never studied beyond high school. Doctor and Professor are not titles. They are his actual first names. Apparently, he was such a funny-looking baby, his parents worried he might not amount to much, so they named him Doctor Professor David. His first name is Doctor just as mine is Harry!"

"The Doc is misunderstood," Ever said, leaping to her guardian's defense. "He's made remarkable discoveries and he's a genius and that's why someone is after him."

"I sincerely doubt it," said Snowize. "No one in the scientific community takes him seriously, so to suggest he is in danger . . . well, forgive me, but it's laughable. He's only famous because of his ridiculous claim that he invented invisible ice cream."

Ever's heart did a twisty lurch in her chest. "Invisible ice cream is not imaginary. The Doc would never lie about inventing something," she said.

"Then he was sadly deluded," said Snowize.

Ever was fed up. "If you don't believe me, then why don't you taste it and see for yourself? Melschman, three bowls of invisible ice cream, please." She smiled triumphantly as she waited for the robot fridge to deliver the goods.

Melschman shuffled his feet. He twiddled his robot thumbs. He nervously plugged himself into an electrical outlet and made ice cubes noisily, to drown out the awkward silence. Then he opened and closed his doors a few times and finally confessed that he had entirely forgotten to bring any invisible ice cream with him. Ever sighed. She felt the frustration that her guardian must have felt all those years ago when he was mocked and ridiculed, and no one would believe him.

"Right," said Snowize. "We don't have time to argue about the existence of invisible ice cream. Snitch, pack your pouches. We leave immediately for the scene of the crime on Mount Fuji, Japan." He turned to Ever. "Well, best of luck in your bid to find the Doc. I'm sure he ran off to get a much needed break from the two of you. He'll be back before you can say—" The detective clutched his head in midsentence. "Excuse me a minute," he said. "Incoming t-mail from the dreaded Deodora. Why I ever agreed to thought mail, I'll never know. . . ." He rolled his eyes several times and stamped his foot angrily before breathing deeply and counting to ten. After a pause, he began pacing up and down, occasionally mumbling, "Send!" and "Yes, yes, accept incoming!" followed by, "Oh, for the love of pernicious periwinkles, why did I have to go and tell her that?" All of this seemed to be directed at someone who wasn't there. Ever watched with deep confusion.

"Okay," the detective said, turning to Ever. "You, girl, are coming with us. I made the mistake of mentioning your presence to my Secret Secretary, the Mighty Miffingpin, who has informed me that we have to take care of you. Apparently abandoning a child would not be just plain wrong, but also against the code of the SSSA."

"What's the SSSA?" Ever asked, but her question was drowned out by the cacophonous rattling of Melschman springing up and down with glee.

"Yippee!" he cried. "Tokyo, here we come!"

"Oh no. No. No. Absolutely not," said Snowize. "Just the adverb. Not the robot. I have my limits."

"Please," begged Melschman. "I've always wanted to fly. Pretty please with a bowl of cherries on the top, take me with you." He reached inside his fridge section and held out a bunch of very ripe cherries.

"Negative," Snowize said. "Traveling with a robot fridge would draw unwanted attention." But Melschman would not give up. He whined and pleaded and then started to snort and stomp. He threw himself angrily about the room in the clumsiest of fashions. Snowize warned Melschman that if he did not control himself, he would wait for his battery to run flat and have him reprogrammed with a more pleasant personality. Predictably, Melschman cried tears from his water dispenser.

"That's not going to work on me," said Snowize. "I'm not going to be tricked into believing that a machine has feelings."

"The Doc says Melschman might be temperamental, but his heart is in the right place," said Ever.

"How could its heart be in the right place, when it's a fridge? It doesn't even have a heart."

"I do, too," said Melschman dispassionately. "I have a computerized component that gives me feelings just like you have."

"I sincerely doubt that," countered Snowize.

This angered Melschman. "I will get you for that, you no good, half-baked defective detect—" Melschman froze. His robot arms dropped limply to his sides, and the bunch of cherries splattered on the floor. His battery had apparently run out of juice.

"Crazy machine," said Snowize. He turned to Ever. "We'll reactivate him when we get back. I can see you're fond of him, although I can't fathom why."

"He's the only family I have right now," said Ever, feeling both a little sad for Melschman and a little sad for herself.

"You certainly know how to pick them," said Snowize. "Parents who abandon you; a guardian who disappears; and a deranged robot fridge."

And that's not all, Ever thought to herself. *Now I've found myself some defective detectives.* Out loud she muttered, "I guess I'm a magnet for bad luck. Bad luck follows me wherever I go. I brought it to my parents. I brought it to my guardian." She found her voice breaking as she spoke.

Ever noticed Snitch signaling to Snowize. "See what

being so tactless does? You've upset her. Now she's going to start crying and then what?" asked Snitch.

"I'm sorry," said Snowize, trying to make amends. "I am not good with children. Having none of my own, I find them confusing and inconvenient."

With that Snitch clapped his paws over his eyes and shook his head in despair.

Snowize held the office door open, and Ever followed Snitch as he began making his way up a set of stairs carved into the red earth.

"I'm merely speaking the truth," continued Snowize as they reached the cool, natural hollow inside the massive trunk of the baobab tree. He poked his head through the narrow archway that led outside and sighed. "For example, it's not as if she's going to help us navigate our way through the pride of lions that has taken shelter under the shade of the baobab tree. The very lions, that is, that stand between us and the jeep that is our only way of getting to the airport."

Ever could see from the rat's reaction that this latest morsel of information was no exaggeration. Snitch was already shaking. With trembling paws, he told her it was in his blood to fear cats. Ever peeked through the opening in the tree trunk and found herself blinking into the African sun. Veld stretched out in every direction, dotted with the occasional thorn tree and termite hill. No more than twenty feet away was a green jeep, and draped over its hood was a large male lion, its golden face framed by a black-tipped mane. *Panthera leo leo.* Ever could see the entry in *The Encyclopedia Brittanicus* in precise detail. *Of the family Felidae. Order: Carnivora. The male stands four feet at the shoulder and can weigh up to five hundred pounds. His role is to protect the pride.*

The lion was asleep; its breathing seemed to match

the rise and fall of the song of the cicadas. It was not alone. Scattered in the limited shade provided by the baobab were seven more lions, bringing the total to eight. A second male lay lazily on top of a large termite hill. Its amber eyes opened sleepily and for a moment it took in its surroundings with disinterest. Then it allowed its heavy lids to close again. Lions, Ever knew, spent about twenty hours a day in slumber.

"Remember the most important thing: no sudden moves," said Snowize, carefully making his way out of the trunk. He first stretched out one leg and then the other until he had fully emerged and could survey the scene. "Here's the plan. We approach the vehicle slowly, imperceptibly, as if we're not really there. And whatever you do, don't have an adrenaline rush. If you show any fear, they'll be drawn to you like bees to honey. Like moths to a flame. Like sharks to a feeding frenzy. Like leeches to lychees—"

"Enough!" signed Snitch. "Enough with the similes. A simile is not going to get us out of this predicament!"

"Then perhaps a proverb will help? We'll let sleeping lions lie."

"It's dogs. The proverb is, 'Let sleeping dogs lie.'"

"Dogs, cats. Why are you always splitting hairs?"

Snitch had no comeback. He was distracted by the formidable lions and their perilous proximity.

The thing about lions, Ever thought, *is that they are much bigger in real life than you can ever imagine. All muscle. All tooth and claw. Beautiful from a distance. Terrifying up close.*

"Is there really no other way?" asked Ever. "I mean, they're bound to wake up. Then we're done for." Her heart was already pounding.

"We have no choice. Remember, if one confronts you,

stand up tall and shout loudly. Stand your ground, but don't look him in the eye. Whatever you do, don't run."

Ever knew this was standard advice, but it seemed very flimsy against the veritable king of the animal kingdom. She jumped involuntarily as a lion twitched its tail to swat off a fly.

"I'll lead the way. Ever follows and then Snitch," commanded Snowize in a low whisper. "Hands at your sides. Try not to breathe."

With that he took three steps out onto the plain. Three silent and slow steps that Ever could not help but admire. He was either mad or exceptionally brave. She could not decide which, and right now it didn't matter.

Snitch nudged Ever, and she instinctively took his paw in her hand. With her other hand she pressed her silver locket against her heart. The faint smell of cinnamon and roses gave some comfort. Ever kissed the locket for good luck, and then, together, she and Snitch followed Snowize into the brightness.

The lions slept on.

Then they heard it. At first, Ever thought the sound was solely in her head, that her fiercely beating heart was causing the blood to rush to her ears in a deafening whoosh. But the lions had heard it, too. They were opening their eyes, looking extremely vexed at being disturbed, and Ever saw Snowize raising his eyes skyward. By now he was halfway between the baobab and the jeep. He seemed even more ticked off than the lions as he gazed up at a helicopter that had appeared out of nowhere. Silver and sleek, it hovered above them like a strange bird of prey, its blades whipping around in a repetitive *thuk-a-thuk-a-thuk* that drowned out the song of the cicadas.

The two male lions were now fully alerted to the humans among them. A female stood up warily and stretched. Above, the helicopter door swung open, and Ever saw a square object tumble out and land next to Snowize with a *whump*! A parcel, wrapped in string and brown paper. As the helicopter took off toward the East, Ever noticed the letters SSSA shimmering on its side.

"Timing is everything," said Snowize, "and the SSSA has the worst possible timing. Those are our disguises in that package, but somehow I suspect we might never get to use them." As if on cue, the two male lions rose to their feet. The one with the black-tipped mane pawed the dusty earth and then it opened its mouth to give a roar of discontent that would be heard miles away. Snitch curled into a ball on the ground and clamped his paws over his ears.

"If anyone has any suggestions," said Snowize as the second male lion dropped down off the hood of the jeep and sized him up, "now would be a good time."

There was a slight edge to his voice that belied his calm demeanor. On the ground, Snitch curled up even tighter, trying to pretend that nothing bad was about to happen. Ever watched helplessly as the lions closed in around the detective.

"I have a plan," said Ever, surprised at how the solution came to her fully formed. It would involve some coaxing and a lie, and she wasn't sure they had enough time. But it was their only option.

"Don't go anywhere," she said, realizing too late how ridiculous that might sound to a man surrounded by lions. "I'll be back," she added. Then she spun on her heel, raced back into the trunk of the baobab tree, and thundered down the dusty stairs to the office below.

A breathless Ever reemerged three minutes later followed by an enthusiastic robot fridge. Snowize, still frozen to his spot, raised an eyebrow to express either his surprise or his bewilderment. The dominant male lion was now snorting and growling a low, menacing growl. An attack was imminent. There was no time to waste.

"Okay," Ever said nervously. "Melschman, go!" She knew the backup battery that she had hastily activated downstairs would give Melschman ten minutes of power. Ever hoped it would be enough to pull off a small miracle. "When I shout 'run,' we run for the car," she called to the detectives.

Snowize gave an almost imperceptible nod of approval. The lion pawed the ground one more time, and then its growl deepened. It tensed its muscles in preparation for a charge but seemed confused as Melschman, shouting monotonously at the top of his voice, marched into the veld and positioned himself right in front of the detective. Snowize backed away as Melschman took another step toward the lion.

Ever then clapped her hands, and the robot fridge started dancing. It was a jerky, uncoordinated dance. Melschman flung and swung his robot arms as rapidly as he could. The lions' natural instincts were instantly triggered. Their eyes locked onto the dancing fridge, entranced by the flurry of activity. Melschman made a sudden move to one side and three lions all made a lunge for him. He feinted and went in the other direction, leading them away from the car.

"Run!" yelled Ever, and she picked up the ball of fur that was Snitch and sprinted toward the jeep. It was not a great distance, but with lions involved, it felt like every step was a mile. Her lungs burned with the effort. Snowize met her halfway, pulled her along and then swung her up and over into the jeep. Then he jumped into the driver's seat and shut the door.

Through the windshield, Ever could see Melschman emptying out the contents of his freezer section. An old steak. Some cherry pie. A lump of lard. He flung them fiercely and with precision, and the lions gave chase. It was his best performance yet.

"Keys?" asked Snowize, patting his pockets.

"Oh no," signed Snitch, who had finally uncurled himself and now sat between the two humans. "Don't tell me you for—"

But Snowize was smiling as he reached into his pocket and withdrew a single key that he placed into the ignition. The engine roared to life, and Ever found herself grinning back at the detectives. They all high-fived, hand to paw, paw to hand, hand to hand.

"Young lady," said Snowize, as he straightened out the wheel, "how did you get that rambunctious robot to agree to save my life?"

"I lied to him," said Ever, feeling a terrible sense of shame and guilt. "I promised I'd take him to Tokyo." It was the worst kind of lie, Ever knew. It was a promise like the one her father had made. When a promise like that is made to you and then broken, it takes something away from you. It eats away at the hope and spark inside of you, leaving you feeling hollow and empty.

"A lie. That's bad," said Snowize. "Did you at least cross your fingers?"

Ever shook her head. "Crossing your fingers doesn't count. It's still lying. It's just lying about making the promise in the first place."

"Then you'll keep your promise," signed Snitch.

"I will?"

"Certainly," said Snowize, giving her a reassuring pat on the shoulder. "When, or rather, if we get back here, you'll make it up to him and take him to Tokyo."

Ever allowed this reasoning to make her feel better. She would make it up to Melschman. She would! She hadn't specified when they'd go to Tokyo, so technically, she hadn't broken her promise.

"Or better yet, with his battery dead, you'll be able to have him reprogrammed so that he doesn't remember this little incident, and voilà, problem solved."

"I could never do that," said Ever. "Robbing him of his memories would make him less than Melschman. That would be cruel and unkind and wrong." In the rearview mirror she could see Melschman standing on top of a termite hill, waving wildly, giving them the thumbs-up. It was a pitiful sight. "I can't just leave him like that. Standing on a termite hill with his heart broken," she added.

So Snowize drove around the waving robot a few times. He stopped to lean down and pick up the parcel that the helicopter had dropped earlier. Melschman waved one more time, took two steps toward them and then, to Ever's relief, his battery died and he froze in a waving position.

"Perfect timing," said Snowize. "Now you won't have any explaining to do."

Ever insisted that they wheel Melschman back into the hollow of the baobab tree to protect him from the elements. The pride of lions observed with mild curiosity from beyond the termite hill, but didn't dare approach again.

Once they were back in the jeep, Snowize stepped on the gas, and Ever watched the baobab tree receding into the distance. *Step one accomplished. Detectives saved*, she thought to herself.

But something bothered her. It felt too easy.

"Detective Snowize," she wondered out loud, "earlier, you said *if* we get back here . . ."

The detective sighed. "When you step into the unknown, especially with a case as dangerous as I believe this one may be, there can be no guarantees about anything."

9

Curiouser and Curiouser

It was with wonder and fear that Ever found herself boarding a plane bound for Tokyo, Japan, along with two highly effective defective detectives. Her faith in the detectives and their sleuthing methods had sunk a little lower. The pair were now dressed in the questionable disguises that had been thrown from the helicopter. A very unhappy Snitch was disguised as a cat, while Snowize was disguised as an elderly Japanese man. Unfortunately, Snowize kept forgetting to act elderly.

As they made their way down the aisle of the plane, avoiding the curious stares of their fellow passengers, Snitch and Ever constantly reminded Snowize to walk slowly, hunch his shoulders and speak either in Japanese or with a Japanese accent.

"All we need," said Snowize, buckling his seat belt and turning on his overhead light, "is one reasonably good clue. That would serve us better in solving this case than what we have right now."

"What do we have right now?" signed Snitch, fidgeting in his cat suit and checking three times to see if a life jacket was, indeed, under his seat.

"No clue at all," said Snowize, forgetting his Japanese accent. "All we have is a strong hunch. That's why I'm hoping you'll sniff out something substantial at the scene of the crime."

Snitch sniffed the air through his rubber cat suit. "I'm picking up something right now," he signed. "A whiff of . . . something evil." The rat shivered involuntarily.

"Nonsense," said Snowize. "Your smell receptors always go haywire on planes due to your debilitating fear of flying. All you can smell right now is the glue holding that cat suit together."

As they prepared for takeoff, Ever patted Snitch's paw.

"I don't understand why you have to be in disguise," Ever said. "It looks very uncomfortable."

"Not to mention hot, scratchy and humiliating," signed Snitch as he wriggled beneath the layers of rubber. "Or the fact that these ears keep slipping over my eyes so I can't see a thing."

Ever leaned over and with much stretching and tugging, helped Snitch pull the ears back into place.

"We opt for discomfort when we have no other choice," said Snowize, tapping his pen against his notebook. "When the world's worst people have you on their eliminate-and-obliterate list, you quickly realize that a herd of lions is the least of your troubles."

"Pride," said Ever. "It's a pride of lions."

"I'm not proud of the fact," Snowize continued, ignoring her, "that I've spent so much time in hiding. Ironically, the only thing that's keeping me alive, besides this disguise, is the fact that most people think I'm already dead."

As the plane raced down the runway and lifted off, Ever's thoughts turned to her guardian. Were the Doc's pursuers getting closer? Was he safe? Or was he frightened and alone, waiting for someone to come to his rescue?

And what had he meant when he'd tapped his head and said that they wanted what was most precious to him? It nagged at her. After all, what was in the Doc's head besides his brain?

Snitch pulled the life jacket out from under his seat and placed it around his middle, while still complaining bitterly about the very insensitive choice of disguise. Cats were his biggest enemy, and he'd lost two close relatives to large felines back in Gambia. Furthermore, he pointed out, he didn't feel adequately prepared for this mission.

"Put away that life jacket. You'll make the other passengers nervous," said Snowize. "And stop worrying. On this mission, there will be no mistakes. We'll get back into the SSSA's good graces and all will be well." With that, cool as a cucumber, he closed his eyes and popped on his sunglasses. "Wake me up when we're in Tokyo," he said, and a few seconds later he was fast asleep.

Ever turned to Snitch. "What is this SSSA I keep hearing about?" she whispered.

The rat twitched slightly and glanced around nervously. "The Secret Society of Spies Anonymous," he signed surreptitiously. "It's an organization so secret that nobody can prove it exists, and only the Secret Secretaries know who the members are."

"If it's so secretive," asked Ever, "why are you telling me about it?"

"Firstly, my nose tells me I can trust you. Even through this rubbery cat suit, you have the odor signature of a good, kind person. Secondly, if you repeat this information, no one will believe you. And if you say you heard it from a rat, your credibility rating will be zero," signed Snitch.

Ever thought about this for a moment and then asked, "Who is Deodora Miffingpin, and what exactly is a Secret Secretary?"

"Every spy has to have an approved Secret Secretary. For security purposes, the spy and the Secret Secretary never meet in person. So, in theory, Snowize has no idea where Deodora Miffingpin is located, or what she even looks like. Deodora, though, knows much more about Snowize. Part of her job is to monitor his activities and assist him in his missions. She has also taken on the additional task of keeping tabs on his mistakes."

"Mistakes?" asked Ever, slightly alarmed. "What mistakes?"

Snitch sighed and explained that Snowize had almost messed up their last mission. Now there were rumors circulating that his memory was faulty, that he was no longer the man he used to be. Snowize had broken several Society rules when he used Yoshinobu Azayaka's experimental procedure to conceal himself in the left lower incisor of a man who was rumored to be stark raving mad. And although he'd outsmarted the evil Brothers Weiss by doing so, when he finally reemerged, it soon became obvious that he had damaged himself in the process. Damaged goods were not welcome in the SSSA; and for reasons that included both professional and unprofessional jealousy, there were those waiting for him to slip up so they could kick him out of the organization for good.

"Snowize has no idea about the degree to which Deodora is checking up on him, or that I have to report any strange behavior directly to her," he signed to Ever.

"So," said Ever, "you're actually spying on Snowize for Miffingpin."

"It's for his own protection," signed Snitch. "That's why I do it. That's why Deodora does it. We're on his side, trying to stop him from slipping up. "

"But why is Deodora so protective over Snowize?" wondered Ever aloud.

"She has her reasons," signed Snitch vaguely.

"There!" he suddenly signaled. "I caught a whiff of it again."

"What is it?" asked Ever.

"Something rotten. A human being. But with all this glue interfering, it's hard to tell exactly how rotten, or where he's seated."

"You can smell degrees of rotten?" Ever asked. She knew African giant pouched rats have such an acute sense of smell they can sniff out explosives buried deep beneath the ground and even detect disease, but Snitch's skill seemed extreme.

"That's why Snowize hired me," Snitch added. "Because I'm a supersniffer."

Ever glanced over at the detective, who was still in a deep sleep, resting his head against the window. She caught a glimpse of blue sky and clouds so white and fluffy they barely looked real. Snowize shifted in his sleep, revealing his sleuthing notebook open to a page not meant for anyone else's eyes. Ever quickly looked away, but it was too late. The detective's cool, flowing cursive floated up before her, exactly as it was inked on the page:

> . . . I know it's ridiculous, but sometimes I get the sneaking suspicion that Snitch is checking up on me. Am I becoming paranoid? Perhaps, but in truth, that's not what troubles me most. What keeps me up at night is a terrible nagging feeling that I've for for can't remember something of utmost importance.

This feeling gnaws at me during the day, and it wakes me in a cold sweat in the middle of the night. It's the sense that something that was once there, something of vital importance, is now missing from my life. Yet, I have absolutely no idea what it might be. At times it's as if a great gaping hole has been torn through my very soul.

The words made Ever feel inexplicably sad. She shook her head vigorously, trying to loosen the picture of that page from her mind. It was of no use; there was no way to unsee what had already been seen.

"Now it's your turn," signed Snitch as the flight attendant poured them lime cordials. "I want to know all about the invisible ice cream fiasco and how it ruined your guardian's reputation. I suspect this might be important for our investigation."

"Then you do think my guardian's disappearance is connected to this case?" Ever was relieved to see Snitch nodding.

"But of course. Your unusual arrival in our office was no coincidence. I just wish my partner would see it that way." Snitch settled as best as he could into his seat. "Please tell me the story."

"It's not a story," insisted Ever. "It's the absolute truth." She took a deep breath, already agitated at the thought of how her guardian had been mocked and humiliated. "Invisible ice cream is the one thing the Doc regretted inventing. He always said it was a spectacular flop, from the moment it was unveiled to the moment it almost killed him."

The way it had almost killed him was that burglars had dropped some invisible ice cream at the top of the spiral staircase that led to his laboratory. The ice cream had melted, and the Doc had slipped on the invisible puddle and tumbled down the stairs, very nearly breaking his neck. But that was not the worst part, he always told her. It was nothing compared to the humiliation he suffered when he unveiled invisible ice cream to the world.

The great unveiling had taken place at the International Inventors Conference before a packed auditorium. People were expecting to see a truly great invention and when the Doc drew back the curtain there was a hushed silence. The audience held its collective breath in anticipation.

"Behold," the Doc said in a voice filled with pride, pointing to a clear glass bowl on the table in front of him. "My finest and most important invention to date: invisible ice cream."

His revelation was met with stunned silence that was interrupted by nervous titters and some grumblings as people turned to each other to ask if this was perhaps a joke.

"Are there any questions?" asked the Doc.

After more nervous giggling, a hand shot up. "If you eat too much invisible ice cream, do you put on invisible pounds?" asked a man with a smirk on his face. This resulted in hoots of laughter that started to spread throughout the audience.

"If it drips, does it leave invisible stains on your clothes?" asked a lady with a flower in her hair.

"You don't understand," said the Doc. "There are other uses for invisible ice cream." But no one was listening.

They were too busy wiping away tears of laughter and coming up with more jokes.

"Waiter, waiter, there's an invisible fly in my invisible ice cream!" someone yelled.

"Don't knock it till you've sampled it!" the Doc called out, which led to more laughter and a series of knock-knock jokes.

Those who had paid for the Doc's research filed out of the auditorium, their noses turned up in disgust.

"Wait," cried the Doc to his disappearing audience. "This discovery could lead to so much more." But his appeals fell on deaf ears. The idea of invisible ice cream was so ludicrous that no one dared to be seen trying it.

Eventually only one little old lady remained behind. "I would love to sample your invisible ice cream," she said. The Doc was grateful for this request. He gave the woman a teaspoon and allowed her to sample it right from the bowl. The woman exclaimed it was the most delicious ice cream she had ever tasted and that anyone who had left without trying it was a fool. However, after she ate every last drop, she mentioned that the true genius of invisible ice cream was wasted on her, because she was blind.

That night, to make matters worse, the supply of invisible ice cream was stolen out of the Doc's freezer, along with the book in which he'd written the formula. The Doc called the police and reported the theft only to be met with further humiliation. Inspector Will D. Deuce arrived to take a statement. But every time he asked a question, he burst into uncontrollable laughter.

"So," he began again, "you claim that this invisible ice cream has . . . *disappeared*?"

"Yes. Completely and utterly. It was right in the freezer,

and now it's been stolen. Along with my notes for its formula."

The inspector dutifully made a note in his book, trying to hide the smile that was creeping across his face.

"Please," said the Doc. "Invisible ice cream is one of the most important inventions of this century. We need to find the stolen batch and get it back. Urgently."

"Of course," said Inspector Will D. Deuce, not feeling any urgency at all. "Now, can you describe this stolen ice cream? If my men stumble across it, what would be its distinguishing feature?"

"Well," began the Doc. "First . . . they would not be able to see it, because it is invisible." He regretted the words as soon as they were out of his mouth.

"So," continued the inspector, "you want my men to look for something that they cannot see?" The question was rhetorical, and the inspector snapped his notebook shut. "We'll call you the moment we don't see anything suspicious," he added with a wink. Then he turned abruptly to leave, his shoulders shaking with very visible laughter.

After that incident, Doctor Professor Ezratty was branded a charlatan and a joke. His reputation was destroyed, and he could not find any scientific work. No one would employ him.

"He became a recluse," Ever concluded. "He kept his research strictly to himself. He seldom appeared in public, and he didn't discuss his work with anyone except me."

"Fascinating," signed Snitch.

"I find it hard to believe," said Snowize, opening an eye. "Although I do have one question. If the formula was gone, how did he ever manage to make more invisible ice cream? How did he get the formula back?"

"You won't believe that, either," said Ever and was about to explain further when Snitch held up a paw to silence her.

"What is it?" asked Snowize, instantly on alert.

"The smell," signed Snitch. "It's coming from the man in front of us. He's up to no good. People who are cruel have a very distinctive smell. It's subtle, but quite unmistakable. A sour smell blended with something sharp, like vinegar; a hint of sulfur, not unlike rotten eggs; and decaying banana peels."

Ever sniffed the air. She couldn't smell a thing. But Snitch's sensitive nose gave rise to a terrible fit of sneezing that lasted three minutes. Even though he frowned on superstition, Snowize felt obliged to bless him after each sneeze. Ever giggled at the two of them.

The man in front of them was less amused. He slowly turned around and glared at Ever.

"You might want to keep it down," he said as he studied her with icy eyes that chilled her to the bone. Ever could not tear herself away from his poisonous gaze. She noticed a silver pin on the lapel of his sleek suit jacket. It was engraved with a logo that read ColdCorp Corporation, and below that was written *Mater artium necessitas*.

"Necessity is the mother of invention," Ever translated out loud.

"Keep your Latin smarts to yourself," said the man as he pulled his sleep mask over his eyes and turned back sharply in his seat. Ever felt as if she had just stared into the face of malevolence itself.

In his seat, the clone shifted ever so slightly. *That might look like an old man and a cat*, he thought to himself, *but I smell a rat*. He'd been listening to their every word and now his suspicions were confirmed: Rumors of Snowize's death had been greatly exaggerated. If he could have smiled, he would have, but he didn't know how. In his hollow heart, he desired only to please his Master. He would follow these misfits, learn all their secrets and then, at his leisure, destroy them.

10

The Sock and the Snowman

Three hours after landing in Tokyo, Ever, Snowize and Snitch stood at the base of Mount Fuji, ready to begin the arduous task of climbing its frosty slopes in search of the exact spot where Yoshinobu Azayaka had lost his life.

"It says here in fifteen languages that the path is closed and treacherous at this time of the year," said Ever, pointing to a sign that also depicted a stick figure slipping over the edge of a steep crevasse and tumbling into the abyss below. Ever felt a little light-headed. Heights were not her strong point, and the trio hadn't even begun their ascent.

"Excellent," said Snowize. "That means we'll have the crime scene all to ourselves."

"I'm not so sure," said Ever. "I have the strangest feeling that we're being watched."

Snowize surveyed their surroundings. "I don't see another soul out here."

It was true that there didn't appear to be anyone else around, but Ever couldn't shake the nagging feeling that they were not alone. Something had caught her eye earlier, the flash of something reflective. A signaling mirror, perhaps? Or the lens of a telescope?

"Speaking of crime scenes," signed Snitch, "where is the sock?"

As if by magic, Snowize produced a smelly old sock from his sleeve. He dangled it in front of Snitch, who approached it and breathed in deeply to memorize the scent. The sock, it turned out, belonged to Yoshinobu Azayaka. It had been waiting for them at the reception desk of the hotel in Tokyo, in an envelope marked:

SNOWIZE & SNITCH: . . . --- . . .

The dots and dashes, Ever quickly recognized, was Morse code for the universal distress signal. It also spelled out the letters SOS, which has come to mean Save Our Souls. In this case, however, it stood for Smelly Old Sock.

"I don't know how she got hold of Yoshi's old sock, but sometimes that Miffingpin can be marvelous," said Snowize, with a hint of admiration in his voice. The admiration didn't last long. Detective Snowize suddenly gripped Ever by the shoulder. He grabbed Snitch by the scruff of the neck.

"All right, all right!" he shouted. "I'll open it. I'll open your urgent t-mail! Just stop the noise! *Stop the noise, Miffingpin!*"

He turned to Ever. "I spoke too soon. This woman is trying to kill me with her urgent t-mail alarm." To alleviate his pain, he began repeatedly slapping his forehead with the palm of his hand.

Thought mail, Snitch hastily signed to Ever, was a lot like e-mail, only it went directly from one mind to another. You didn't need a computer; you just need a brain and a small chip. The reason Snowize was in such pain was because the t-mail had an alarm attached to it that would only stop once the message was opened. Snowize nodded to confirm this was the case.

"Incoming t-mail," he said, reading the t-mail aloud in a mocking tone. "You have one new message. To listen to your t-mail, think *yes*, followed by your secret password."

Snitch surmised that the only reason Snowize was struggling to open the message was that he had forgotten his password. He signed his suspicions to Ever.

"Nonsense," snapped Snowize, who was watching. "I have it right here, at the tip of my tongue. It's . . . it's . . ." Ever watched him frown as he struggled to recall the password.

"Nazgurath!" he whispered loudly, sighing with relief as Deodora's voice appeared in his head: *Harry, just a reminder that your t-mail password is nazgurath. Keep it safe. D.*

As soon as he processed her words, Snowize was instantly annoyed. "Does that Miffingpin woman think I'm a complete idiot? I've never in my entire life for—I've never failed to remember anything. Never. *Ever.*"

Snitch, still in his misshapen cat suit, raised a drooping eyebrow. He gave Ever a knowing look.

"She is without a doubt the most annoying woman I've ever had the misfortune of not meeting," added Snowize.

"You've really never met her?" asked Ever.

"Of course I haven't," said Snowize. "What kind of Secret Secretary would she be if I knew who she was?"

Snitch sighed and nodded in agreement as the trio began trudging along the zigzagging path that led up the mountain. The detectives were hampered by their cumbersome disguises, both of which were starting to look a lot worse for wear.

"What's it like, this thought mail?" asked Ever as the volcanic scree crunched beneath her feet.

"Horrible," said Snowize, adjusting his traditional Japanese robe that limited his usual long strides. "And ghastly, too. It's like having someone else's voice in your head. It's as if someone else is thinking their thoughts to you. No matter where I am, asleep or awake, dreaming or comatose, someone can interrupt my peace of mind with a message. It is possibly the most annoying thing ever to be invented," he added. "It's more annoying than children who arrive unannounced through tunnels that didn't exist the day before, claiming their guardians have disappeared and their deceased parents named them after an adverb of frequency like Sometimes, Often, Always or Ever." He gave Ever a wink to show he didn't really mean any offense by this.

Ever paused to take in a deep breath. The air was definitely thinning as they climbed higher, and she was struggling to get enough oxygen into her lungs. The volcanic scree was now covered in powdery snow that came up to her ankles.

"There is an old Japanese proverb," said Snowize, stopping to take in the view and to adjust the rubber mask of his disguise. "He who climbs Mount Fuji once is a wise man. He who climbs it twice is a fool."

"I wonder," signed Snitch, "what they would say about those who climb Mount Fuji searching for a crime scene while dressed in itchy disguises and holding up a smelly old—" Snitch froze. He held up his paw and sniffed the air. "We're getting closer. I've picked up Yoshinobu's scent." It was a struggle to sniff properly through the nostril holes of the rubber cat suit, but the scent was unmistakably there.

"And Ever's right. We're not alone," he added. "There's someone else on one of the other paths."

"Perhaps it's the criminal returning to the scene of the crime," suggested Snowize, his eyes lighting up with excitement at the prospect.

Ever couldn't explain why, but she still had a horrible

sense of foreboding. If someone was indeed following them, the detectives were at a disadvantage in their clumsy outfits. Snitch was struggling to walk under the additional weight of the awkward disguise, and there was also the growing threat of altitude sickness.

As they completed another switchback, Ever stopped. Just off the path stood a large snowman. It had coins for eyes and a silk tie and top hat as adornments. On closer inspection, Ever saw the coins were fifty-yen pieces, with holes at the very center. *Strange*, she thought, noting that while there were footsteps leading up to the snowman, there didn't appear to be any leading away from it. As the Doc would say, something didn't add up here. That's when she noticed that there was a pin on the tie. Moving closer to examine it, she almost shouted out in surprise. It was the exact same pin as the one worn by the creepy man on the plane, inscribed with the ColdCorp Corporation logo and the Latin motto: *Mater artium necessitas. Necessity is the mother of invention.* Something about the words themselves troubled her.

But before Ever could express further misgivings, Snitch started signaling frantically.

"We're here!" Snitch made his way excitedly through the snow to a spot about twenty feet from the peculiar snowman.

"Yoshinobu Azayaka stood here, in this very spot. I can smell the whole scene. . . ." Snitch's nose twitched rapidly from side to side. "In one hand, Yoshinobu carried a sword and in the other . . . in the other hand, he held either a chameleon or a rose."

"Perhaps both?" suggested Snowize. Snitch shook his head. He wasn't sure. Fresh snow had fallen and muffled some of the scents.

"It smells like it's half chameleon and half rose. It was

definitely not one or the other; it was a mixture of the two," he declared.

Ever carefully made a note of this in the little notebook that she'd picked up at the hotel. Since these were not the most effective detectives, it wouldn't hurt for her to practice her own detecting skills. She added some further thoughts: *What do you get if you cross a chameleon with a rose? A rose that catches flies? A chameleon that smells like a rose?*

"Go on, Snitch," urged Snowize. "What else do you pick up? The scent of his killer, perhaps?"

"There was no one else with him," signed Snitch. "He was alone when he died."

"Impossible," concluded Snowize. "He did not take his own life. Someone or something took it from him."

"But there are no signs of foul play," signed Snitch. "No scent belonging to anyone else. Except," and here he turned around and pointed, "for that snowman. Built just hours ago by someone with malice as pure as the driven snow in his wicked heart."

"Forget the snowman. We're not looking for smells from today, we want clues to the past," said Snowize as he paced up and down too energetically for an old man. Ever reminded him to slow down and act the age of his disguise, just in case they were being watched.

Snitch shifted uncomfortably and complained that it was getting really hot and itchy under his ill-fitting cat suit. The itchiness was reaching unbearable proportions. He wriggled around and around as he desperately tried to get comfortable. Ever grew dizzy watching him.

"Your cat appears to be having some sort of seizure," said a stranger's voice. Ever turned around sharply. The voice belonged to a concerned English tourist who was carefully making his ascent and staring in vague horror at the wriggling Snitch.

"The cat is fine," Snowize answered in English with a poor Japanese accent. "Just a little bit crazy. Loopy of the loop."

"Oh dear," said the tourist, who now turned to look at Snowize. It was a fortunate move because Snitch's ears were now sliding over his eyes, and his nose and mouth had migrated down to his neck. Ever tried to readjust the disintegrating cat suit, but as she pulled at it, an ear came off. She quickly hid it behind her back and smiled sweetly at the tourist. But the man was staring at Snowize with an awestruck look upon his face.

"Dare I ask, are you perhaps the ancient and wise mountain man Akido-San?" he asked.

"Er . . . yes," said Snowize a little bit too quickly. "That's me. I kid you not. I am Akido-San. Wise beyond my years." He moved to block Ever from the tourist's view as she frantically tried to push Snitch's remaining ear back into an earlike position.

"I have been seeking you for years, wise Akido-San," said the tourist, bowing deeply. Snowize bowed back even more deeply. The tourist politely bowed again, and the detective responded with an even deeper bow. They remained bobbing up and down until Snowize thought the tourist looked sufficiently dizzy and confused.

Behind him, Snitch had stretched the cat suit so badly that his tail appeared to sprout from the back of his head, and his cat paws were splayed out in a very odd way.

"I would be honored to hear your words of wisdom, Akido-San," said the tourist.

Snowize cleared his throat as he searched for something wise to say. "No man is a mountain," he said slowly.

He closed his eyes and breathed out a great big sigh. The tourist smiled in admiration. By now, Snitch's cat suit was in such a convoluted tangle that the rat's only choice was to tear his way out of the disguise. As the tourist turned to see what Ever was trying to hide, Snowize blurted out more words of wisdom. "When the rat emerges from the cat, it will be a year of great turmoil."

The poor man's eyes almost popped out of his head as Snitch burst out of his cat suit. The tourist fell to his knees and began to sob, believing he had just witnessed a miracle.

"Sorry," Snitch signed to Snowize. "It was so hot in there I had no choice."

Snowize was not impressed. "We'd better get out of here before our cover is totally blown," he whispered back.

The tourist watched in amazement as the old man and a rat raced down the steep slopes of Mount Fuji. They were followed by a young girl who could barely keep up with them. He thought it remarkable that a man so old could move so quickly. The tourist was still marveling at the sight when he heard a strange muffled sound. That's when he noticed the snowman just a few feet away. It seemed to be trembling and shaking. Then it fell apart completely to reveal a man in a suit who stepped right out of it, shook clumps of snow off his jacket and placed the snowman's tie around his own shirt collar. Then he peeled the yen from his eyes and blinked them open.

"Are you all right?" the man in the suit asked the tourist. "I see you are sobbing, a clear indication of emotional distress in the unengineered human."

"Oh, I am well!" The tourist beamed. "I'm blessed. I've just seen a miracle!"

"Is that so?" the man commented, but his gaze was fixed on the hasty footprints left by Ever and the detectives.

It was then that the tourist noticed the pallor of the man's face and the icy malice in his disturbing eyes— electric blue eyes that shone with an eerie glow. The tourist backed away and hastily resumed his climb.

The former snowman didn't even notice. He was too busy staring at the three sets of footprints. Then he bent down and scooped up a handful of snow from the nearest one. He tasted it with the tip of his tongue and his eyes blazed. "Snowize," he whispered, and almost smiled at the irony. "Not so wise after all. And not so long for this world, either." Then he speed dialed a number on his cell phone and whispered, "The falcon has landed. Activate Operation Avalanche."

11

Secret Thoughts of a Secret Secretary

Far away in an undisclosed location somewhere on the planet, Deodora Miffingpin was at her wit's end. She wanted to tear her hair out. Being the Secret Secretary to Harry Snowize, Private Investigator, and most eloquent spy, was by far the most frustrating and challenging assignment ever. She tugged at a few strands of her hair in sheer desperation.

"Ouch!" she muttered to herself. "That's it. Another two weeks and then I'll resign. I'll admit that I've failed in my mission, and I'll accept the consequences. I'll accept that . . ." But her voice trailed off, and she couldn't bring herself to say the words. She wasn't ready to believe that Harry Snowize was a lost cause. She was not ready to write a letter recommending that he be kicked out of the Secret Society of Spies Anonymous.

Working with him was absolutely infuriating. It was also heartbreaking. Every time she t-mailed or spoke to him, she hoped that would be the day he remembered her. But it never happened. She tried not to take it personally, but that was impossible under the circumstances. Of all the people in the world, surely he couldn't have forgotten who she was? And now there was a young girl who had arrived mysteriously, and Deodora felt she had to be there for the sake of the child. Just the thought of the little girl in peril made tears spring to her eyes. Snowize had given her no details. All he'd said was that the girl was asking for help. Deodora wiped the tears away and told herself to be strong. She could be of no help to any of them if she fell apart at the seams.

Almost every member of the elite group of spies who belonged to the SSSA had told her to give up on Snowize. He had spent too much time squished inside a tooth. The experimental procedure that had put him there had been dangerous, and Snowize had paid a high price for the risk he'd taken. It had cost him a chunk of himself, and it might yet cost him his career as a spy.

Whenever the rumors flew, Deodora always sprang to his defense, reminding everyone of the brilliant work he'd done in the past. She spoke of the lives he'd saved, the impossible missions he'd made possible. Unfortunately, in spy circles, you were only as good as your last mission. And if your last mission had gone horribly wrong because you forgot a very simple password and almost lost your partner to an error in judgment, then your capabilities were brought into question.

A vote was taken at a very hush-hush meeting of the SSSA. Deodora was the only member who stood up for Snowize. Everyone else voted to have him expelled from the group.

"He deserves another chance," Deodora stated, to which everyone responded that he'd already been given a second chance and messed it up. That's when Deodora reached up her sleeve and produced a copy of the Society's hidden rules. She triumphantly read out rule number 877. "A spy who has shown exceptional ability in the past should be given a second, second chance."

There was a lot of grumbling and mumbling about this, but eventually it was agreed that Harry Snowize was entitled to a second, second chance to prove his worth. Rules, after all, were rules and as much as they disliked this one, they would have to obey it. They insisted that during this trial period, Snowize would have to be secretly monitored. Deodora volunteered for the position because it was better for her to check up on him than have some stranger do it. It was also a way for her to be close to him.

If Snowize failed in his mission, he would be thrown out of the SSSA and lose his reputation. Reputations, once lost, are extremely difficult to get back. All Snowize knew was that there were those in the SSSA who whispered behind his back and who wanted him kicked out. He was not particularly bothered by this. In fact, he'd conveniently forgotten that he'd messed up his previous mission and that Snitch had saved the day.

"That's not the only thing he's forgotten," sighed Deodora, playing absentmindedly with her wedding band and fighting back tears.

Stop wallowing in the past, she told herself, *and concentrate on the fact that Harry Snowize is not responding to your latest thought mail.*

In the last half hour, she had re-sent the same t-mail three times, and he had failed to open any of them. The t-mail contained vital new information about the kidnapping of Professor Gustav Cadiz. Either Harry was ignoring her, which he sometimes tried to do, or something might be terribly wrong in Tokyo. Or he was just angry about their last t-mail exchange. She flipped through the messages and replayed them in her mind. Even though some of it was particularly mean, she secretly liked hearing his voice in her head.

DEODORA! his last t-mail shouted in his most annoyed voice. *For Heaven's sake, stop trying to kill me with your urgent alarm. Why send me a ridiculous message reminding me of my password?* Then he'd added, quite thoughtlessly, *How did I end up with a Secret Secretary who is so very irritating and clearly not very bright?*

That was one of the problems with t-mail; it allowed thoughtless thoughts to slip through. The Telepath® network was working on a filter that would allow you to think twice before sending any unkind thoughts.

Deodora had given an aloof and businesslike reply.

Detective Snowize, you may find me annoying and irritating, but the message I sent was the coded message we agreed upon. It's really a reminder to change your password every two weeks for security reasons.

This was a plan they'd decided on together, to confuse anyone trying to tap into his t-mail or steal his password. The fact that he'd forgotten about it made her anxious about his state of mind. So she'd sent him the only threat she knew that would make him take her seriously and watch his step.

Sigh If you slip up again I'm afraid . . . I'm afraid I will have to report it. And we both know that means a visit to the Spychiatrist. ☺

This had made Snowize even more furious, and he'd let a bunch of extremely angry thoughts slip through, ones that were too unpleasant to replay, but which expressed his horror and disgust at the thought of visiting a spy doctor.

That was the last she'd heard from him, and that had been a while ago. If he didn't respond soon, she'd have no choice but to attach a more alarming alarm to this next t-mail. She needed to be kept in the loop. Something told her the detectives and the girl were not safe, that this case was leading them into deeper trouble than they could handle.

12

Avalanche

As they ran down the mountain, Ever heard a rumble and a whooshing sound that filled her heart with dread. *Don't look back,* she told herself, but she couldn't resist. She had to know what was making the muffled, roaring noise behind her. *Curiosity killed the cat,* a little voice in her head warned, but she turned around anyway. What she saw made her freeze like a pillar of salt.

"Keep moving," yelled Snowize. Ever could tell from the urgent note in his voice that he had never been more serious, and for good reason. A gigantic wave of snow was bearing down on them, moving at what had to be at least eighty miles an hour.

Even as Snowize yelled, "Avalanche!" Ever struggled to overcome the terror that firmly rooted her to the spot. She watched as Snowize leaned down to pick up Snitch, his robes flapping around him as he ran. With growing dread, Ever realized that even if she could persuade her feet to move, there was no way they could outrun the approaching wave. It was going to swallow them whole.

In an amazing feat of both athleticism and courage, Snowize ran five steps back up the slope toward Ever,

grabbed her hand and pressed a small disc-shaped object into it. "Hold on to this for dear life!" he commanded above the deafening roar. "Do the backstroke once the snow hits, and if we're buried, cross your hands in front of your face to create an air pocket," he yelled.

And that's the last thing Ever heard as the snow bore down on them.

She tried her best to do the backstroke, but that helped for only a few seconds before she was carried away and then completely overwhelmed and engulfed. With great difficulty, she pulled her hands in front of her face, creating a small pocket of air. And then all was dark.

An eerie quiet replaced the roar. The silence was deathly. *Experts advise taking in a deep breath before the snow freezes. This will expand your chest and give you more room to breathe.* Ever was once again glad she had read the entire *Encyclopedia Britannicus* from A to Z, even if it had been an old edition from the 1970s that had been collecting dust in a corner of the Doc's laboratory. She breathed in as deeply as she could while the snow around her set like concrete. It pressed on her chest, squeezing the breath out of her, while the cold numbed her face and hands.

She tried to slow her breathing so that she wouldn't use up her limited supply of oxygen, but she could sense her brain already growing weird and sluggish as it was deprived of life's most necessary element. As the cold seeped in, Ever wondered who would miss her. Certainly not her missing parents. If they were alive, as the crow had suggested, they hadn't put any effort into finding her. The Doc, she imagined, would be devastated under normal circumstances, but right now he was too busy fleeing evil pursuers. Perhaps Melschman, once he was switched back on, but she realized that was just wishful thinking. He was a robot and not a very sentimental one, and he'd still be very angry at her for leaving him midwave under a baobab tree. It had been only days ago, but it felt like a lifetime, like a distant dream that had happened to someone else entirely. She wanted to reach for her locket, to smell the cinnamon and roses one last time, but it was now physically impossible for her to move. She could no longer feel any part of herself at all.

Images flashed before her: The strange snowman with the yen coins for eyes. The pin with the words, *Necessity is the mother of invention*. The creepy man on the plane wearing the same pin. The Doc pointing to his head, repeating over and over, *They want what is most precious to me.*

That's when she made the connection. Ever could have sworn she heard a *click-click* in her head as it fell into place. It was his *inventions* and ideas that were most precious to the Doc. That's what he feared—that someone was after them. And somehow, something told her, the ColdCorp Corporation was involved. *The great pity*, thought Ever, *is that this important clue is going to be buried along with me in a snowy grave.*

But the *click-click* she'd heard was not just in her head, because now she heard it again. Which meant she was still alive, if only just barely. It was followed by a repetitive *scritch-scritch-scritch* sound. Within seconds something had dug a small tunnel from her nose to the surface. Ever felt the air rushing in. She inhaled hungrily, filling her lungs. After more *scritch-scritching*, she was blinking snow from her eyes and looking up into the bright blue sky. A metal insect, about the size of a very large beetle, was moving snow from her face with specially designed spadelike digging appendages.

Suddenly a set of hands and paws were also helping to dig her out. An old Japanese man and a rat lifted her up into a sitting position. The silver insect, its work now done, folded its legs inward like a Swiss Army knife and once more became a smooth silver disc that fitted into the palm of a hand.

"The Diggadisc," said Snowize. "I never leave home without a few of these in my pocket. They'll dig you out of any premature burial situation. What saves you is the tunnel that establishes vital access from your nostrils to the air supply. They can dig through sand and snow, or chew their way through metal and concrete. Terribly handy little fellows." He scooped up the disc and put it back into his pocket.

"Inventions!" was the first word out of Ever's mouth once she stopped chattering with cold. "That's what they're after." And as the three of them, slightly battered and bruised, moved slowly down the mountain, she told the detectives about the clue she'd recognized while buried beneath the snow.

"I'm sorry, but it's a bit feeble, young lady," was Snowize's response as the bedraggled trio finally entered their suite at the Hotel Okinawa. "Perhaps the lack of oxygen to your brain interfered with your power of reasoning. It's a bit of a stretch to say the ColdCorp Corporation is somehow connected to our case just because their company pin was worn by an evil-smelling man on a plane and an odd snowman at the scene of a crime."

Ever's shivering was replaced with annoyance. It wasn't as if the detective had come up with any better deductions himself, but she didn't say this aloud because, just then, it appeared that the same itchiness that had plagued Snitch in his disguise was now attacking Snowize.

"Holy macaroni!" Snowize exclaimed. "It's so hot in here. And itchy!"

He wriggled around in discomfort and, in desperation, stuck his thumbs up his nose and proceeded to rip off his old-man face.

"Now what are we going to do? We don't have any backup disguises," signed Snitch.

"Never fear," Snowize assured him, "I have a brilliant plan. Take note and learn from a master of disguise."

Snitch and Ever watched as he removed the remaining bits of his costume and disappeared into the bathroom. When he returned, he had changed into a suit with a bright green tie.

"Ta da!" he exclaimed. "So? What do you think?"

"That's it?" Snitch asked in disbelief. "*That's* your new disguise?"

Snowize grinned a boyish grin. "Well, what do you say? Brilliant or just plain incredible?"

"Incredible," said Ever, finding it hard to believe that Snowize was being serious.

"But you look exactly like yourself," signed Snitch. "Technically, it's not really a disguise at all."

"Oh, but that is where you're dead wrong," said Snowize. "It happens to be the perfect disguise because no one is expecting to see Harry Snowize alive. Rumor has it that I'm dead. My best friends don't even know I'm alive. So, if someone does recognize me, they'll simply think I'm a Snowize look-alike."

Snitch scratched his ear nervously, signing to Ever behind his back that he worried that Snowize's condition might be far more serious than he or Deodora had originally thought.

Before they could say anything further, a look of pain and annoyance darkened Snowize's expression.

"Miffingpin!" he roared. "Are you trying to kill me? Using a high-pitched dentist drill as a t-mail alarm?" He danced around the room in agony, sporadically smacking the palm of his hand against his forehead to ease the pain. "Snitch, what's my new password?" he yelled.

"You never told me," signed Snitch.

"Yes, I did! I most certainly did!" shouted Snowize, struggling to hear himself.

Desperate to end his pain, Ever and Snitch threw out a few suggestions.

"What about *password*? Could that be it?" Ever asked.

"Do I look like a fool?" snapped Snowize.

When they ran out of options, Snitch tentatively signed, "Perhaps you for—failed to change it?"

"That would be most unlike me," Snowize mumbled. "Nothing ever slips my mind."

Ever noted the look of momentary panic that flitted across the detective's handsome face. She recognized that feeling of helplessness—she had felt it so many times herself when sheer panic prevented her from answering exam questions. She wished she could help him somehow, especially now as he stood banging his head against the wooden door.

In desperation, Snowize tried his old password, *nazgurath*, which instantly opened the t-mail. "Seems I didn't change it after all," he muttered, adding, "I'm sure I had my reasons. No doubt, very good reasons." But it was clear to Ever that he had no idea what those reasons might be.

Snowize read the t-mail out loud for their benefit. "Harry, I have good and bad news. The good news is they've found Professor Cadiz. He's safely back home with his wife. The bad news is he's suffered some sort of breakdown and is acting very strangely. It's as if a big part of his mind is missing. I've arranged for you to travel to Spain as soon as you're done in Tokyo. Please reply as soon as possible. D."

Snowize responded immediately. *Nice touch with the*

dentist's drill, Deodora. Really charming. Sometimes I wonder whether you might want me dead. Or mad. Or both, in no particular order. The ridiculous disguises you sent have fallen apart. Great choice on your part.

As soon as he tried to send the t-mail, a computer-generated voice entered his mind. *The t-mail you are about to send contains heavy sarcasm and may be offensive. Are you sure you wish to send it?*

"Yes!" Snowize said out loud, noting that the t-mail system had been upgraded in the most annoying way.

You might wish to breathe deeply and count to ten before sending.

No, he thought, *I want to* send. *Now!*

This was just an automated suggestion brought to you by the Telepath® network. Your thoughts are with us. We are always in your mind!™

Before he could say anything else he might regret, Snowize was interrupted by an urgent knocking at the door. He put a finger to his lips, flattened himself against the wall and motioned for Ever and Snitch to do likewise. Then, very slowly, he reached for the handle and eased the door open, all the while remaining hidden behind it.

The floorboards creaked ever so slightly as a man tiptoed into the room. Snowize blinked his eyes a few times to make sure they weren't deceiving him. Standing before him was the last person on earth he ever expected to see.

13

Yoshinobu, Noshiyobu and the Man Who Melted

Ever held her breath as the man inched farther into the room, brandishing a dazzling sword. He was dressed in all black, somewhat reminiscent of a ninja, with his long hair tied back in a single plait.

"Show yourselves!" cried the man in English, as he cut the air with a stroke of the deadly blade.

"Yoshinobu!" cried Snowize exuberantly, tears of joy welling up in his eyes. "Ever and Snitch, meet Yoshinobu Azayaka. Scientist. Inventor. Genius. And dear friend. Dear *alive* friend!"

But Yoshinobu did not seem to share the detective's joy. Instead, he whirled around, sword clasped in both hands, muscles taut, ready to slice his enemies in half. A delighted Snowize moved forward to embrace him. Yoshinobu did not lower his sword.

"No," he said, shaking his head sadly, "Yoshinobu is very much dead."

The detective leaned forward and touched Yoshinobu's arm. "This is a living arm. Blood runs through these veins, does it not?"

Yoshinobu leaped forward in a dramatic somersault and pinned Snowize against the wall, pointing the sword directly at the detective's throat. Ever could see both their reflections in the highly polished metal blade. Snitch covered his eyes, afraid to witness his partner's final moment.

"My friend," Snowize tried to reason.

"I'm not your *friend*," the man spat. "I have never met you before." The man's eyes burned with anger as he increased the pressure of the blade against the detective's skin. "But I did see you on Mount Fuji, sniffing around, sneaking about in devious disguises."

"You were the one watching us from afar!" Ever blurted out. She pointed to the binoculars hanging around his neck, realizing it had been light reflecting off those lenses that she'd seen.

"Yes," the man admitted, not moving the sword even a millimeter. "I've been watching the crime scene for days. After you survived that unusual avalanche, I followed you here, convinced you were not what you appeared to be."

Snowize took advantage of Yoshinobu's momentary distraction. He closed his eyes and breathed in deeply. Then he did the impossible. He pushed his body into the wall, creating a space between himself and the sword where there was none to create. Ever watched in wonder. She had never seen anything like it before. For a second, the wall rippled liquidly, and Snowize slipped away from the sword. Then, quick as lightning, he did a backward somersault through the air away from his opponent, avoiding the blade of the sword and landing perfectly balanced on one leg, arms ready to deflect any blow that might come his way.

Yoshinobu's jaw dropped. "Where did you learn that?" he demanded.

"Yoshinobu-san, we both know that it was you who taught me the ancient techniques of The Way of The Way," said Snowize solemnly.

The man lowered his sword. "I am not Yoshinobu. I am his identical twin brother, Noshiyobu."

Ever could see the disappointment in the detective's eyes and the deep sadness etched into Noshiyobu's face.

"I believe you must be a friend of my brother's, for only he could have taught you how to master that move," he added with a sigh.

"Yes. Your brother taught me many things. He also saved my life by helping me hide in the unlikeliest of places."

Noshiyobu was astonished. "Are you telling me you're Harry Snowize? The spy who hid in a human tooth?"

"Yes. Your brother thought it was sheer madness, but nevertheless, he complied with my wishes. And he never once turned his back on me."

Noshiyobu nodded. "That is what my brother was like. Loyal and wise to the very end."

"And secretive," added Snowize. "I never even knew he had a brother."

"We were rivals for a long time," sighed Noshiyobu. "For over twenty years."

"Why?" asked Ever, opening her notebook and writing, *Can we trust rival brother?*

"Ah," replied Noshiyobu. "For the silliest of reasons: We both fell in love with the same woman. She couldn't decide which of us to marry and it created a terrible rift. Even after she ran off with a trapeze artist and joined the circus, we still did not speak. I left for America, fool that I was, and severed all contact with my brother.

Then, five months ago, our lives crossed paths. Little did I realize that I would lose him again so soon, this time forever."

"Murder most foul," said Snowize.

Noshiyobu nodded in agreement and then spoke in a whisper. "We must leave immediately. You're not safe. The avalanche that almost devoured you was not solely the work of Mother Nature."

"Are you saying it was deliberately triggered?" asked Snowize.

Noshiyobu nodded. "We cannot talk here. The walls have ears. The mirrors have eyes." He motioned for them to be silent. "Follow me. We're going on a trip down Memory Lane."

Noshiyobu led Ever and the detectives through the Tokyo traffic and beyond the daunting high-rises, until they found themselves weaving through an intricate network of narrow alleyways lined with noodle bars. Delicious smells emanated from every direction.

The bustling Omoido Yokocho district, whose name literally means Memory Lane, is located just north of busy Shinjuku station. Ever recalled the exact page of the *Encyclopedia Britannicus* where she'd once read this seemingly useless information.

"Stay close," whispered Noshiyobu as they wound deeper into the maze of tiny eateries. He came to a stop at a noodle bar and directed them inside to plastic chairs at a small table. Soon, they were being served plates of vegetables, fish and noodles. Ever hadn't realized how hungry she was until the plate of steaming ramen was placed before her. As they slurped up noodles, Noshiyobu recounted how he and his brother had been reunited months before.

"It all began at a genetics conference in Las Vegas, Nevada," he told them. "I was meditating by a water fountain when a man approached me. The man was very nervous and sweating profusely. 'Listen,' he told me. 'Your life is in terrible danger.'

"I was taken aback. I could think of no reason that my life would be in danger. I was even further perplexed when the man told me that someone was after my latest invention. The truth was, I had not recently invented anything. The man whispered anxiously that he was referring to my work concerning the chameleon and the rose. Again, I had no idea what he was talking about."

Snitch perked up at this and nudged Snowize in the ribs.

Noshiyobu continued. "The sweating man became frantic. He urged me to trust him, dabbing at his brow with a handkerchief that was instantly soaked through. I watched in fascination as a pool of sweat began collecting at the man's feet.

"'They're coming for you, and they have no mercy,' he said. 'They will take what is most precious to you.'"

Upon hearing these words, Ever slurped down a noodle and put down her chopsticks, riveted. Those were the exact words the Doc had used.

"I thought about what my most precious possession might be," said Noshiyobu. "'My blue suede shoes,' I wondered out loud. 'Why would anyone take my blue suede shoes?'

"The sweaty man became agitated. 'This is no time for jokes,' he said. 'I'm running out of time. If they find me now, they'll kill me.'

"My eyes were drawn to the pool of sweat at the man's

feet, which was by now a large puddle. 'What is wrong with you?' I couldn't help asking.

"'There's no time to explain,' answered the man in a liquid voice. And with that, to my astonishment, he melted and disappeared. All that was left was a puddle, a shiny patent-leather shoe and a wide-brimmed hat."

14

The Name of the Rose

"You're saying that this man actually melted before your eyes?" asked Ever, trying to be sure she'd heard correctly.

"Yes," insisted Noshiyobu. "I know it's hard to believe. It was hard for me to believe at the time. But the man had truly melted. I felt a chill down my spine as I realized he must have mistaken me for my twin brother. It was my brother's life that was in danger."

Snowize and Snitch looked at each other, each with an eyebrow raised. And then they both looked at Ever, whose heart was racing. She had written down in her notebook under the heading Peculiar Facts the following peculiar facts:

1. Man warned of danger.
2. Man sweated profusely.
3. Man melted!!!
4. Man left behind hat and shoe.

"I believe you," Ever said to Noshiyobu. "It's just like the crow that brought me a message from the future. The crow also melted. No one would believe me, either."

"You're the first person who has not doubted me," said Noshiyobu with a grateful nod in Ever's direction.

"I think," said Snowize, "we can conclude that the Doc's disappearance and Yoshinobu's death are somehow connected."

Ever had to bite her tongue to stop herself from saying she'd been telling him that all along. Instead, she urged Noshiyobu to continue with his story, eager for more details and hoping there might be some clue among them that could help save the Doc from a similar fate.

Noshiyobu then told of how he immediately returned to Japan to warn his brother of the evil forces that were plotting against him. It was a bittersweet reunion because there was no way to recover the many years they had lost over a silly argument. But happily, a delighted Yoshinobu was eager to forgive and forget. He invited his brother to his laboratory where he showed him the most exciting thing he'd ever invented.

"What was it?" asked Ever, unable to contain herself.

"To describe it would be to diminish it," said Noshiyobu. "That's why I've brought you here to see for yourselves."

Noshiyobu led them to a door in the alleyway behind the noodle bar. It was a plain red door with no markings on it. He drummed on the door with both hands, tapping out a very specific rhythm. The drumming turned out to be a code that released an intricate security mechanism in the door. Seven hundred and seventy-seven locks within the mechanism released, one after the other, and as they did, they each struck a bell that sang out an ancient Japanese lullaby.

Ever was the first to step through the open door. She found herself in a surprisingly large, sparkling room that was perfectly white, from floor to ceiling. Behind spotless glass cabinets were bottles and test tubes, pipettes and flasks, all precisely organized according to their various shapes and sizes. Everything had its place, and nothing was out of place.

Once they were all inside, Noshiyobu directed their attention to a sterile, white table in the center of the room. In a clear glass vase was a single white rose that was perfect and beautiful in every way.

"Behold, the Chameleon Rose," said Noshiyobu. He stepped over to the flower. From his pocket he pulled a blue handkerchief and held it gently against one of the petals. Within a few seconds, the entire rose became a deep blue, the exact hue of the handkerchief. Next, he held a silver spoon against a petal. The blue faded and was replaced by a shimmering metallic silver. Ever was astonished by its loveliness. Even Snowize was at a loss for words.

"That was it," signed Snitch. "That's what smelled half chameleon and half rose on the mountain." Ever quickly translated the sign language for Noshiyobu's sake.

"Yes," said Noshiyobu. "By inserting the genetic material from a chameleon into the cells of a rose, my brother created his masterpiece. It took years of hard work to perfect. And the rose not only changes color; it can mimic texture and pattern as well."

"A rose like this," said Snowize, "would be extremely valuable. Who would not want to buy magical roses that could be any color you desired?"

"Exactly!" agreed Noshiyobu, and once again his eyes filled with sadness. He told them how excited Yoshinobu had been to share his success with his long lost brother. His plan was to introduce his invention to the world the next day, with Noshiyobu at his side.

"Of course, I wished I could have been as excited as

my brother," said Noshiyobu wistfully. "But the moment I saw the Chameleon Rose, it called to mind the warning of the man who had melted, and I could not help but fear for my brother's life. Yoshinobu, however, was not at all concerned. He reassured me that the details of his invention were safely stored inside his head, where no one could get to them. He insisted that no one else knew about the Chameleon Rose, except for one big company that had made an offer to buy his invention. An offer he had refused because he knew it was worth far more."

"By any chance," asked Ever, "was this company the ColdCorp Corporation?"

Noshiyobu stared at her as if she had suddenly grown tentacles.

"Oh, please ignore the child. She's overenthusiastic, and she's got it into her head that she's actually an investigator on this case," said Snowize with an apologetic laugh.

But Noshiyobu's expression did not change. "How could you possibly know that?" he asked Ever.

Ever smiled shyly. Her powers of deductive reasoning had long been sharpened by her guardian, and now they were paying off. "Just a hunch," she said demurely. Snitch gave her a thumbs-up while Snowize continued to look perplexed.

"The day after our celebration," Noshiyobu continued, "when he was supposed to reveal the Chameleon Rose to the world, my brother disappeared. He was nowhere to be found. Eventually, I broke down the door to his laboratory and found it empty and untouched. The smell of roses lingered in the air, but there was no sign of him. I searched everywhere for my twin, but to no avail." Noshiyobu bowed his head in deep sorrow. Ever could see how difficult it was for him to relate what happened next. In her notebook, she scratched Noshiyobu's name from her list of suspects, leaving only one:

Suspects

1. ~~Noshiyobu, jealous brother~~

2. The ColdCorp Corporation

With a heavy heart and through several awkward pauses, Noshiyobu described his brother's untimely demise. A week after his disappearance, he found Yoshinobu wandering around a Tokyo fish market, lost and confused, balancing a dead fish on his head. He was a changed man. He could not remember where he'd been. In fact, he could not even remember his own name, and nothing he said made any sense. Finally, he stopped talking altogether.

Day after day, Yoshinobu sat staring at nothing in particular, refusing food and water. Then a headline appeared in the *Tokyo Sun* that shocked Noshiyobu: COLDCORP CORPORATION ANNOUNCES THE INVENTION OF THE CHAMELEON ROSE. Noshiyobu went pale as he read further.

"No," he whispered. "It's not possible. It can't be." But it was. ColdCorp Corporation was proud to announce that its scientists had come up with an amazing invention. Noshiyobu didn't show the upsetting article to his brother, who sat staring into space. The next day, Yoshinobu's lifeless body was found on the slopes of Mount Fuji.

"As you can imagine, I was beyond devastated. I wandered the streets wracked with grief, trying to understand what had happened, convinced that ColdCorp had stolen my brother's invention and passed it off as its own. But I had no evidence, no proof, and everyone I spoke to thought I was mad."

Noshiyobu reached into a fold in his robe and brought out a worn copy of a newspaper article. He read it aloud with great sadness.

TOP SCIENTIST SLAYS HIMSELF IN WAKE OF BITTER DISAPOINTMENT

Yoshinobu Azayaka, one of our nation's top scientists, took his own life today. It's suspected that he suffered a nasty blow when a rival team of scientists beat him in the quest to develop the ultimate rose. Cold-Corp Corporation, under the leadership of Laszlo Coldwell, announced its perfection of the Chameleon Rose earlier today. It had no idea Yoshinobu was working on a similar invention. ColdCorp expressed sadness at the untimely passing of such a brilliant mind.

Yoshinobu's twin brother, Noshiyobu Azayaka, would not confirm reports that his brother had shown signs of mental instability in the past week. Police said a note found next to his body was cryptic and deranged. Noshiyobu suspects foul play after he was warned that his brother's life was in danger by a man who mysteriously melted. The police found this hard to believe and noted that insanity tends to run in families. Police concluded that Yoshinobu had suffered bitter disappointment and had sufficient motive to end his life. He remains the only suspect in this fatal act of violence against himself.

Tears now ran freely down Noshiyobu's face. He refused to believe that his brother would give in to disappointment.

"The note he left was addressed to you," he said, handing a small piece of parchment paper to Snowize.

"He addressed it to me? Even though I hadn't seen him in years. . . ? Even though there was no reason to believe I was alive?" asked Snowize.

"Yes," answered Noshiyobu. "The police thought he was crazy addressing this note to a man who was presumed dead. Now you will prove them wrong by shedding light on the meaning of this note."

Noshiyobu bowed deeply in gratitude as Snowize unfolded the piece of paper. The detective stared at the words in complete and utter disbelief. Then he cleared his throat and read them out loud. *"Midori desu. Pinkugakatta shiro desu."*

Noshiyobu nodded his head as each word was spoken. Snowize paused, lowering his eyes to avoid Noshiyobu's penetrating gaze. Ever leaned forward as he quietly translated the words into English: "It's green. It's a pinkish white."

"That's it? That's all he had to say?" signed Snitch, perplexed. Snowize nodded gravely as Ever jotted the words down in her notebook.

"That's it. *It's green. It's a pinkish white.* That's all he wrote," said Snowize.

"But sometimes, one sentence can mean much more than the sum of its words," said Noshiyobu, with a touch of desperation in his voice.

A long silence followed, during which Snowize avoided the hopeful eyes of Noshiyobu Azayaka. Ever could tell that he had no idea what the words meant. They were cryptic, enigmatic and made no sense at all. Absolutely none whatsoever.

15

The Strangest Lunch

It's green. It's a pinkish white.

Ever turned those six words upside down and inside out. She helped Snowize translate them into fifty-three languages. She could only contribute Latin, Zulu and Spanish, while Snowize skimmed through the fifty other languages that he had once spoken fluently. When nothing was revealed, Ever suggested studying the words in a mirror, backward. She tried not to laugh as Snowize stood on his head to better contemplate the words while upside down. But even with the rush of blood to his brain, he had to confess that nothing became clear. No secret meaning revealed itself.

Wondering if the letters of the six words might contain a hidden message, Ever jumbled them all up, shuffled them around and created new sentences. She diligently wrote them down in order of decreasing absurdity.

1. *Ire is in the spaghetti's wink.*
2. *He spit wishes at tiger in ink.*
3. *Is it a white king in her steps?*
4. *Wise in risk in the spaghetti.*

They were all rather silly sentences, but Snowize and Snitch found them intriguing, and Noshiyobu was convinced they were on to something. So they all thought long and hard about what these reconfigured words could mean. Was Snowize being warned against eating spaghetti? Could they be in danger from a white king? Was there a clue hidden in Gan Ku's famous portrait of a tiger that hung in the British Museum? The possibilities were endless.

Snowize suddenly snapped his fingers and announced that he had come to a conclusion. "We are not paranoid conspiracy theorists, we are detectives. We will take the most logical explanation. Quite simply, Yoshinobu's note contains no hidden meaning. He was in no state of mind to send out hidden messages. He was mostly out of his mind. His words mean exactly what they say. He saw *something* that was both green and a pinkish white. That *something* is the mystery we have to uncover, because whatever it was left a lasting and deadly impression on poor Yoshinobu."

Ever found herself agreeing wholeheartedly with this type of reasoning. She also urged the detectives to get going. Another t-mail had come from Deodora that worried them all: *Professor Cadiz is exhibiting increasingly strange behavior. He's stopped talking gibberish and now refuses to say anything at all. Situation dire. The sooner you get over there, the better.*

The signs were all too ominous and all too familiar. Even Noshiyobu urged them to leave before another scientist succumbed to a fate similar to his brother's. Ever started trembling. She kept pushing the thought away, but it kept popping up. Would they be able to get to the Doc before someone got to him? Or would they get to him only to find him speaking nonsense and staring into space? Surely if he were safe, he would have gotten word out to them by now, wouldn't he? In her heart, she feared that the longer he remained silent, the worse the outcome was going to be.

Noshiyobu insisted on driving them to the airport, so Ever and the detectives squeezed onto the back of his motorbike. It was an awkward and terrifying ride as Noshiyobu drove at high speed, whipping around other vehicles in an attempt to elude anyone who might be following them. After a while, above the drone of the traffic and the roaring of the bike's engine, Ever heard another sound, coming from overhead. It sounded like a giant mosquito, high-pitched and whiny. She looked up and then prodded Snitch in the ribs. The rodent looked up in astonishment. They were being followed after all. Something the size and shape of a pizza box was hovering in the air above them. The high-pitched buzzing came from a set of high-tech diaphanous wings. Snitch covered his head with his paws, closed his eyes and hunkered down. Ever urgently tapped Snowize on the shoulder. The detective squinted up with mild curiosity. Then he shrugged and politely rapped his knuckles on Noshiyobu's helmet three times and pointed up.

As soon as he saw they were being followed by an unidentified flying object, Noshiyobu revved the engine and applied maximum speed. He zipped across lanes of traffic, careening and careering as the winged box gave chase. It didn't let them gain even an inch. Ever winced as the edge of the box almost clipped her ear. That's when she caught sight of the letters SSSA in tiny print on its side. It was a special delivery by the Secret Society of Spies Anonymous.

Noshiyobu pulled over near the entrance to the airport to allow his passengers to disembark. The pizza box still hovered above them. As he bade them farewell, he handed Snowize a silver briefcase.

"Look after this," he whispered. "It might help with your investigation." And with that, he roared off, and soon his bike was just another glittering speck in the river of traffic on the highway.

The hovering box carefully landed itself on the pavement beside them. Inside were new disguises and fake passports, courtesy of Deodora. Snowize ushered them all behind a tree where he quickly stuck on a false moustache and a hat. Now he was Señor Benalta from Malta traveling with his niece, Señorita Bonnita. Ever groaned as he handed her a pink dress.

"Oh no, I don't wear dresses," she insisted.

"Which means it's a good disguise," said Snowize, tossing her a pair of silver ballet shoes and a pink bonnet.

"Good thing I don't have any friends, because I wouldn't want them to see me now," said Ever, growing indignant. "I might be small for my age, but I'm almost thirteen. This is humiliating."

"Young lady, a sleuth makes sacrifices. You'll come to learn that dignity is never a prerequisite for a disguise. Now you will slip all of this on quickly before we attract any attention, and I don't want to hear another word from you, is that clear?" He turned his back to give her some privacy.

Ever didn't appreciate his tone, but she stopped complaining when she emerged to find Snitch holding up his disguise and squeaking in utter disgust. She held back her smile. The plan was for Snitch to be passed off as a battery-operated stuffed toy that Ever, aka Bonnita, would carry. He had to wear a silver-studded collar and an embarrassing T-shirt that said, Hug Me, I'm Adorable.

Snowize helped Ever with her bonnet while she adjusted Snitch's collar. Then the disguised trio, two thirds of whom were extremely disgruntled, headed into the airport and over to the security check-in line. Snitch lay down stiffly as he was placed on the conveyer belt along with the hand luggage. As he passed through the X-ray machine, he held his breath and tried not to move, but there was no way to prevent his bony skeleton from showing up brightly, along with his pulsing heart. These were not things you expected to see inside a stuffed toy. The security official stared at the X-ray image in wonder.

"I don't believe it," he said, shaking his head in time to Snitch's heartbeat.

Ever felt panic rising, but the detective, or rather, Señor Benalta from Malta, remained as calm as a clam.

"It's amazing how sophisticated toys are today," he remarked. The security guard nodded in agreement as he let Snitch slide through to the other side, muttering that when he was a boy, he was content to play with simple wooden blocks.

Other than that minor hitch, they had no problem boarding the plane, and the flight to Barcelona via a connection in Paris looked set to be uneventful—that is, until thirteen hours into the journey, when smoke started seeping out of one of the overhead luggage compartments. Ever was busy writing a list in her notebook under the heading *The Case of the Man who Melted—Things to Consider* when she saw the smoke. She had to shake both the detectives awake while a flight attendant quickly put out the small, inexplicable fire with an extinguisher.

Thirty minutes later a slightly rattled flight attendant called over the intercom, asking if anyone knew how to fly a plane. Snitch nudged Snowize in the ribs and implored him to volunteer to fly the plane, but Snowize whispered that he didn't want to draw unnecessary attention to himself. He was certain there was someone more capable who would step up to the challenge.

As the plane banked violently to the right, a panicked Ever pulled at the detective's sleeve.

"Please," she begged. "We can't rely on anyone else." Snitch was of no help. The terrified rat had pulled down his oxygen mask, placed it over his nose and mouth and assumed the brace position.

"Oh, all right," said Snowize grudgingly as Ever, in her pink frock, led him down the aisle to the cockpit. There they discovered that the pilot and copilot were both suffering from severe food poisoning. They were so sick they were having difficulty breathing and could barely manage to drag themselves out of their seats before collapsing in the aisle. At the sight of them writhing on the ground, Snowize sprang into action and took over the controls.

He sang a soothing song over the plane's intercom system, hoping to calm both the frightened passengers and himself. "The rain in Spain falls mainly on the plain," he sang. Ever was surprised by what a deep, comforting voice he had. She even started humming along with him, until she heard the detective praying under his breath that his memory would not fail him in this dire situation. Worse yet, she heard him quietly dictate an urgent t-mail: "Deodora, I'm currently flying a passenger jet. Will possibly be deemed a hero and draw unwanted attention. Please send new disguises. Oh . . . and if you happen to have a copy of the flight manual for a Boeing 747, please t-mail that to me ASAP. Thanks. Harry."

Ever was suitably horrified. "You've never actually flown a plane like this before, have you?" she asked.

"Let's not get caught up in specifics," said Snowize. "If you've flown one plane, you can fly them all. Although, truth be told, I've never flown a plane of any description, Ever. But I did practice very intensely in a flight simulator once."

He stared intently at the array of instruments and buttons on the control panel before him. "Fortunately, we seem to be quite close to our destination," he mused.

Ever turned to the detective and in her most calm and commanding voice said, "Okay then. Reduce altitude to fifteen thousand feet and prepare to release the landing gear." She didn't know who was more surprised by this, she or the detective.

"Thanks for reminding me," he said, reaching up to click a switch.

Ever would later explain to Snowize and Snitch that the Doc had all sorts of journals, manuals and books that he encouraged her to read. She would sometimes curl up in the armchair in the corner of his office, the one that was so soft it almost swallowed her, and flip through notebooks filled with the Doc's uninvented inventions. She browsed the blueprints for singing washing machines, robot fridges, tap-dancing toasters and more; and quite recently, at the Doc's insistence, she had also read up on the mechanics of elevators, cranes, cargo-ship operations and flight instruction manuals for several planes. She could recall them word for word.

Snowize was amazed and grateful. He and Ever made quite a team, with Ever reciting instructions she didn't quite understand and Snowize executing them as if he'd been flying planes all his life.

Half an hour later, the plane landed safely in Barcelona to huge applause and much relief. Ever had to admit that for a defective detective, Harry Snowize was extremely effective. And this time, not that she was keeping score, she wasn't sure if she had saved the detectives or if they had saved each other.

Unfortunately, when they stepped into the terminal, there was a TV crew waiting to interview the hero who had saved the day. It was just the kind of attention they didn't need. Ever was grateful for the pink bonnet that hid her face. She kept Snitch tucked under her arm like a toy and held on to Snowize's hand. Señor Benalta from Malta lowered his hat so that it cast a shadow over his face as cameras flashed. He brushed aside the praise, answered a few questions and then quickly slipped past the microphones.

If they had not been in such a hurry, Snowize, Snitch and Ever might have noticed the man with piercing blue eyes and a very pale face who stood watching the proceedings from a distance. Snitch should have picked up the scent of the cruel man, but his senses were overwhelmed by the smell of chocolate wafting out of the candy store at International Arrivals.

"Master Coldwell, I don't know how, but they made it," the man said softly into his phone. "Neither the fire nor the food-poisoned pilots brought down the plane."

"Are you telling me," came an angry voice over the phone, "that Snowize, the rat and that girl are still alive?"

"Yes," said the clone, feeling deep shame at having failed his Master.

"It's just as well," said the voice. "After searching the Doc's house, we discovered part of a holographic message that mentioned a mysterious growling box that must be in the girl's possession. I want whatever is inside that box." At this, the voice paused. "By the way, do not think for one moment that just because your mistake worked to your benefit, you will not be punished." There was an unhappy hiss on the other end of the line, then complete silence. The man with the cruel blue eyes snapped his fist shut. His knuckles whitened as a dangerous rage surged through his body. The detectives and the girl had made a fool of him. There would be a terrible price to pay.

Blissfully unaware of the extent of the danger they were in, Ever and the detectives made their way to the Barcelona train station where they ditched their disguises and boarded the train to Alicante, which would stop in Valencia. In the comfort of a private compartment, they fell into an exhausted silence. Soon they were lulled into deep sleep by the gentle, rhythmic motion of the train.

Ever began dreaming of her missing guardian. In her dream, he stood before her holding a small silver box. The Doc offered the box to her, but she was too afraid to take it because the box growled every time she reached for it.

"Open it up," said the Doc. He repeated this several times, and his voice became louder and more demanding in a way that was most unlike the Doc. Dream and reality blended as Ever was startled awake by an insistent knocking on their compartment door and an unfamiliar voice shouting in Spanish, "Open up! Open up!" Before Ever could gather her thoughts, the voice yelled, "Fine, I'm coming in!"

The door opened up and in stepped a very agitated conductor. He didn't apologize for barging in. Instead, he stared at Snitch with loathing and revulsion.

"Señor," he said, puffing up his chest with self-importance as he turned to address a groggy Snowize in heavily accented English. "Sir, there are rumors that you are traveling openly with a big rat. I now see with my own eyes that this is true beyond any reasonable doubt. Do you concur that this is a rat?"

"Indeed I do," said Snowize, perhaps a little too calmly for the conductor's liking. "You are quite correct.

Your powers of observation are astounding. Snitch is most certainly a rat. Thank you kindly for barging in here and pointing that out to me. Or else I might have been sitting here for the entire journey thinking he was another creature entirely."

The conductor straightened his tie. "Are you making fun of me?" he asked with growing annoyance.

"Oh no," answered Snowize. "I can see you are a man of little humor, and I sincerely doubt that you would appreciate fun in any form at all."

The conductor let out a little snort of contempt and then continued with his questioning. "Are you the owner of this rat?"

Snowize gave Snitch an apologetic look. "Yes, of course. He's my . . . pet."

"Neither pets nor vermin are allowed on this train." The conductor fixed Snowize with a suspicious eye and then stared hard at each of them in turn. "By law I am required to search your luggage for further vermin." He pointed to the metallic silver briefcase. "Open your case. Now."

Snowize tried to act as if the briefcase held nothing of interest at all. He took his time searching for the key and then slowly opened it.

The conductor peered at the contents. Inside there was a shiny, black-leather shoe and an exquisite rose. The Chameleon Rose.

Ever held her breath. She was dazzled by the beauty of the rose, but it was the shoe that really grabbed her attention. She knew that shoe. "Oh my," she said, unable to stop herself. Snitch, Snowize and the conductor all turned to look at her.

"Does the girl with the generous gap between her teeth have something to say?" asked the conductor.

"No," said Ever, "I don't. I just . . . I'm just admiring the rose."

The conductor, suddenly struck by its beauty, reached for the Chameleon Rose with his plump, sweaty hand. The rose was turning a shimmery silver where it had touched the metallic briefcase. Before the conductor could hold it up to his nose, Snowize deftly swiped it out of his hand. Then, to the complete astonishment of everyone present, he bit into its soft, delicate petals and began to eat it. He methodically munched it up, much as one might an ice-cream cone.

"My lunch," he proclaimed without missing a beat. "I hate it when people put their grubby hands on my lunch."

"Are you also going to devour this shoe?" asked the conductor, taken aback by the detective's strange behavior.

"Oh no," said Snowize. "I'm a vegetarian. I avoid leather."

The conductor gingerly lifted the shoe with his pen. He held it up to his nose and sniffed it. Then, with the utmost disdain, he dropped the shoe back into the briefcase.

"I am fining you for smuggling an animal on board," he said, handing Snowize a small yellow slip of paper. "If I receive any further complaints, I will be forced to terminate your travel. Do I make myself clear?"

"As crystal," answered Snowize. "Any false moves, and you'll kick us off the train."

With that, the nonplussed conductor warily backed out of the compartment, closing the door behind him with a smart, firm click.

16

Secrets, Lies and Vitmo

As soon as the compartment door was shut and she was sure they were alone, Ever turned to Snowize.

"Why?" she asked. "Why did you *eat* the Chameleon Rose?"

"I have my reasons," he said enigmatically with a twinkle in his eye. "Reason one: I didn't want it to fall into the wrong hands. Reason two: I was hungry. Reason three . . . is a secret."

Snitch shook his head in dismay. Ever could tell that he was worried about the detective's increasingly strange behavior. "It's just not normal to go ahead and eat an experimental flower," he signed.

"Calm down," said Snowize. "I'm already burping roses, and I don't want indigestion."

"Good thing you skipped the stem and the thorns," signed Snitch.

"Moving on to more important things," said Snowize, "Ever, please explain your reaction to the shoe. You were definitely startled when you saw it."

"That's because I am absolutely positively certain beyond a shadow of a doubt that it's the Doc's shoe!" she replied.

"How can you be so sure?" asked Snowize. "There are thousands that look just like it."

"Look on the inner sole," said Ever.

Snowize studied the inside of the shoe. "There are letters stamped in yellow ink. DPDE. What could they possibly mean?"

"Doctor Professor David Ezratty. They're the Doc's initials," said Ever. "Which proves that the man who melted is actually—"

"Bingo!" exclaimed Snowize, before she could finish her sentence. "We must conclude that the melty man who came to warn Yoshinobu was none other than Doctor Professor David Ezratty, your irresponsible guardian. The question is, Where did he come from, why did he melt, and where he is now?"

"The crow told me he was sweating because of the effects of time travel," said Ever. "He also brought a message from the future. Do you think it's possible that the Doc is hiding in—"

"Of course, now it makes perfect sense," said Snowize. "Your guardian is hiding in the future. It's the only place where he can be safe from those who are after him. I only wonder why I didn't think of this sooner."

"Perhaps because I thought of it first and because you find it hard to believe anything I tell you," said Ever.

"Perhaps because you make all sorts of strange and unbelievable claims. By way of example, you claim to have eaten invisible ice cream and that you're a magnet for bad luck," countered Snowize.

"Which I have and I am, and so there," said Ever, tempted to stick her tongue out at him.

"Well, it's hard to believe you when, by way of a more telling example, you claim that there's a picture of your parents in that locket around your neck, when any fool can tell that's simply not true. Tell one tall tale, and then nothing you say can ever be taken at face value."

Ever stared at Snowize in astonishment. "But they *are* my parents," she insisted. She opened the locket for Snitch to see. Snitch gave her a pained look and shook his head sadly.

"Honestly, do you expect us to believe that the late Princess Diana of Wales and Prince Charles are your parents?" asked Snowize solemnly. "Surely, Einstein, you could have come up with a more believable claim."

"I don't know any prince or princess. The Doc told me these are my—" Ever swallowed her words. She stared at the grainy picture as the truth slowly sank in. For some reason, the Doc had lied to her. And now she looked like an idiot. Worse, she felt hurt, confused and betrayed all at the same time. She also felt foolish. The picture was grainy because it had been cut out of an old newspaper. Only now did she notice the reason for the poor quality was that it was flimsy newsprint.

"The question is, Why would the Doc lie to you?" wondered Snowize.

Ever snapped the locket shut. She felt like pulling the silver chain off her neck and flinging it as far away as possible. Everything about her past was shrouded in half-remembered truths or based on outright lies. She was tired of the mystery, of the not knowing. She wasn't sure if her parents were dead or alive, what they looked like or if she could trust anything her guardian had told her about herself. The only thing she was sure of was that the locket smelled of cinnamon and roses and that, based on one hazy memory, she knew her mother had loved her. When you feel loved, you never forget it, and Ever clung to that memory as if it were the only thing she had left in the world. As angry and confused as she was, she didn't have the heart to get rid of the locket.

"My dear girl," said Snowize, "you are a total mystery. As soon as we complete this mission, I will open a file on you and help you to answer some crucial questions about yourself. The effective detectives will be at your service. I'll waive my fee, and Snitch, who will only accept payment in chocolate, will work for just a single bar. What I'm saying is that together, we will find out who you really are and what happened to your parents."

Ever nodded quietly, fighting back tears. She had already made a list in her notebook under the heading, *Who Am I, Really?* with the word "really" underlined several times. Under the heading she'd written:

1. *Parents' yacht missing and both presumed dead.*
2. *Suspicious crow suggests parents still alive.*
3. *If alive, why have they not bothered to find me? At least if dead, they had an excuse for forgetting about me.*
4. *Why did they leave me with the Doc in the first place?!!! Who or what was after them?*

Snitch hated to interrupt at such an awkward moment, but he had something urgent to say. "There was something suspect about that conductor's behavior. Underneath all his anger, he actually seemed a little frightened," he signed. "Fear has a slightly sour and acrid odor that cannot be disguised. It oozed from his pores and hung in the air around him. But we weren't the ones he was afraid of."

Snowize agreed with Snitch. "You're right. There was something peculiar about him. I found his interest in my briefcase suspicious. Snitch, you'd better sniff out what he's up to," Snowize urged. "You're the only one small enough to do this unobserved."

"Be careful," whispered Ever, suddenly afraid for her rodent friend.

"And no curling up and acting dead when things get scary," added Snowize. "You're not even in the same family as an opossum, so don't behave like one."

Ever watched as Snowize eased open the compartment door just a crack. Snitch remained rooted to the spot. Snowize nudged him gently with his foot.

"Move!" whispered Snowize. "Now!"

Snitch edged carefully out the door, sniffing the air. He followed the sour scent of the conductor along the corridor toward the dining car and finally spotted him sitting opposite a man in a dining booth. The man's face was hidden behind a newspaper. Snitch, an excellent scurrier, scurried beneath a nearby table and tried to catch what the men were whispering about.

As bad luck would have it, at that very moment a family of four moved into the dining booth under which he was hiding. Snitch rolled over just in time to dodge the spikey heel of a pink stiletto that almost impaled him. Then he had to roll in the other direction to avoid being trampled by a black leather boot belonging to a heavyset man. Snitch's eavesdropping opportunity was ruined by the family's chitchat.

Through the maze of feet, he caught a glimpse of the conductor accepting a brown envelope from the man with the newspaper. The man had put the newspaper down, but his face was now blocked from Snitch's view by the owner of the pink stilettos, a blonde-haired woman with a pinched face. Her expression seemed to say that she found everything, from her husband to her two morose children, utterly distasteful. In fact, it looked to Snitch as if she'd

once eaten something very bitter and had never quite gotten the taste out of her mouth.

When a waitress arrived with a tray of breakfast goodies, the woman snapped at her, "We did not order that!"

"It's a free sample of a new cereal that's quite delicious," said the waitress. "Vitmo cereal is low in calories and high in fiber. I find it quite addictive. Would you care to try it?" She put down the tray with the bowls of cereal.

"It looks like bits of paper smooshed together," said the woman, curling up her lip in distaste. Snitch noticed that it did indeed resemble clumps of gray paper. Nevertheless, the woman's husband thanked the waitress and handed over bowls of Vitmo to the rest of his family. They slurped up the cereal in silence.

"Wow!" exclaimed the woman after a moment. "There's something . . . something quite scrumptious about this Vitmo." An expression not unlike a smile crossed her face, and for the first time in a long time, she looked as if she were truly, blissfully happy.

"Roma," said her husband with a grin, "you're not complaining, honey. Are you sure you're all right?" The children started laughing, and their father beamed. Snitch marveled at how the cereal seemed to have transformed them completely. They were all smiles and joy as they munched it up.

Then, all at once, the entire family reached for the box of Vitmo. Four hands gripped and pulled in opposite directions.

Snitch took advantage of their distraction. He dashed across the aisle to hide under the conductor's table, straining to hear what he was saying to the mysterious man who was once again hidden behind the newspaper.

"Are you telling me," snapped the mystery man, "that

he managed to eat the rose right under your nose? And that the only other thing of interest in his briefcase was a smelly old *shoe*?"

The conductor nodded fearfully.

The mystery man slowly lowered the newspaper to reveal an incredibly pale face and eyes that shone eerily blue behind his dark glasses. He showed no expression, but Snitch could sense that he was seething with anger. That's when he caught a whiff of something highly toxic, tinged with a hint of rotten eggs and boiled banana peels. It was the smell of cold-blooded cruelty, and it set his teeth on edge.

"I paid you good money to do a very simple task. You were to find a small growling box and bring it to me," the man whispered.

The conductor whispered back, "I did as I was told. I checked the briefcase as you asked. There was no little box. Nothing growled at me. Not even that rat. And as for the rose, how was I to know he would eat the darned thing? Why would anyone eat a rose?"

"Oh," said the man, "I have a very good idea why he ate the Chameleon Rose. But I won't be sharing that reason with an imbecile like you."

Snitch missed the rest of their conversation because a great commotion erupted at the next table. The family of four had started fighting over the last serving of Vitmo cereal. Everyone in the dining car turned to stare, but this did not stop the family's loud and ugly bickering. Snitch had never seen anything like it. He knew that humans could behave poorly, but this was outrageous. They scratched and clawed at the cereal box until it was completely shredded; and then, quite shockingly, they started munching up not only the remaining cereal, but bits of the cardboard box as well. Snitch knew sewer rats who behaved better.

While the youngest child happily munched on the corner of the box, Snitch noticed that the man who smelled of evil was enjoying the spectacle, as if he found the family's behavior particularly pleasing. The mother snatched the last bit of the box from her child's hand and gobbled it up greedily. This didn't seem to concern the father, who was too busy licking the tablecloth to care. Snitch was astounded when the older child accidentally swallowed his spoon in desperation.

Sensing this was a good time to make his getaway, Snitch stealthily crept down the aisle. When he glanced back, the pale-faced man had risen from his seat. For a brief moment the man lowered his dark glasses. Snitch felt the hair on the end of his tail prickle. The man's luminous blue eyes were staring straight at him. Very slowly he lifted up his hand and pointed directly at Snitch. *"Cricetomys Gambianus,"* he said.

A deathly silence ensued, broken by a woman's voice. "Rat!" she screamed. "There's a gigantic rat in the train car!" And Snitch knew he had to run for his life.

17

The Not-so-Great Escape

A breathless Snitch arrived back in the compartment. In a panic, he locked the door and then tried to explain what had happened. Ever and Snowize frowned as they tried to read his frenetic signs, but Snitch's paws were all over the place, pointing, shaking, signing frantically.

"You saw the conductor eating cereal with a man . . . who swallowed a spoon . . . while wearing pink, high-heeled shoes that almost trampled you?" asked Ever, trying to make sense of it all and take down relevant notes.

Snitch shook his head fretfully. "No, that's not it!" His nose and whiskers were all atwitch, and he was hyperventilating.

Ever took his paws in her hands and urged him to breathe deeply. Snitch finally regained his composure and told them what had happened in the dining car.

"There's no doubt," he warned them solemnly, "that we are being followed by this cruel man. The very same man who sat in front of us on the plane to Tokyo. The man who built the snowman on Mount Fuji."

Snowize didn't seem troubled by this at all.

"It's hardly a surprise that we're still being followed,"

he said. "In fact, it's good news. It means we are definitely on to something." He scowled as he was interrupted by an incoming t-mail. Deodora's voice sprang into his mind.

Harry, I've left directions and a package under a bench at the station in Valencia. Regrettably, there was no time to replenish your disguises. I also have a request from the SSSA. They want a progress report ASAP. They demand to know how far you've gotten with your investigation into Yoshinobu's death and the attack on Cadiz. It's imperative that you comply.

Snowize rolled his eyes. Only his Secret Secretary used words like *imperative*. He imagined Deodora to be as dull as dish water, a dreary woman who smiled on rare occasions. Unfortunately, Deodora was still connected to her t-mail at that moment. Snowize realized too late that he had sent her his unkind thoughts.

Deodora, I'm under a lot of pressure. I didn't mean to think the things I thought about you.

There was a pause. Deodora responded in a clipped tone. *Never mind what you think about me, just follow my instructions so that you don't get kicked out of the SSSA. As it is, I've been ordered to set up a visit with a Spychiatrist for you.* Snowize let out a howl of deep dismay.

"Absolutely not!" he thundered. "There will be no visits to the spychiatrist and no spychotherapy for Harry Snowize!"

"There are doctors specifically for spies?" asked Ever in disbelief. Snitch signed a quick explanation. Spychiatrists, it turned out, deal with all sorts of spy-related disorders, the most common being the dreaded Double Identity Disorder in which the spy starts to forget who he really is and takes on the identity of his disguise.

"Like poor Agent Trumbledot," said Snowize, shaking his head with pity. "He still runs around thinking he's

Julius Caesar. Around the fifteenth of March every year, he becomes terribly anxious and screams that the ides are upon him. He has to be physically restrained for his own safety."

Ever had never thought that spying could be so dangerous for one's mental health.

"Everyone knows that once a spy starts seeing a Spy Doctor, it's the beginning of the end of his career," said Snowize. Snitch nodded his head in agreement. "I would rather be shot full speed from a cannon than see a Spy-chiatrist," Snowize said gloomily. At that moment, Ever froze. The door handle to their compartment was moving ever so slightly. She raised a finger to her lips and quietly pointed this out to Snowize and Snitch.

Snowize carefully pushed open the window and signaled for Snitch and Ever to follow quickly as he climbed out of the moving train. Ever was terrified, but someone was jiggling the door handle quite forcefully now, so she took a deep breath and followed Snitch out of the window. Soon all three of them were dangling on the outside of the train, with Ever and Snitch clutching on for dear life as the wind whistled in their ears.

Ever watched with fear as the compartment door was kicked open and in stepped the man with the pale face and disturbing blue eyes. For a second he looked confused as he surveyed the empty compartment, but then he approached the open window where all that could be seen of Ever and the detectives were their sets of fingers.

"Close your eyes," yelled Snowize. "Perhaps he won't see us."

Ever wanted to say this was no time for jokes, but the wind was so forceful she could not open her mouth to speak. Every muscle in her body ached as she used all the strength she had to hold on. The man was now peering down at them as they hung precariously from the speeding train. He considered them with a cruel and knowing look. In a remarkable show of strength, Snowize held up one hand and waved politely. The man did not wave back. Instead, he breathed onto the window and then drew a question mark and a square in the area he'd misted up. Snowize shook his head to indicate he didn't know what the man was talking about. This irked the creepy man. He stared at their exposed fingers and slowly started to close the window.

This is it, thought Ever as the metal edge slid closer to her fingers. *We're doomed.* But they were in luck. The train, which had been slowing down as it approached the Valencia station, came to a full stop for a moment, and the trio leaped down to safety just in time. Snitch's handsome whiskers were plastered against his face, and his ears were flattened against his head. Ever couldn't stop her legs from shaking as the train pulled off again, taking with it their irate enemy, who hadn't had time to make it to the door. Ever met his gaze as the train gained speed. He was still staring fixedly at them with his evil eyes.

"Well," said Snowize, "it seems we'll be rid of him for a while." He smiled his charming smile as if he didn't have a care in the world. "Nothing quite like having the wind in your hair and a little bit of high-speed adventure to work up an appetite. Now the question is, Under which bench did Deodora leave our care package?"

Snowize sent Snitch to sniff out the possibilities in one direction while he went off in the other. Ever was to search under the benches in the middle section, but her legs were still wobbly, and she found she had to sit down for a moment. Her hand reached instinctively for the locket around her neck, and she began to wonder once more about the mystery of who she really was and whether the detectives would be able to help unravel it. She opened the locket and stared at the picture of the Prince and Princess of Wales. Their gentle smiles seemed to mock her.

Just then, Ever got the strangest feeling that someone was watching her. The back of her neck tingled in a most peculiar way. She looked up slowly and caught sight of a man in a black cloak standing on the other side of the platform. His face was hidden in shadow, but she knew immediately who he was because he was wearing a shiny, black patent leather shoe on one foot, and nothing but a simple white sock on the other. It was the Doc! He was beckoning to her. She could make out his shock of wild, white hair sticking out in multiple directions and even his unruly eyebrows.

Ever made a mad dash across the double set of tracks, despite the warning bell announcing an oncoming train. As she reached the other side, her foot got caught under the rail and she couldn't get it unstuck. The approaching train sounded its alarm. Ever hadn't realized how fast it was traveling, and she winced as the lights grew brighter and bigger. She desperately tried to lift herself up onto the platform. All of a sudden the Doc was there, reaching down for her. He lifted her with surprising strength and pulled her to safety. Then he led her by the hand toward a row of trees, away from the crowd. Ever didn't think twice. She would have followed her guardian to the ends of the earth. She was so relieved to see him again.

"You've come back to the present," she said, out of breath and overwhelmed with happiness. The Doc grabbed her wrist. Ever was unable to stop the tears that were already spilling from her eyes. "I was so worried . . . I thought I might never see you again. I have so many questions for you, I don't even know where to start! Who is after you? What do they want? Do they know that you've been hiding in the future? Why did you lie to me about my par—" Ever stopped speaking when she felt the icy grip around her wrist tighten.

"Do you have the growling box?" asked her guardian. Ever recalled the man on the train. How he'd drawn a square in the misted up part of the glass. Only it hadn't been a square, she realized. It was the box. He was after the box, and now the Doc desperately needed it. She could tell by how tightly the Doc was gripping her wrist that it was of vital importance, and she felt overwhelmed by guilt. Protecting the box was the one thing she'd been asked to do, and she had failed miserably.

"I left it behind. . . . I was in such a panic, and by the time I was in the tunnel, it was too late. I'm so sorry I failed you. I've brought all this bad luck to everyone." Ever gasped as flashes of pain soared up her arm. The skin on her wrist, where the Doc held her, burned as if acid was eating into it.

"Where is it? I know you have it," said the Doc, except that this was not her guardian's voice. It was harsh and cruel; and when she looked up, she was staring into icy blue eyes that did not belong to the Doc. Ever tried to scream, but the man clamped his hand over her mouth and pulled her behind a stone pillar. She watched as his facial features transformed from her beloved Doc to the creepy man who had been following them. She vaguely wondered how this man, whom they had left behind on the train, could be at two different places at once.

She couldn't breathe and as much as she tried to struggle, she couldn't move.

Suddenly there was a blur and a flurry of feathers and a screeching sound. "Always go for the eyes," said a familiar voice.

It was the crow. Ever recognized him by his glittering

black eyes and the missing toe on his right foot. Now that right foot clawed at the man holding her prisoner, scratching his cheek. The man shielded his face with one hand while his other hand remained tightly gripping Ever's wrist.

The crow flew past her, flapping his large wings so vigorously that she could feel a breeze as he circled upward. Once he was high enough, he folded his wings behind his back and dived straight down toward her attacker. This time the man had to let go of her to defend himself. The crow was relentless. His beak left a gash above the man's eyebrow. Any closer and the bird would have plucked out his eye. The man backed away, but before he merged into the shadows, he pointed to Ever's arm and hissed at her.

"That wound will never heal. You've been touched with a deadly poison. Slowly, it will take all your strength until you are too weak to breathe, and then it will kill you."

"Why are you doing this?" asked Ever. "What have I done to you?"

"Give me the box, and I'll give you the antidote," he said.

"But I just told you, I don't have the box," Ever pleaded.

"We know he gave you the box," said the man. "Only the box can save your life."

Ever suddenly felt cold all over. She dropped to her knees as the man slipped into the darkness and was gone.

"It's not true," said the crow as he landed next to her. "What he said about the poison. He was messing with your mind."

Ever stared at the wound on her wrist. It was circular in shape, about the size of a large thumbprint, and it burned unrelentingly. While it wasn't deep, it was slowly

bleeding, where the skin had been eaten away. "How can you be so certain?" asked Ever.

The crow shifted his weight from one foot to another. "I'm not certain, but I'm trying to put a positive spin on this. You see, I don't think they want you dead. At least, not yet. Not while they're still searching for the box," said the crow. "Not while you still might lead them to the Doc. Not while they know who your parents are."

"They know who my parents are?" Ever asked, astonished. "What do my parents have to do with this?" she asked.

"Everything and nothing," answered the crow.

"Thanks," said Ever, exasperated. "That explains it perfectly." A great wave of weariness washed over her. She was tired of being left in the dark, tired of being afraid, tired of all the mystery. Her whole body felt exhausted, as if a slow poison were making its way through her system. Ever shivered. The crow stretched out a wing and plucked a folded piece of paper from between his feathers. He dropped the note into her hand, winked at her and then slowly melted away. Ever sat shivering and too weak to move for what felt like the longest time.

"There you are. Finally!" The shadow of a man and a rat fell over her.

"You had us running around like legless chickens looking for you," said Snowize.

"I think he means *headless* chickens," signed Snitch.

"No," said Snowize, covering his forgetful slipup. "I deliberately used the image of legless chickens to emphasize what an extremely difficult task it has been for us. It's far more difficult for chickens without legs to—"

The detectives stopped arguing as they noticed the wound on Ever's arm and the fact that she was trembling uncontrollably. She told them what had happened, leaving out the part about the poison; and by the time she finished, they were both furious and eager to go after her attacker. Ever was touched at how fiercely protective they were of her. She told them how the crow had saved her and showed them the note he'd given her, which she now unfolded.

"It's the Doc's handwriting," she said, instantly recognizing his nearly illegible script and squiggly signature.

"Ever, above all else, you have to find the growling box. And remember this: Your betrayer is your friend," she read aloud, not knowing quite what to make of the Doc's warning.

"Ah, betrayal," said Snowize, peering at the note. "The closer the friend, the worse the betrayal. . . . Now take a deep breath and tell me again exactly what happened to you."

Ever repeated the story, once more leaving out the details about the poison. She wasn't entirely sure why. Maybe it was because she didn't want to worry them too much. Or perhaps it was because, if she kept it secret, she could pretend that it had never happened; that there wasn't any possibility of a deadly poison coursing through her veins.

But secrets have a weight and a dreadful power all of their own, and she would later realize that it was not wise or safe to keep one of this magnitude all to herself.

18

A Begubbled Mind

"Who ate our destination point?" asked Snowize as he consulted a map that had been carved into the underside of a loaf of crispy bread. The ingenious Deodora Miffingpin had included it in the care package she'd sent to the station. The hungry trio had been eating parts of the loaf as they trudged along the road, careful to eat only what they no longer needed for navigation purposes.

Snitch signed an apology. "I'm sorry. I ate the destination." Reading was clearly not Snitch's strong suit, and he readily admitted that he was hopeless with maps.

"I'm afraid that until you can read a map, you'll never make it to partner," said Snowize.

Snitch winced at this slight, but this was no time for that old argument.

"Fortunately," said Snowize, "I had Ever commit the entire map to memory before you committed it to your belly. I'm putting this photographic memory of hers to the test. You see, the only other person I've ever met with such a gift is myself. So, Ever, any suggestions?"

Ever could picture the recently eaten map perfectly in her mind's eye. She pointed up to a house on the hill.

"Over there. The home of Octavia and Gustav Cadiz. We follow this road, make two lefts and we're there."

"Excellent. Exactly as I recall. And my hunch tells me that therein lies the key to solving this case."

Ever certainly hoped that he was right. The wound on her arm burned beneath the makeshift bandage that the detective had made by dramatically ripping off the sleeve of his white shirt. She bit her lip, determined to ignore the pain and forget the poison, as they headed up toward the charming house on the hill.

Inside the charming house, Octavia Cadiz, the loving wife of Professor Gustav Cadiz, sat next to her husband on the sofa, watching infomercials. From time to time, she turned her gaze from the TV and looked at her husband, who stared unblinkingly at the flickering screen. To see him in such a mindless state was terribly distressing. He was no longer the man he had once been. Before his disappearance, Gustav had refused to watch television. He found the flickering images disturbing and hated commercials with a passion so deep it sometimes made him weep.

"The sole purpose of a commercial," he would say, "is to make people want something they don't need. This I find deeply upsetting."

He believed that excessive television-watching was especially damaging to the developing mind. Professor Gustav Cadiz valued the mind above all else. He would tap his head and say that it was his greatest blessing. And now, in a cruel twist of fate, his mind was gone. When the doorbell rang urgently, he did not even turn his head. Octavia sighed.

"Who is it now? Who is calling on us at this difficult time?" Since her husband's return, Octavia had been visited by an endless stream of doctors and scientists, all trying in vain to figure out what had happened to Professor Gustav. Now, when she opened the front door, she was confronted by a most peculiar sight. Before her stood a tall, handsome man in a shirt with only one sleeve; a young girl of about twelve; and an African giant pouched rat. The young girl had a makeshift bandage on her right forearm. She looked pale and exhausted.

"Harry Snowize at your service," announced the man. The rat gave a little bow, and the pale girl gave a shy smile that revealed a charming gap between her teeth.

"Harry Snowize . . . that's impossible," Octavia protested. "Harry Snowize is dead. Murdered by the evil Brothers Weiss. It was all over the underground news sites."

"Mrs. Cadiz, since it's clear that I am not dead, I will not waste your precious time explaining how it is that I am alive, or debating the merits and demerits of hiding in a human tooth. Nor will I explain why I am in cahoots with a rat of superior intelligence named Snitch, who aspires to be a partner in my detective agency, or why we are traveling with this adverbially named orphan girl, Ever, whose guardian has disappeared into the future with only one good shoe, and whose only real friend is, oxymoronically, a robot fridge with homicidal tendencies. I'll spare you these inconsequential trivialities and get right to the point: I am here to offer my assistance in solving your husband's case. I am at your service, Señora. I, and my very bright assistant, and this girl whose only talent, besides her photographic memory, is her claim that she is a magnet for bad luck. We are all completely at your service. And we are backed by the Secret Society of Spies Anonymous who so value the fabulous technological inventions of scientists that they have made this a high-priority case."

Octavia gave them a warm smile. "That is quite an

introduction. I remember the rumors of your eloquence, Mr. Snowize. But before you make so bold an offer, I suggest you take a look at what's left of my husband. You'll see very quickly that this will not be an easy case to solve."

Ever and the detectives followed Octavia into the living room where Professor Cadiz was now watching a documentary on the life cycle of fleas. Snowize held out his hand in cheerful greeting, but Professor Cadiz continued to stare listlessly and openmouthed at the television screen. Ever observed an ant as it crawled over the Professor's chin, up over his lip, along his front teeth and onto his tongue. It must have tickled, but Gustav showed absolutely no reaction. He blinked and swallowed the ant, quite by accident.

Ever made a note of this in her notebook, to which she added a small drawing of an ant crawling over a set of teeth.

Snowize took out a small voice recorder and started making comments. "Observation one: The subject's eyes have lost their intelligent sparkle. They appear dull and lifeless. Even his magnificent mustache looks droopy," he said. When he waved a hand in front of Gustav's face, the scientist showed no response. "Observation two: The jaw is slack and an expression of mild confusion is plastered on the subject's face." Snowize stood directly in front of Gustav and pulled a very silly face. Still no response. He pulled several more ridiculous faces. Ever stifled a giggle. Then she saw tears welling up in Octavia's eyes.

"As you can see," said Octavia, "my husband is hardly with us at all. He has lost his presence. He has lost his mind."

"Indeed," Snowize was forced to agree. "He has completely lost his presence of mind."

Octavia wiped away another tear. "Even if you track down the people who did this to him, what use will it be?

How will it help him to recover? Is it not clear my dear husband is beyond repair?"

Snowize kept very silent. He paced up and down.

Ever felt sick to her stomach. Whatever had happened to the Japanese scientist was happening all over again to the Spanish inventor, and she had no idea how they were going to save him. "We have to do something," said Ever. "This is exactly what happened to Yoshinobu Azayaka. He stopped talking after his return and just stared into space."

Snowize stopped pacing. "I'm inclined to agree," he said. "Something has to be done. The poor man is showing every sign of having a mind that is completely and utterly . . . begubbled."

"Begubbled?" asked Octavia. "My English is not perfect. What is a *begubbled* mind?"

"I've never heard of such a word," added Ever, who had once read the *Oxford English Dictionary* from A to Z and could page through it in her mind and call up the definition of almost any word. *Begubbled* was nowhere in the B section.

Snitch shook his head in dismay as Snowize explained. "Oh, it's a word I made up. Sometimes I find the English language lacking, so I invent a word to better suit the situation. A begubbled mind is one that has gone into complete shock and can no longer function. A begubbled mind is one that is confused beyond confusion."

"I see," signed Snitch, not really seeing at all, indicating to Ever that he worried about his partner making up silly words and using them freely. Octavia dabbed at the corner of her eye with a silk handkerchief.

All of a sudden, the Professor let out a low groan and pointed to the TV. Something in the flickering images was causing him severe distress. He groaned again.

"I'd better turn it off," said Octavia.

"Yes," agreed Snowize. "He seems agitated."

"Wait!" said Ever. "This could be important. Why did he start groaning at the exact same time that this commercial came on?"

"I'll ask the questions," snapped Snowize. "As lead investigator, I don't think this is anything more than coincidence."

Ever pointed to the television. Three cute cartoon bunny rabbits were singing about a new vitamin-enriched breakfast cereal. "More vital, more Vitmo! There are more vital vitamins in Vitmo than in anything else at all," they sang. This appeared to be torture for Gustav, who rocked back and forth, groaning.

"Perhaps it's the bunny rabbits," whispered Octavia. "Three of his were killed when his lab was ransacked." Octavia dabbed her eyes some more.

"Maybe," Ever said hesitantly. "Or maybe it has something to do with this Vitmo . . ."

At the mere mention of the word *Vitmo*, Gustav Cadiz made the noise of an animal in anguish. Then very slowly and quite softly, he uttered six words that made the fur on the tip of Snitch's tail bristle. It made the wound on Ever's arm sting and burn.

Gustav Cadiz spoke in a voice etched with pain. "It's green," he said. "It's a pinkish white." On his face was an expression of absolute horror, as if he were reliving the moment when his very last thought was ripped from his brain, leaving him with nothing but a sense of terrible blankness.

19

A Love Story, A Terrible Cook and Compound 37d

As soon as she heard those all-too-familiar words, Ever had to sit down. Her body felt weak and shivery all over. The wound on her arm burned as if it were on fire, and it took every ounce of strength for her not to cry out in pain.

"Did he just say, 'It's green. It's a pinkish white?'" asked Snowize, scratching his temple.

"He did," signed Snitch. "Sure as sugar, he did."

"It's proof that he's gone soft in the head. It makes no sense at all. What's green and a pinkish white?" asked an unhappy Octavia.

"We have no idea what it means, but it's an important clue. You see, those were precisely the last words of Yoshinobu Azayaka." Snowize set down his glass of mineral water and met Octavia's gaze. "Octavia," he said in a voice filled with compassion, "I don't think your husband has taken leave of his senses. I think his senses have left him. And I don't think they left of their own accord. I believe they were taken by force. Excised without his permission." Snowize paused to allow this to sink in. "I don't know how else to say this: I believe your husband's mind was *stolen*."

"Stolen!" gasped Octavia. "Stolen? By whom? And for what? And how?" Octavia was so overwhelmed, she promptly burst into tears. Snowize handed her his silk handkerchief and assured her once more that he would do his utmost to retrieve her husband's mind.

"We're convinced someone is after scientific inventions and stealing minds to get them," said Ever.

"Precisely," said Snowize. "And in order to find out who is behind this, we're going to need your help, Mrs. Cadiz. Like Yoshinobu Azayaka, I suspect your husband may have invented something that someone else wanted. Do you know what projects he was working on?"

"My husband kept much of his work in his head," said Octavia. "Not because he was worried about anyone stealing it, but mostly because he forgot to write anything down."

"I see," said Snowize. "And in the week before his disappearance, did your husband at any point run around the house shouting Eureka! or Yes, by Jiminy Cricket, that's it!? Those would be sure signs that he'd come up with a new idea. Something worth stealing."

Octavia shook her head. She recalled nothing like that. But Ever noticed her sigh and hesitate for a moment, as if she had something more to say. "No," added Octavia, scratching her nose and then her eyebrow, "I don't recall anything like that."

Ever sensed Octavia was holding something back. It was in her gestures and the way she averted her eyes that tipped Ever off. Now that she had a secret of her own, Ever seemed to be able to read the telltale signs in someone else.

Octavia put on a smile. "Before any more questions,"

she said, "let us eat. You must be hungry after all your travels."

Ever's head felt thick and foggy as they sat down at the heavy wooden dining table that was set with dazzling silver cutlery, each piece engraved with an ornate dragon. Snitch handed her a napkin; and as she placed it on her lap, she suddenly noticed that she could see not one, but two Snitches beside her. There were also two Snowizes opposite her, both equally irritated as they hastily composed a progress report and prepared to t-mail it off to the head of the SSSA. Ever blinked her eyes vigorously to get rid of her double vision. But she couldn't ignore it any longer. Something was seriously wrong with her, undoubtedly caused by the slow poison that was working its way through her system. Still, she said nothing, hoping against hope that the worst was over.

Professor Cadiz was wheeled in and positioned at his place at the head of the table where he sat transfixed by the white tablecloth. Meanwhile, Octavia removed silver lids from the dishes she'd prepared. She smiled as she urged her guests to help themselves.

Ever took just one sniff and froze in horror. The food smelled absolutely vile. Perhaps the poison had damaged her sense of smell? But then she noticed Snowize holding his nose while taking a bite of something gray and lumpy. He looked stricken. Before he could stop himself, he let out a cry of disbelief, and for a moment it appeared as if he was about to spit the food back onto his plate. Ever and Snitch didn't know where to look. But Octavia was watching Snowize's reaction with immense interest. He hurriedly swallowed his mouthful and washed it down with a gallon of mineral water.

"I'm afraid," said Snowize, almost choking on his words, "this dish is a little bit too spicy for my liking."

Octavia pushed forward the red herring surprise. "My specialty," she said. "Try some."

"Ever will try it. I'm allergic to fish, and thankfully also a vegetarian," said Snowize, trying not to gag.

Ever glared at the detective, but with Octavia watching, she was forced to sample a small portion. The instant the food was on her tongue, she felt positively dizzy with revulsion. It was certainly the most horrible concoction ever created. "I don't have much appetite," she said, reaching for the water jug as her stomach grew queasy.

Octavia pushed the mushroom soufflé forward. "Go on," she insisted to Snowize. It seemed more like a direct challenge than a suggestion. Ever could read the reluctance on the detective's face as he took a bite.

"You've outdone yourself!" he spluttered in sheer horror. "Just as I thought that nothing could be viler than the very smell of your red herring surprise, I discover that the mushroom soufflé takes the cake, so to speak."

"So, you don't like the food?" Octavia asked, beaming.

"Not only do I not like it, I don't think anyone in their right mind could possibly tolerate it," said Snowize with a frankness that Ever found both shocking and refreshing. The detective continued, "Perhaps somewhere, in a distant galaxy, there exists an alien life form with a completely different set of taste buds and a digestive system of steel. It's possible these beings might be able to stomach your cooking, but right here, on earth, this food is not edible. Not even a starving sewer rat would eat this food."

Snitch, who was covering his sensitive nose with a napkin, gave an apologetic nod in agreement. To Ever's surprise, despite the insults, Octavia sighed with relief and then smiled.

"I know the food is terrible," she said. "I know it because I cooked it, and I happen to be the worst cook in the world."

None of them felt moved to disagree with this statement.

"I'm sorry I inflicted this meal on you, but I needed to know that I could trust you. Your brutal honesty proves that I can. Now I can tell you what I didn't before." She looked meaningfully at each of her guests. "My husband did, in fact, invent something quite remarkable."

"I knew it!" said Ever, forgetting her manners and her fragile condition. "I had a hunch you were hiding something. Was it an invention worth stealing?" she asked, getting ahead of herself.

"Yes, I believe so," said Octavia. "But I'll let you decide for yourselves." And with that she brought out what looked like a glass saltshaker filled with clear crystals that she began to sprinkle over the dishes of food. Ever noticed that the individual crystals shimmered with all the colors of the rainbow. Professor Cadiz, who had almost been forgotten as he nibbled on the end of his napkin, let out another groan at the sight of the crystals, a fact that was not lost on Ever.

"Now try the food," Octavia commanded.

"Oh no," said Snowize. "The addition of salt will not remedy your terrible cooking."

"This is not salt," said Octavia as she pushed the dishes toward them. "This is Compound 37d."

"While I'm known for both bravery and recklessness, I cannot revisit the depths of revulsion I found in those dishes," said Snowize.

That's when Snitch threw caution to the wind and took one bite of the red herring surprise. Ever and Snowize waited with bated breath. Snitch took another bite, and another. He was beyond delighted. In fact, he ate with so much gusto and such deep relish that it was convincing enough for Snowize to follow suit with the mushroom soufflé. They both gave Ever the thumbs-up as they dished up generous portions of the food that had just moments before been deemed too awful for sewer-rat consumption.

Ever ignored her dizziness and took a bite. To her astonishment, the food was completely transformed. What had tasted quite ghastly was now exquisitely delicious—so delicious that it made her forget about the poison coursing through her veins. There were no words to accurately describe how delectable the food was. She had no doubt that she would eat it raw or cooked, and worse yet, she knew she would happily fight both the detectives for the remaining scraps. But when she looked up she saw that there was nothing left in any of the dishes. In a manner quite unlike him, Snitch had given up on good behavior and had crawled onto the table to lick the bowl. Now both the detectives gazed at Ever's plate where there was one remaining blob of food.

"*My* food," Ever said protectively, holding up her knife and fork as if they were weapons. The scary thing, she realized, was that she was more than prepared to use them as such. And even scarier was the way that both Snowize and Snitch were eyeing her food. The look of desperate craving on their faces was like nothing she'd ever seen before. It frightened her, but then she caught a glimpse of something that struck fear right into her heart. It was her own reflection in the shiny surface of her knife, and on her face she saw that very same look of desperation.

Octavia, sensing that things had gone too far, quickly whisked away Ever's plate before anything could happen. Both the detectives and Ever stared after her, robbed of the most delicious thing they had ever tasted.

"This . . . this is quite an invention," sputtered Snow-ize, coming to his senses. "You must tell us what these crystals are and how your husband came to invent them, and how we might be able to get some . . . so that we might improve our own cooking."

Ever coughed politely. "I'm sure he didn't mean the last part. That stuff is dangerous. It made the food delicious . . . but it made us all crazy."

Snitch nodded in agreement. He was still mortified by his own behavior and apologized profusely to Octavia for climbing on top of the table.

"Well, you won't believe it, but to understand the origins of Compound 37d, you must first hear a love story," said Octavia, taking her husband's hand in hers. There was something so tender in the way she looked at him that Ever suddenly felt terribly sad for the two of them, a brilliant man with his mind missing and his wife who missed him despite the fact that he was right there beside her.

"Oh no," said Snowize. "Time is of the essence, so please skip the mushy love story and cut straight to the matter at hand. We need to focus on these divine crystals, this compound that could enslave the world."

"I'd like to hear the love story," said Ever, even as a fiery pain gripped her entire body. "The Doc always said the small details are where the truth hides. And the great Sherlock Holmes said there is nothing so important as trifle," she added, for she'd gone through a Sherlock Holmes phase in which she had memorized his every quote.

"Well, if you insist, I'll make it as brief as I can," said Octavia, smiling gratefully at Ever.

"Perhaps briefer than that," said Snowize. "We don't really have time to listen to mere trifles." He glared at Ever, who glared back and briskly opened up her notebook to the page on which she'd written, *The Case of the Stolen Minds: Professor Cadiz's Story*. The pain had subsided briefly, but her whole body felt as heavy as lead.

"The great love story is the story of how we met," Octavia began. "Many years ago, back when Gustav was a young scientist, he quite literally tripped over his feet and was flung head over heels right into me, Octavia di Benezia. As much as I don't like to share this, the truth is that in those days I was described as one of the most beautiful women to have ever graced the planet. From the moment I was born, I heard about nothing but how beautiful I was."

To illustrate this point, Octavia brought out an album filled with photographs. She pointed to the image of a young woman with an olive complexion, long, black hair that cascaded down to her slim waist, and big, green eyes. Ever had never seen anyone so lovely.

"By the time I was eighteen," continued Octavia, "my legendary beauty had inspired many young men to send me appalling poetry. However, I regarded my beauty as a curse. Everyone I met loved me because of my looks, when all I wanted was someone who liked me just for who I was.

"I was determined to prove that I was more than just a pretty face, so I took up archery, astronomy and chess. I also learned to speak twenty-nine languages, including sign language, and to play the harp. But it made no difference, no one paid attention to my accomplishments; they were too impressed with my beauty to notice.

"On the day that Gustav knocked me off my feet, I hit the back of my head on the concrete stairs of the library and ended up in the hospital with a fractured skull. My father was outraged. He did not believe that the incident was an accident, so he refused to let Gustav see me or to apologize. Instead, he filed a charge of attempted murder against Gustav and promised that he would be locked away for good if he came near me.

"Back in the hospital, while I drifted in and out of consciousness, I received over three thousand terrible poems from lovesick young men around the country. Poems so terrible, they kept me in a coma for longer than was necessary. There was also one very wealthy young man who sent me a rose for every second that I was unconscious. Seventy-five thousand six hundred roses in total. When I woke up, I was highly embarrassed to discover that someone had wasted so much money on me. The roses clogged the corridors of the hospital and made it difficult for the doctors and nurses to move about the place. Much to my father's dismay, I refused to see the man who had sent the flowers."

"Do you remember the name of this man?" asked Ever, not wanting to miss a single detail.

"I'll never forget it," answered Octavia. "Salvador L. Pozodelfrio. He was determined to win my heart at any cost. The fact that I didn't want to see him made him even more determined. He swanned into my room uninvited and told me that I was the only woman who deserved him and that our wedding would be the most extravagant that Spain had ever seen. The nerve of it!

"In the meantime, Gustav was still desperate to apologize to me. Unfortunately, my father had put his picture up at the hospital entrance along with a warning full of lies that he was vicious, depraved, armed and dangerous. My father also hired a bodyguard to stand outside my room day and night, and never let me know of Gustav's pleas for an audience with me.

"Fortunately," Octavia said, pausing briefly to squeeze her husband's hand and plant a kiss on his cheek, "Gustav was not one to give up easily. He knew there had to be a way in to the hospital. One night, as he lay in his bed, he saw a gecko crossing the ceiling and realized that the answer was staring him in the face. He leaped into action and set to work.

"Three days later, having not had a wink of sleep, he arrived at the hospital. He looked up at the eighteenth floor where I lay in my sickbed and knew what he had to do. He slipped his hands and feet into a set of gecko gloves that he had fashioned and adapted according to the unique design that allows geckos to stick so effortlessly to walls and to rest so calmly upside down on ceilings. It was no easy task and highly experimental. Fortunately, as he started to climb the outside of the building, he was delighted to discover that the gloves worked beyond expectation.

"When he reached the seventeenth floor, he made the mistake of glancing down and was overcome by an attack of giddiness. Worse yet, his gecko gloves started to lose their grip and he suddenly felt himself slipping. The gloves, it turned out, worked perfectly when he moved quickly, but they started to lose their stickiness when he was still.

"Inside, I was writing to Salvador L. Pozodelfrio, refusing another of his obnoxious marriage proposals in which he declared that he would never take no for an answer. I was interrupted by a weird sound and looked up to see a crazed man stuck to my window, tapping frantically on the glass. I watched him flail about at my window, with no idea he was in grave danger of falling. To make matters worse, his thick glasses slipped off his nose and hurtled down to the pavement. Without his glasses, he was legally blind.

"Somehow he managed to open the window and tumble inside. My first thought was that he might be dangerous, so I slowly moved out of bed and backed away toward the door. Gustav politely addressed my pillow.

"'My name is Gustav Cadiz,' he said. 'I am the man who is to blame for your injury.'

"'I see,' I replied, now only three steps from the door, ready to flee if I had to.

"He squinted at the white pillow on the empty bed. 'I can tell by your pallor that you are not well, and I apologize a thousand times for the pain I caused you,' he said.

"Puzzled, I asked, 'Why do you apologize only now?'

"Gustav approached the bed and felt foolish as he realized that he had been speaking to a pillow. He turned to me and explained how his many attempts to see me had been thwarted by my father. Then he showed me the gecko gloves. That was the moment he won my heart. I was impressed by his sincerity and intelligence. We talked for hours, and by the end of the conversation, we were both deeply in love.

"I would later discover that at that exact moment, my father was back home lighting a cigar for none other than Salvador L. Pozodelfrio, who had arrived on our doorstep and offered him a large sum of cash for my hand in marriage.

"'Never mind just her hand,' my father told a delighted Salvador. 'You might as well take the rest of her as well.'

"That night, while my father and Salvador discussed wedding plans and toasted the future, I snuck out of the hospital to have dinner with Gustav. We were halfway through our gazpacho when I impulsively proposed to him. Gustav was so surprised that he knocked over his bowl of soup, splattering us both. We were married the next day in a secret ceremony, unaware of the fury we were about to unleash."

Octavia shivered involuntarily, and Snitch played nervously with his whiskers. Even Snowize looked full of trepidation. "When Salvador found out the news of our marriage, he was so outraged that he burst a small blood vessel in his brain and could not move for three days. Once he'd recovered, he swore that if it was the last thing he did, Gustav would pay for stealing the woman he loved."

"And did he?" asked Ever. "Did he ever try to get revenge?"

"Funny you should ask," said Octavia. "As it happened, a week after we married, we were at the opera one night, in front row seats, watching a performance of *Carmen*. At the point where the beautiful Carmen chooses one suitor over another, Salvador appeared onstage with the opera singers. He looked crazed and demented. As the music reached a crescendo, he leaped down from the stage and tried to strangle Gustav with a bootstrap."

"That must've been terrifying," Ever said, secretly terrified for herself as she realized she now couldn't feel her hands or feet at all.

"It was. And I believe that incident ruined Salvador's reputation," said Octavia. "Once he came to his senses, he packed his bags and fled. Rumor has it he went north and joined a tribe of Inuit in the farthest reaches of the Arctic Circle. All I know is that he has never bothered us since."

"Interesting," mused Snowize, "but quite irrelevant, I believe. We need to move on to this Compound 37d."

Ever wanted to stop the detective right there, but she

discovered, to her dismay, that she could not move at all. Every time she took a breath, it felt as if the air was not reaching her lungs. The poison had paralyzed her. It was like being caught in a bad dream, where you scream for help, but no sound comes out of your mouth.

20

The Deliciousness of Deliciousness

"Compound 37d," Octavia declared, "is part accident, part discovery, and partly my fault. You see, back then I had no idea that I was the worst cook on the planet."

"How is that possible?" asked Snowize. "Surely you tasted your own food? Or were you in deep denial?"

"Oh no, I honestly had no idea. The truth is, I have a rare condition where my tastebuds are severely underactive. I can't taste very much at all."

"That would explain it," said Snowize, and then he caught sight of Ever, slumped over the table. "Ever, sit up. It's rude to slouch over like that," he said.

It was a relief to finally be noticed. Ever made an attempt to move, but nothing happened.

"Poor thing is exhausted," said Octavia. "Leave her be."

No, thought Ever, *whatever you do, don't leave me be!* Her eyelids were the only part of her body that she could still move, so she tried desperately to blink out a Morse code message.

"Really, Ever, fluttering and rolling your eyes is not appropriate behavior right now," said Snowize. "I'm sorry.

She was abandoned by her parents, and her guardian clearly didn't teach her any manners."

Ever fluttered her eyelids some more, but her SOS message was lost on her audience. Snitch, who was usually more astute, was not paying any attention because he'd secretly stashed some food in his cheek pouches and was slowly savoring the remains of his delicious mouthfuls. There was no distracting him.

"So," said Snowize, returning to Octavia's story, "surely your husband flat out refused to eat your awful concoctions?"

"That's the tragedy. You see, even though everything I made was perfectly dreadful, poor Gustav never had the heart to say the food was inedible. Rather, he added two letters and said it was incredible. He was not lying; he did find it incredible that anything could taste so horrendous."

Ever would have nodded along in agreement, but her mind was now focused on trying to save herself. *Move, move, move!* she commanded her jaw and her tongue, but they were no longer under her control. Darkness was closing in on her.

Octavia continued, oblivious to Ever's plight. "At the time, Gustav was working as a flavorist for WHIFF, the famed World Health Institute for Fabulous Flavor, where it was his job to invent new flavors for sodas, cakes and candy. Late one night, as he was shaking up a mixture of chemicals, trying to create a chocolate-berry-mint flavor, he reached for a vial of ethyl acetate, but mistakenly picked up a bottle of soy sauce and added a dash to his experiment. Then he accidentally spilled some phosphorous, which found its way into the mixture. The effect was explosive. Gustav was knocked off his feet. The test tube shattered, spilling its ingredients to the floor and forming a gooey gloop that shimmered with colors he had never seen before. An instant later there was a blinding flash of white light and a tremendous amount of heat, and the gloop was transformed into a pile of clear crystals. He scooped up the crystals and placed them in his pocket.

"When he arrived home, I was putting the final touches on a Spanish omelet. I am told it smelled dreadful. In desperation, Gustav took the crystals from his pocket and sprinkled them over his food, hoping they would at least give the disgusting omelet a chocolate-berry-mint flavor. He took a mouthful of his egg dish and was so amazed by the taste that he almost fell off his chair. It did not taste like chocolate or berry or mint. Instead, it tasted like an omelet, and it was absolutely delicious. Beyond delicious."

"So," said Snowize, "you're saying that your husband, quite by accident, created an unknown compound, and then, out of sheer desperation, he discovered that it could miraculously transform any dish into something so delicious it was instantly addictive?"

"Yes," said Octavia. "He had discovered the super-flavor of ultrascrumptiousness: the very deliciousness of deliciousness. And its unique properties made it colorless, odorless, tasteless and totally untraceable.

"Gustav knew that he could have sold his discovery for a huge fortune, but instead he vowed to himself that he would use it only to improve my cooking. So he quietly stored the formula in his head and told no one of its existence."

"Not even you?" Snowize asked.

"Especially not me. It was the only secret he ever kept from me and would have remained so if I hadn't gotten it into my head to enter a baking contest. You see, the trouble started with a batch of muffins."

Octavia described the muffins in question. They were cauliflower-and-orange-peel muffins, created from a truly revolting combination of ingredients she had thrown together. Out of self-preservation, Gustav secretly added Compound 37d so he could choke them down, and the muffins, of course, became so delicious that anyone who ate one would poke someone's eye out to get a second helping. Octavia decided to enter them in the National European Baking Contest. When the judges saw the disgusting-looking, misshapen muffins, they recoiled. However, when they tasted Octavia's creation, it was so spectacularly delicious that they pronounced her the winner.

"The biggest upset was that I beat the famous chef, Sergei Sergeiovski, who had created a seventy-layered chocolate cake for the competition.

"Poor man. When he heard that I'd beaten him, he demanded to taste the winning muffin. It was reported that when he bit into it, his face crumpled in sheer dismay, for he knew he could never make anything that tasted so scrumptiously delicious. He fell instantly into a state of despair and sadly declared that he would never bake again.

"I, on the other hand, went on to win a string of awards for my cooking, completely unaware of the real reason for my success." Here Octavia paused and looked fondly at Gustav. "By this time, Gustav had started to feel guilty about what he was doing," she continued. "He knew his interfering was not right, but he'd started something that he didn't know how to stop.

"One day, as I was creating a dessert that consisted of tinned sardines, caramel whip and pickled cucumbers, he decided it was time to confess.

"'My beloved,' he said to me, 'I've been adding a chemical to your cooking to make it taste delicious. I am so sorry for deceiving you, but I was in over my head. I thought I was doing the right thing, but it was wrong. So very wrong.'

"To his alarm, I didn't believe him. I laughed and told him to stop being silly. I was so convinced it couldn't be true that, without his knowledge, I entered the awful dessert into yet another contest. By this time, the organizers of any contest I entered automatically engraved my name on the gold medals. In fact, such was my reputation that judges would fight for the chance to taste my cooking. In this case, of course, they were in for an unpleasant surprise. Gustav would not come to the rescue with Compound 37d.

"The first judge took one bite of the dessert and let out a bloodcurdling howl of horror. Then he began to run around in circles, gnashing his teeth like a man possessed. It was then that I learned the truth about my cooking and the extent of my husband's deception.

"It almost destroyed our marriage, but our love was too strong, and his remorse was so great that eventually I forgave him. Gustav vowed he would never again hide the truth from me or use Compound 37d. I vowed in return that I would take cooking lessons and that the magical compound would remain our secret."

There was silence as Octavia finished telling her story. Snowize seemed lost in thought, while Snitch wiped away a tear with his white paws. He always cried during a good love story. Or perhaps, thought Ever, who was still fighting the encroaching darkness, he was crying because he'd finished his last stashed-away bite of the most delicious food he would ever taste. Ever's eyelids felt extremely heavy, and she could no longer fight to keep them open. Blackness pressed against her lids, but before she succumbed to it, she had one very clear and final thought. She suddenly knew exactly why Gustav Cadiz had groaned when he'd seen that breakfast cereal commercial. It was all too obvious to her, but now that vital clue would be lost. As darkness embraced her, Ever slipped off her chair and onto the floor.

"I . . . I can't breathe," she managed to say as Snowize knelt down beside her. "I've been poisoned. I'm sorry." And with that said, she closed her eyes and passed out.

21

A Meeting Underground

Meanwhile, in the city of Rome, a secret meeting was underway—way, way underground. Deodora Miffingpin was running extremely late for it. She was running late because, to get to the meeting's secret location, she had to decipher a series of cryptic clues sent to her by the Secret Society of Spies Anonymous. Each clue required extensive research and fluency in at least five languages. If anyone asked her, Deodora would say that this was another indication of the ridiculous inner workings of the SSSA.

The entrance to the secret location turned out to be beneath one of the oldest *gelaterias* in Rome. To get to the entrance, Deodora followed the instructions sent to her by the SSSA. First, she ordered an ice cream cone with seven scoops. Then she hastily ate the ice cream, which took ten minutes and gave her several excruciating brain freezes. Once she'd finished, she stared at the owner of the shop and winked at him three times, which was part of the secret code. Then she asked the secret question, "Somewhere over the rainbow, bluebirds do fly, don't they?"

The owner looked back at her blankly and asked if

she was feeling all right. Deodora's face flushed as she realized that she must be at the wrong ice-cream shop. As it turned out, the oldest *gelateria* was actually across the street. She paid for her ice cream and hurried over to repeat the procedure, brain freezes and all. This time, the owner gave her the secret response.

"So, you're off to see the wizard, are you?" he asked, returning the winks.

To which Deodora gave the expected reply, "It would be wonderful to look into that nut's hazel eyes." After this she had to bow three times. She felt a little foolish doing this; but security was tight, and if she didn't get it right, she would not be allowed in.

The owner beckoned for her to follow him into a refrigerated room at the back of the shop. The room was filled with great silver vats, each containing a mixture of semi-liquid ice cream. The owner gestured to the closest vat and motioned for Deodora to climb inside. She reluctantly submerged herself in the icy, yet quite delicious creamy hazelnut mixture.

As she sank deeper, it soon became apparent that the vat did not have a solid bottom. The bottom gave way, and she was deposited into a cavelike chamber made of stone. Deodora stared at the moss-covered walls and shivered uncontrollably while trying to wipe the hazelnut ice cream from her face. She was greeted by her fellow spies, some of whom were still covered in ice cream.

It was going to be a tricky, sticky meeting, that was for sure. Deodora already knew she was going to have to fight for Harry Snowize. The committee had read his progress report and found it to be so shoddy that they wanted Harry off the mission and out of the organization immediately. He was considered no longer competent. The unfortunate report was projected onto a screen for all to see.

Secret Mission Progress Report
Submitted by Agent Harry Snowize

Aims and Objectives

1. To investigate the death of Yoshinobu Azayaka.
2. To find out who kidnapped Professor Gustav Cadiz and why.
3. To ascertain whether Doctor Professor David Ezratty (the Doc) is really missing, or whether he has merely misplaced himself somewhere in the future.

Clues and Conclusions

Based on a strong hunch, I must conclude that Yoshinobu Azayaka was murdered. Only time will tell how this was carried out. There is no doubt that his murder is linked to the kidnapping of Professor Cadiz. This link has been established beyond a shadow of a doubt by these words: *It's green. It's a pinkish white.*

Yoshinobu wrote these words in a final note, and they are the only words that Professor Cadiz has uttered since his return.

It's my belief that Professor Cadiz's mind has been stolen. Furthermore, I maintain that Yoshinobu Azayaka's invention, the Chameleon Rose, was stolen from his mind and sold to the ColdCorp Corporation. Perhaps it was even stolen by ColdCorp. This may not make sense, but time will prove me right. Speaking of time, Doctor Professor David Ezratty is hiding in the future, most likely to protect his own mind and inventions from such thievery. He has sent messages from the future instructing his young ward to find a mysterious growling box. We have no idea why.

Unfortunately, we can't prove anything just yet. We can only be sure that the mastermind behind all this deviousness is cold, calculating and cruel. In the meantime, scientists around the world should be warned to watch their backs, their fronts, their sides and, most importantly, their minds.

Greetings and salutations,
Secret Agent Harry Snowize &
Assistant Snitch

"I know the report looks inconclusive," said Deodora, before anyone could start attacking Harry's questionable work, "but I believe it was written . . . in a hurry. Snowize and Snitch are really close to a breakthrough."

This statement was met with derisive laughter from everyone present. Deodora stared at her feet as Harry's report was ripped to shreds. No one had a good word to say.

"He's based all his conclusions on hunches. He has no evidence to back anything up," said the SSSA President. Everyone nodded in agreement.

"His hunches are hardly ever wrong," said Deodora, desperately trying to save the situation.

"He's lost his touch, Deodora, and you're in denial because . . . because of the past," said Agent Trumbledot, who was dressed in a toga and accompanied by his Spychiatrist.

"Trumbledot, I thought you were suspended," Deodora responded.

"I prefer Hail Caesar! when you address me," Trumbledot replied as he was led away by his despairing Spychiatrist, mumbling, *"Et tu, Brute?"* under his breath.

"Order, please! Quiet!" said the President. "The point is that Snowize is making wild assumptions about minds being stolen and has fanciful notions that big corporations are involved. Frankly, Snowize is beginning to sound paranoid." At this, a heated argument arose among the group about what should be done. Voices were raised, and they echoed in the underground chamber. Deodora twiddled her thumbs nervously, fighting her own frustration.

"That does it," said the President at last. "He was given a second, second chance, and he's blown it. I want him off this case pronto. The case must be reassigned to someone who has all their wits about them."

Everyone nodded in agreement, except Deodora, who jumped to her feet and pointed out that according to the rules, Harry still had three more days in which to solve the case.

"All right," said the President. "We will wait three days before striking him officially from the register."

"Thank you," said Deodora, wondering how on earth she was going to save Harry this time.

"You should stop fighting for him and move on with your life, Deodora," said Agent 007, who had always been secretly jealous of Harry's quick wit and cool sense of style. "He doesn't even remember who you are," he continued.

"It's temporary," Deodora snapped. "It's a temporary loss of memory."

"It's been several years, Deodora. We don't call that temporary," added the President in a more gentle tone. "He's damaged goods. Surely, as his wife, you have to see that's the truth."

Deodora felt her cheeks glow red with a mixture of shame and anger. There was no denying that cruel truth. Ever since coming out of hiding, Snowize had no recollection of her or of having been married in the first place. It was inconceivable that he could forget her; but forget her he had, and it hurt in a way she could not describe.

At first she had thought he was pretending not to know her for security reasons. After all, it was for security reasons that they had decided to go into separate hiding places to escape the Brothers Weiss, whose criminal activities they'd been trying to stop. Snowize had gone into hiding in the same tooth in which he'd hidden once before, and Deodora went underground. It had been the most difficult decision they'd ever made, but it was the only way to ensure the safety of all involved.

The plan was that a year later they would come out of hiding and meet at a specific time and place. Deodora arrived at their rendezvous point, only to find that Harry was not there. She waited ten minutes, wondering what could be keeping him. Harry, on the other hand, had written the time and place of their rendezvous in invisible ink in his daily planner. But all it said was: *Secret rendezvous with you-know-who to plan return of you-know-what.* Harry didn't remember what any of it meant, so there was no sense of urgency. He arrived ten minutes late and greeted every stranger he saw in the hope they'd turn out to be the person he was supposed to be meeting. Deodora, meanwhile, was about to give up and leave when thugs working for the Brothers Weiss surrounded her. They dragged her right past Harry, who didn't recognize her, and merely waved back at her with a smile when she tried to signal for help.

The kidnappers kept Deodora imprisoned on a remote island for five years. But Harry made no attempt to find his wife. It was as if he had forgotten she existed. Later, after the SSSA announced that its agent, Deodora Miffingpin had escaped captivity with the help of a highly intelligent, genetically enhanced rat named Snitch, Harry shouted, "Bravo!" and promptly submitted an application for the rat to be installed as an assistant in his detective agency. His failure to acknowledge his wife made Deodora realize that the warnings she'd received about Harry's mental health were not exaggerated. In fact, they were far worse than she'd imagined.

Even so, it hurt deeply when she called to tell him that she was his newly appointed Secret Secretary and he didn't recognize her voice. He was curt to the point of rudeness over the phone, irked at being interrupted during a chess match. Deodora wanted the job because it was the only way she could be close to him and monitor his state of mind, yet it was a constant source of pain for her. Especially at moments like these, when her SSSA colleagues forgot themselves and spoke so thoughtlessly.

Just as Deodora was thinking up a good excuse to leave the meeting, Agent Zed came shooting through the entrance, shouting that he had urgent news.

"Extremely urgent news!" he shouted emphatically as hazelnut ice cream dripped from his nose. "Harry Snowize sent me a t-mail. I guess there is no reception down here so he contacted me instead of his Secret Secretary." He took a deep breath and looked at Deodora.

"It's the girl traveling with Snowize. Ever."

"Ever?" asked Deodora. "Did you say her name's *Ever*?"

"Yes," answered Agent Zed. "She's been poisoned. It looks bad. Very bad." Deodora grabbed Agent Zed's sticky arm for support, afraid her legs were about to cave in. She felt an icy grip on her heart. Without any further explanation, she dove headfirst into the vat of icy, semiliquid lemon sorbet, marked EXIT, and was gone.

22

The Disappearing Detective

While a panicked Deodora boarded a plane in Rome, back in Spain frantic efforts were being made to revive Ever. It took the strongest smelling salts to wake her. When she came to, she found herself staring up into three sets of worried eyes, one of which belonged to a rodent. Through her labored breathing, Ever was able to tell the detectives and Octavia how her attacker had poisoned her and that she needed the growling box in order to exchange it for the antidote.

"Listen to me, Ever," said Snowize, shaking her slightly to help her remain conscious. "This is an old trick that's been used through the ages. People tell other people that they've been cursed, or that a spell has been cast on them and that they will die. The mind is a powerful thing. People convince themselves that this is true, and then they just die because they believe they've been cursed or enchanted or . . . poisoned."

"Now I know why I never told you," said Ever, barely able to get the words out. "I knew you'd never believe me." She slowly pulled the bandage off her arm to reveal the coin-sized wound beneath it. It was red and raw, and to her eyes, it glowed strangely.

"Does it look like this is all in my mind?" she asked weakly. Her tongue felt thick and clumsy. Snitch shot Snowize a warning look. Octavia was instantly alarmed.

"I'll call for an ambulance. We have no time to waste," she said, reaching for the phone.

"No need," said Snowize nonchalantly. "She'll be dead by the time they get here."

Ever was too weak to be stunned.

"You monster!" exclaimed Octavia. "We have to do something to save her."

"Of course," said Snowize, calmly. "I have just the thing for her." He then removed the silver ring he wore on his middle finger and twisted it open into two halves. The lower half was hollowed out and inside was a white powder.

"The Universal Antidote," said Snowize. "No spy worth his salt travels without it. It will stop the effects of any poison both known and unknown to man."

Now Ever understood why the detective was being so calm. He stirred the powder into a half glass of water and held it gently to her lips. She drank slowly, taking tiny sips. For a few minutes, nothing happened. The darkness still loomed, but it seemed as if something was holding it at bay. All eyes were upon her. And then, after ten minutes, she started to cough, deep coughs that wracked her entire body and made her feel as if her insides were raw. Just as suddenly as the coughing started, it stopped. Ever's hands and feet tingled, as a comforting warmth filled her from head to toe. She was flooded with an incredible sense of well-being. It was as if she could feel the poison draining away and her strength returning. She smiled broadly, paying no thought to the gap between her teeth, happy just to be able to smile.

Octavia immediately rechecked Ever's vital signs and found them to be in perfect order. The girl was the picture of health.

"Detective Snowize, I owe you an apology," said Octavia. "I was wrong to call you a monster."

"Think nothing of it," insisted Snowize. "I've been called far worse by my Secret Secretary. By comparison, being labeled a monster is a compliment. Indeed, amongst her slew of insults, I've been called a venomous toad, a tyrannical troglodyte, an amnesic anemone—"

He was interrupted by Ever, who stood up on strong legs. "I'm cured," she said with wonder and delight, throwing her arms around the detective who was not used to such effusive displays of emotion. "Thank you," she said over and over again. "It seems you were right after all. I got the message wrong. I was never meant to save you and Snitch. You were obviously supposed to save me."

Snowize was uncomfortable with her praise. "I was just doing what anyone would have done under the circumstances," he said. But Ever could tell that there was something that troubled him. He had a look on his face that she now recognized, when he was unable to recollect some important piece of information.

His expression suddenly reminded her of the revelation she'd had just before she passed out. Ever snapped open her notebook and wrote it down.

Snowize, observing absentmindedly over her shoulder, looked startled. "My goodness!" he said, slapping his forehead with the palm of his hand so emphatically that it left a red imprint. "We have a breakthrough!" he announced. "Octavia, I know how they took your husband's mind!"

And as they all leaned forward to hear, Harry Snow-ize did a remarkable thing. Snitch rubbed his eyes with his paws in total disbelief. Octavia gasped, and her knees buckled slightly. Ever blinked multiple times, wondering if the Universal Antidote had side effects that made her unable to see things that were actually there. Because the detective, in a single instant, had completely and utterly disappeared, right before their eyes.

"Well," said Snowize's voice, breaking their silence. "Isn't anybody curious? About the breakthrough?" His voice seemed to come from exactly where he'd been sitting on the sofa. Snitch sniffed the air. His long whiskers twitched. According to his sense of smell, he informed them, Snowize was still sitting on the floral-print sofa. Ever rubbed her eyes again.

"Is something wrong?" asked Snowize, sounding perplexed.

"Er," managed Octavia, "if you're still on the sofa, could you please stand up?"

"Why certainly," Snowize responded. As he lifted himself, it seemed as if a man-shaped portion of the sofa had stood up. Every part of him, his skin, his clothes, his hair, looked identical to the fabric of the sofa.

"What's the problem?" he asked. As he spoke it became clear that even his tongue and teeth were tinged with the color and pattern of the sofa fabric.

"Wow," said Snowize, catching sight of his hands and feet. "It works. Yoshinobu Azayaka's Chameleon Rose works. Just as he suspected it might." He sat down again and once more blended in perfectly with the sofa. Then he stood up and shook out his arms and legs rather vigorously. Slowly, the pattern faded, and his skin and clothes returned to normal. Snitch shook his head in amazement and disapproval.

"That's why you ate the Chameleon Rose," he signed. "You knew it might give you some strange abilities."

Snowize winked at Ever. "Noshiyobu told me that the rose might have these side effects, if eaten. He was afraid to use himself as a human guinea pig because he didn't know for sure what the consequences might be."

"Perhaps," signed Snitch with a frown, "you should have paid attention to that warning and not eaten the rose."

"Jealousy," responded Snowize, "will get you nowhere."

Snitch protested that he was not jealous. He was concerned that Snowize could have harmed himself by eating the altered rose. "Need I remind you that actions like these could necessitate a visit to the Spychiatrist?" he asked.

"Nonsense! I've never felt better," said Snowize. "And now that I know it works, I can learn to camouflage myself at will." Snitch had to agree that this would be a very useful skill for a spy.

If the detectives had happened to look out the window at precisely that second, they might have caught a glimpse of a man moving into the shadows, just beyond the glorious gardens of the Cadiz estate, at the Northern Gate. He looked exactly like the man who had poisoned Ever, except there was no gash above his eye where the crow had attacked. Displeasure seemed to radiate from his entire being as he spoke in hushed whispers into his cell phone.

"Master Coldwell," he said, "Snowize, the girl, and that rat arrived a few hours ago. Just as I predicted."

The person on the other end of the line was not impressed. "I want that detective dead before he stumbles across the truth. He has a knack for not being dead when he's supposed to be, and I want to put an end to that nasty habit."

The clone seemed confused. "Master Coldwell, could you clarify, do you want an end put to the detective or to his habit?"

There was a long, heavy sigh on the other end of the line and the sound of teeth being gritted. "I'll spell it out. As long as he's alive, he could cause trouble. Bring him to me so that I can get rid of him once and for all. And for the last time, get me that growling box. The girl claimed to have left it behind when your good-for-nothing brother interrogated her at the Valencia train station, but I'm certain she was lying. All children are liars. She has it, and I want it. You will find it for me. That is your mission. If you fail, you will be erased and replaced. Understood?"

"Understood," said the clone as he gazed back toward the house, his eyes full of malice. Then he leaned against the cheerful yellow wall and slowly turned its exact color, until it became impossible to tell wall and clone apart. He was like a chameleon on a leaf, almost invisible, except for the occasional blinking of his eyes that revealed two tiny spheres of blue.

23

The MindHarvester™ 005XL

As the camouflaged clone lurked in the gardens of the Cadiz mansion, Snitch, Ever and Octavia waited expectantly to hear Snowize's important breakthrough.

"First," said Snowize, "it's so simple, I don't know why I didn't work it out sooner." As he contemplated this, he suddenly had the disturbing feeling that usually haunted him late at night, the feeling that he'd misplaced something of vital significance. It gave him a horrible sinking feeling in the pit of his stomach; and when he looked at Ever, the sinking feeling got even worse. Ever smiled at the detective. Snowize looked away.

"All right," said Snowize, "Ever, give us your theory."

"Me?" Ever asked. "You want my theory?"

"I saw what you just wrote in your notebook. About the gadget."

"But that was a joke. I wondered if ColdCorp had some sort of gadget that could actually steal minds."

"The unfortunate answer, my dear adverb," said Snowize, "is yes. Ever, your question sparked a memory for me that would have been better left unremembered. It made me recall the MindHarvester™ 005XL, a device of extreme and unusual cruelty and possibly the most ghastly invention since the atomic bomb." He was deeply disturbed. "This devastating device is the brainchild of the Brothers Weiss. Their name is pronounced *vice*, and it's no coincidence. They sell their genius to the highest bidder, and they don't care if their work creates pain and misery. They designed the MindHarvester ™ 005XL to suck out a person's thoughts and memories from the very brain tissue that held them. Several years ago, word leaked out of the Brothers' plan to build this infernal machine, and it became my mission to stop their evil work by stealing the blueprints.

"My mission was a success, and the Brothers Weiss were enraged. They put a very high price on my liver and an even higher one on my head. I was forced to go into hiding: first in a tooth, thanks to Yoshinobu's assistance, and then underground. While I was in hiding, the Brothers Weiss recreated the blueprints. It took them a long time, and it made them increasingly angry at me for having stolen them. My belief is that they finally built the machine, sold it to ColdCorp and now it is being used for the most nefarious of purposes. The ColdCorp Corporation used it to steal the Chameleon Rose and get rid of poor Yoshinobu Azayaka by brainwashing him into taking his own life. Next they set their sights on Compound 37d."

"It's a fine theory," signed Snitch, "but we still have no evidence that ColdCorp has stolen Compound 37d."

"But we do," said Ever, feeling a little more confident about her sleuthing skills. "Snitch, you told us that the family on the train were fighting over that cereal, Vitmo. They found it so delicious they even ate the box. Only Compound 37d could make someone that desperate. We know this from our own experience. I mean, Snitch, even you were prepared to behave atrociously to get more of it."

Snitch looked embarrassed by the reminder, but nodded in agreement. Ever continued. "Also, that same cereal is made by the ColdCorp Corporation. The ColdCorp logo was on the corner of the cereal box, barely noticeable. When Professor Cadiz saw the Vitmo commercial, it made him groan. Now we know why."

Snowize was beaming proudly at Ever. "You make it sound elementary. I couldn't have deduced it better myself. I predict this Vitmo product will fly off the shelves because people won't be able to resist it once they've tasted it. And no one will suspect anything because Compound 37d is tasteless, odorless and otherwise undetectable. That is all the proof we need that the deliciousness of deliciousness has been stolen." As he let this information sink in, Snowize leaned against an old grandfather clock and vanished completely. When he stepped away from the clock his face told the time.

"Impressive," commented Snitch.

"It takes a little practice," replied Snowize, grinning. The camouflage gradually faded, and the detective once more looked like himself and was very pleased, too. But then his expression changed. "*What?*" he asked angrily. "Are you serious?"

Ever could tell from his irritated expression that he'd just gotten a t-mail from Deodora Miffingpin. Snowize shook his head from side to side as he read it.

"Request categorically denied!" he yelled out loud. Then, in his head, he composed an angry reply, oblivious to the fact that he was also shouting it at the top of his lungs. "Deodora, the girl is no longer in danger. I administered the Universal Antidote, so there's nothing to worry about. I strictly forbid you from breaking Rule Number One!"

There was a moment's pause, and then the doorbell rang. Snowize looked both astonished and apoplectic at the same time. Ever thought that if smoke really could come out of people's ears, great volumes would be puffing out of his right now. "Deodora, what part of request-categorically-denied do you not understand?" he fumed.

The doorbell began to ring insistently.

Harry, I'm afraid it's too late, Deodora responded. *I'm here. I'm at the door. So, please let me in.*

"This is an outrage," said Snowize to a bewildered Octavia. "My Secret Secretary has dropped by uninvited and in person. Don't let her in. Tell her to go back to wherever it is she comes from. She knows all too well that meeting with me face-to-face is a violation of a Secret Secretary's code of conduct!"

Octavia hurried off to get the door, leaving Snowize to mutter and fume. She returned with a very anxious Deodora Miffingpin in tow. Ever was completely surprised. From Snowize's comments and complaints, she was expecting to meet a dull, matronly and profoundly mean-spirited woman. Instead, here stood a lady with intelligent eyes who was full of poise and confidence, exuding a quiet authority.

"Where is she?" she demanded. "Where's the girl?" Deodora stopped mid-sentence as her eyes fell on Ever. Her expression, Ever noted, was one of relief and anxiety and extreme concern, and something else that Ever could not recall seeing on anyone's face before.

Deodora moved toward her as if she was going to embrace her; but as she reached out, Snowize leaped forward and gripped the Secret Secretary around the neck in a potentially lethal stranglehold. "Make one false move, and I'll snap your neck before you can say six of one or half a dozen of the other!" Deodora was clearly finding it hard to breathe, let alone say anything quite so verbose.

"Wait! Wait!" Snitch signaled. "Deodora's on our side. Let her go!"

"But how do I even know she's Deodora when I've never seen her before? She could easily be our enemy who's taken on the appearance of Deodora."

With that Deodora twisted to the left and to the right, quickly spinning away from him. "Butterfingers," she said with half a smile.

Snowize whirled around to grab her again. Ever watched in awe as they expertly danced around each other, ready to attack. Deodora glanced at Ever.

"Are you okay?" she asked as Snowize grabbed her hand and twirled her in toward him.

"I'm fine," said Ever, wincing as Snowize attempted to grab Deodora by the neck once more. Fortunately, she dodged him.

Ever was struck by Deodora's eyes, which were the color of the shallow part of the ocean—an aquamarine, greenish-blue that was truly beautiful. She was as lithe as a dancer and as agile as an acrobat. Ever was not the only one fascinated by her. She noticed that Detective Snowize seemed lost in her gaze, transfixed by her graceful movements. When Deodora smiled at him, she revealed a gap between her two front teeth, but she didn't seem at all ashamed of it. She smiled with confidence, and she looked lovely. For the first time, it dawned on Ever that she, too, might one day grow to become that confident in her smile.

"Do I know you from somewhere?" Snowize asked, squinting quizzically at his Secret Secretary. Deodora held her breath. She glanced hopefully at Snitch, who also held his breath. Was this the moment she'd been waiting for, for so many years?

"You tell me," she answered, ever hopeful. "Do I seem familiar?" They were still circling each other, hands at the

ready. Snowize held Deodora's gaze for a moment longer, then he shook his head. "No. Must've been a trick of the light. I certainly would have remembered you if we'd met before."

Snitch winced on Deodora's behalf. He knew how much this hurt her. Deodora lowered her hands and stopped circling. The spark of hope was gone. She sighed. There was no way she could deny it any longer—her own husband had really and truly forgotten her.

Trying to hide her disappointment, Deodora turned to Snitch and nodded. "Hello, Snitch. It's been a while." Snitch bowed in response. Deodora turned to Octavia. "Forgive me for barging in like this, but I had to check on Ever."

"Well, she's fine, and you're fired," said Snowize before Octavia could answer. "You can't go around breaking the rules."

"Fine," said Deodora. "If that's what you want, I won't argue. But right now there are more important things on my mind. We need to get this child to a hospital."

"Why?" asked Snowize. "She's made a full recovery. Ask her yourself." Ever gave a nod to indicate this was true. Deodora looked troubled. She took Ever's arm and looked into her eyes, felt her forehead to check if she had a fever. To Ever, it appeared as if Deodora was fighting back tears. Then Deodora turned to Snowize. "You've forgotten, haven't you?" she asked sadly. "About how the Universal Antidote works?"

"I most certainly have not," retorted the detective. "I'll have you know that I do not for—I do not have lapses of memory. The Universal Antidote can neutralize any poison. I used a full dose dissolved in half a glass of water."

"But clearly you've forgotten the three-day factor,"

said Deodora. "Because if you hadn't, you would be on your way to a hospital right now." Ever was now highly alert. A feeling of dread returned to her.

"The three-day factor?" Snowize looked annoyed, perplexed and, then all of a sudden, ashamed. "Oh. Oh dear. It just slipped my mind momentarily," he said to an unimpressed Deodora.

"Well, what is the three day factor?" asked Ever.

Snowize and Deodora turned to look at her and then looked at each other. An awful silence fell over the room.

"Okay," said Deodora. "This is difficult, but we have to tell her." Snowize raised a finger to his lips, trying to shush her, but Deodora was adamant.

Ever couldn't bear being spoken about as if she wasn't there. "Tell me what? And how come you're so concerned about me?" Deodora froze at Ever's question; and for the first time since she'd walked into the room, she was at a momentary loss for words. She drew in a deep breath.

"I . . . we can't talk about that now. This is a life-and-death situation, and the life in question is yours." She turned to Snowize. "If you don't tell her, then I will," she said. Snowize quickly steered Deodora into a corner of the room and started a heated discussion in hushed tones. From the way they argued, it was as if they'd known each other for years.

"You know," said Snowize, his voice getting louder and his tone exasperated, "you always do this. Whenever we argue, you give me that look."

"I do?" asked Deodora. "Even though you've never laid eyes on me before?" Her tone was hopeful again.

Snowize looked confused by his own comments. "It must be déjà vu," he replied. "That's the only rational explanation."

Deodora stepped in even closer until there was hardly any space between them. Snowize stepped back, flustered.

"This is not fair," he said. "You're not at all what I expected. It's difficult to argue with you in person."

"Do the right thing," said Deodora. "Tell her." Ever was astonished to see that Deodora's eyes once again filled with tears that she quickly blinked away. Snowize was under her spell. He cleared his throat and instructed Ever to sit down. Ever sat down.

"Ever, there is just one small catch with the Universal Antidote." Ever knew from the detective's tone that she wasn't going to like this. "It's an emergency measure to buy time. It's a temporary fix. You can only use it once on any given poison victim and, well . . ."

" . . . It only works for three days," whispered Ever, feeling both afraid and disheartened at the same time. "And once that time is up?"

"The poison will come back even stronger than before. If you don't get the real antidote, then I'm afraid you will relapse and . . ." He couldn't finish the sentence. He couldn't even meet her gaze.

Strangely, Ever didn't feel absolutely terrified at this news. Perhaps she was numbed by shock, she thought. Or she was too preoccupied with the thought that if she died, no one would be looking for the Doc. She would have failed him because she never did find the growling box, and he'd be lost in the future somewhere, hunted down by the most evil people. She also had the sneaking suspicion that Deodora Miffingpin was hiding something from her, something she would not discover if the wretched poison returned and robbed her of her life.

"Don't worry," signed Snitch, who looked extremely worried himself. "We're going to find the box that growls and exchange it for the antidote. You will be saved. The defective detectives will not let you down."

"No, we won't," added Snowize quite solemnly. "You have our word."

Deodora didn't look convinced. She took Ever by the hand and insisted that she be taken straight to a hospital for monitoring. Snowize looked grim.

"Deodora, I will not mince my words even though, at a time like this, I should probably mince them a little. But the truth is that a hospital will be of no use. If they've poisoned her, we can be certain that only they have the antidote. Our best chance is to find the growling box and exchange it for the antidote. So we have a long journey ahead of us, back to the Doc's home to pick up that growling box where Ever left it. We need to get to it before anyone else does."

This did not sit well with Deodora. "I'm coming with you," she said, and there was a resoluteness in her voice that impressed Ever. "All that matters is saving Ever, and I can't leave the responsibility in anyone else's hands."

"No," said Snowize, "we need you as our backup, to come to our aid as you have done so effectively until now. You're our lifeline and the only reliable member of this team who has all her wits about her."

"I won't leave Ever," she said. "I simply cannot. It would be against the rules."

A confused Ever started to protest, but Snowize held up his hand. "That's fine," said the detective. "You won't have to leave her because, on second thought, I would prefer it if she stayed behind with you. Snitch and I need to get down to some serious detective work. We don't need a poisoned child slowing us down. We'll find the box and get the antidote from these dastardly people. We'll return in two days."

"No," said Ever, and she suspected she looked even

more resolute than Ms. Miffingpin. "You're all missing the point. The Doc asked *me* to protect the growling box. He asked me, specifically, and I owe it to him to find it after I stupidly forgot it. I need to do this for him. Because once I was just a little girl stranded on his doorstep; and he took me in and not only gave me a home, but also became my family. He's the only person I have left in the world, and I will not let him down. I will get that box and try my best to help him, even if it's the last thing I do."

There was a long silence, and Ever was surprised to see that a tear was trickling down Deodora's cheek. She didn't even bother to wipe it away.

"Well," said Snowize in his businesslike way, "I suppose that settles that."

24

The Maliciousness of Maliciousness

Laszlo Coldwell, the President of ColdCorp Corporation, stood silently in a meeting room on the top floor of a building made entirely of glass. People in offices on the top floor could see down through the floors below them, and those at the bottom could look up and see their superiors walking overhead. For this reason, the company dress code was strictly enforced and all manner of dresses, as well as skirts, kilts, togas, muumuus and frocks were forbidden. As an added precaution, so was looking up.

Laszlo smiled, glancing across the room at a pair of doors that led from the meeting room to his most favorite place on earth, a large balcony that overlooked the city of Cape Town. From the balcony's lofty heights, he could look down on anyone and everyone, whenever he wished. Laszlo spent a great deal of time on that balcony.

Now, he took his seat at the head of an extremely long glass table. He was immaculately dressed in a sleek suit made of red silk. In his lapel buttonhole was a rose of exquisite beauty; its unusual color had a shifting, musical quality that was like nothing anyone had ever seen before. His smile was cynical, and his heart was as cold as ice.

Also seated around the glass table were twenty men who looked exactly alike. They wore identical black silk suits, and their electric blue eyes blinked in their expressionless, pale faces. This was the dream army of Laszlo Coldwell. They had been genetically engineered to have no emotions beyond rage, anger and hatred. Laszlo surveyed his team of clones and spotted something out of place. One of the clones had a gash above his right eye. Laszlo gazed at it with increasing displeasure. He knew why it was there and what had to be done.

"You!" Laszlo pointed to the clone in question. "You have an imperfection. You must be eliminated and replaced."

"Yes sir," said the clone, betraying no emotion or alarm. Laszlo smiled again. He loved the way the clones were so perfectly obedient.

"Report to the incinerator at once," Laszlo added. The clone rose and bowed slightly.

"Thank you, Master, for having allowed me to serve you." Then he left the room.

Laszlo cleared his throat and began the meeting. "My cruel and loyal workforce," he said, "I'll start with the good news." With a snap of his fingers, the lights dimmed, and the clear-glass table became a flickering screen.

"Behold," said Laszlo, as the TV news appeared before them. The screen showed a reporter standing outside ColdCorp's corporate headquarters. The unusual glass building dominated the Cape Town skyline, with the iconic Table Mountain serving as a magnificent backdrop. Laszlo grinned as a shot of the ColdCorp logo etched into the face of the mountain came into view. "Notice anything different?" he asked the clones. "I had to bribe several officials to get our logo there," he said, pausing the image for a moment to admire his handiwork. "I also had to make more than one environmentalist disappear under mysterious circumstances. But it's the price one must pay for effective advertising, is it not?" He clicked Play, and the reporter stepped forward to make his live report.

"Today shareholders of the ColdCorp Corporation have reason to smile. Sales of the Chameleon Rose have been astonishing. Demand for the rose has risen rapidly, and ColdCorp now dominates the fresh flower market. It seems people are enchanted by the Chameleon Rose's ability to change color."

Laszlo turned the volume down. "Excellent news, but boring. We knew Yoshinobu's rose would bring in millions of dollars." As he spoke, he gently stroked the petals of the rose on his lapel. The rose twinkled and glinted. For Laszlo Coldwell, it was a symbol of how good ColdCorp was at acquiring what was not theirs to take, without getting caught.

"Of course, the real reason the Chameleon Rose is so valuable is because it holds camouflage secrets. I trust you have all mastered your new skills?" The clones nodded, and when Laszlo snapped his fingers, they disappeared altogether. Laszlo smiled at his camouflaged team. They blended in so perfectly with the chairs that they appeared invisible. They even *smelled* like the chairs, to the point that the most sensitive nose on earth would be unable to detect their presence.

"Excellent!" said Laszlo, and as he clapped his hands, his clones instantly reappeared. "And as we have seen, thanks to ideas mined from Yoshinobu's mind, each of you can now take on the identity of another person by merely touching their picture. Of course, I expect better success than your colleague had when he impersonated the Doc at the Valencia station. He was so close to a job well done, and then he entered into combat with a bird and deigned to return here covered in pecks and scratches. He has now paid for his incompetence with his life. I cannot and will not tolerate imperfection! Is that clear?" The clones nodded mutely. "Fortunately, I was merciful and sentenced him to incineration rather than extended torture. After all, he did bring back confirmation that the Doc has been hiding in the future." Once more the clones' heads bobbed in unquestioning obedience. "Good," said Laszlo. "Now, moving on to other positive news . . ." He tapped the glass table, and new images appeared.

A reporter in a supermarket in Plovdiv, a small Bulgarian town, spoke in fearful whispers as he hid behind a display of household detergents. "Around the world, incidents of violence are breaking out as word rapidly spreads that the supply of the new breakfast cereal, Vitmo, has officially run out." The reporter held up a box of Vitmo to show the viewers; but as he did so, a horde of people came crashing around the corner, heading straight for the box in his hand. The poor man tried to make a run for it, but it was too late. The camera went all wobbly as he scrambled offscreen to avoid being completely trampled by the crowd.

News clips from around the world showed similar footage. In a London supermarket, an argument was under way between two very polite old women.

"Oh, my dear," said the older lady in a pink floral dress, "I do believe I reached for the Vitmo first."

"Oh my," said the second woman, who sat in a motorized wheelchair. "I hate to contradict you, but I distinctly recall that my finger touched the cereal shelf just a second before yours did." This carried on for some time, until the first woman whacked the other over the head with her umbrella, snatched the box and made off with it. The other woman gave chase in her motorized wheelchair and was gaining on her when the shop assistant stuck out his foot, tripped the first woman, and grabbed the box of Vitmo for himself.

"Thanks to Vitmo," announced a British journalist, "chivalry is officially dead, and all social niceties have gone out the window as people are prepared to fight tooth and nail for the inexplicably delicious cereal. The makers of Vitmo have assured customers that it will be back on the shelves within days and urge people not to panic over the shortage."

Laszlo Coldwell switched off the TV with a tap of his fingers. The picture faded and the tabletop was once again clear glass. "Gentlemen, this is our latest success. People are completely addicted to Vitmo, but they will never know why it's so tasty. Even when they test and retest and analyze and reanalyze the cereal, they will never be able to find the amazing Compound 37d that is the key to its deliciousness. Let's close our eyes and say a silent thank you to the Brothers Weiss, who gave us the Mind-Harvester™ 005XL. It is indeed our greatest asset, and it is helping us to set a new standard in the acquisition of ideas, leading us on the path to absolute power."

The clones bowed their heads. Laszlo Coldwell watched them, reveling in the authority he wielded. "Of course," he continued sternly after a moment, "the bad news is that Doctor Professor Ezratty is not in our hands. And for us to wield absolute power, we need more than Chameleon Roses and Compound 37d. We need what he has got: the ability to travel through time. If we can manipulate the past, then we will own the future."

Laszlo Coldwell smiled once more, this time showing his teeth. He turned around on his glass swivel chair and picked up a glass remote control. He pointed it at the ceiling and pressed a button. There was a whirring noise as

a metal arm lowered three large glass jars and set them gently on the table.

The first two jars were filled to the top with a green liquid. Inside the liquid floated what looked like a disk, similar to a DVD, except that this disk was made from a thin sliver of a pinkish-whitish material. From the disk itself grew a network of strange tendrils. The label on the first jar read Yoshinobu Azayaka. The second jar was labeled Professor Gustav Cadiz.

"Behold, the fine work of the MindHarvester™ 005XL!" Laszlo Coldwell cried. He tapped the first jar with his glass ruler, and his lips curled into a cruel smile.

"This one is redundant. We don't need it anymore. Yoshinobu is no more, and we have extracted all we needed from his collection of thoughts and memories. Erase it. Permanently. Forever."

As soon as he gave the dreadful command, a metal probe descended from the glass ceiling. It hovered just above the jar and emitted a beam of intense blue light through the top. The green liquid crackled electrically and then the pinkish-white disk flinched as if it were in intense pain. After another burst of light and some more flinching, the disk turned a dull gray and sank lifelessly to the bottom of the jar.

"Mind successfully extinguished," said an automated voice.

"What about Cadiz?" asked a clone, pointing to the next jar.

Laszlo Coldwell ran a manicured fingernail over the jar. "Oh," he murmured, "I won't extinguish his mind just yet. I think I'll hang on to this as a souvenir for personal reasons that are beyond your understanding."

"Ah," said another clone. "A reason involving complex

emotions that we don't have. Like love, empathy and compassion."

"Correct," said Laszlo. "Such weak emotions can cripple your judgment as they once did mine. Love is overrated. Love is the weakness of mankind. You're better off without it." Then he tapped on the lid of an empty jar that was labeled Doctor Professor David Ezratty.

"Within twenty-four hours," he said, "I want the mind of the Doc in this jar. And I want that growling box." He smiled again, running his tongue over his teeth. "Is that understood?"

Nineteen heads nodded in unison. And with that, the meeting was officially over.

25

Something Wicked This Way Comes

"We leave via an underground tunnel that runs beneath the library," said Snowize as he unfurled an ancient map and spread it out across the table. The plan was to surreptitiously leave the Cadiz estate in Spain and head back to the Doc's home in South Africa, where they would retrieve the growling box.

Ever shared a worried look with Deodora, who leaned over the map to review their escape route. The tunnel in question had been built in medieval times. It ran under the Cadiz gardens and eventually wound up in the town of Buñol. While the detectives and Ever sneaked through the tunnel, it was Deodora's task to create a diversion.

"You'll think of something spectacular to distract whoever might be following us," said Snowize.

"I already have," answered Deodora. "We'll set part of the house on fire and call the fire brigade."

"A perfect smoke screen. Excellent," said Snowize. "I couldn't have come up with a better suggestion myself." Octavia started to protest, but Deodora reassured her that it would be a small, contained fire that looked far worse than it seemed and that she'd keep it under control.

Ever noticed the silly way the detective kept staring at his Secret Secretary. He didn't seem able to take his eyes off her. Deodora, on the other hand, was too worried about Ever and the antidote to notice. She held on to Ever's hand as if she would never let go. Ever found this comforting and strange.

Octavia handed Snowize a packet. "You might find this helpful," she said. "I know my husband, if he were in his right mind, would want you to have them."

Snowize held up Professor Cadiz's famous gecko gloves and inspected them. "Only a great mind could have invented these," he said, slipping the gloves onto his hands and feet. He climbed up the dining room wall and then on to the ceiling.

"I want to try," said Ever, staring up at the detective.

Deodora's eyes flashed with anger. "Have you lost your mind, Harry? You have under three days to travel across the world and get the antidote. The clock is ticking. Not proverbially, but quite literally!"

Snowize winked at Ever as he swung down from the ceiling and placed the gecko gloves carefully in his briefcase. "Told you she was no fun," he whispered in her ear; and then added loudly, "When you're better, you can test these out."

Suddenly Snitch stood up on his hind legs, sniffed the air and signaled for urgent silence. "Chameleon Roses approaching," he signed. "I smell a bunch of them. Heading for the front door at three miles per hour. Arriving in three . . . two . . . one—"

Just then the doorbell rang. Octavia pressed the intercom button, and they all waited with bated breath.

"Special Sing-o-Gram for the Cadizes," said a man in a singsong voice. Snowize instantly became very guarded and suspicious. Deodora stepped protectively in front of

Ever. Snitch's nose twitched as he sniffed the air. He could detect no malice, so he gave Octavia the go-ahead to open the front door, which she did cautiously.

A tall, skinny man entered and bowed deeply. He handed a bunch of exquisitely beautiful roses to a surprised Octavia. Each rose was a different hue of shimmering blue.

"Blue is my favorite color," said Octavia in wonder.

"Violets are blue and now roses are blue, too, there are things that are lies, and things that are true, the answer is found in one little clue," sang the tall man as he awkwardly danced a silly jig. There was a card attached to the roses. In a trembling voice, Octavia read it out loud.

"Some say life is like a pouring rain,

And all of the madness quite insane.

Like the straw that broke the camel's back,

Vilified forever and painted black.

And the rhyme of the reason is the reason of the rhyme.

Does the punishment ever fit the crime?

Oh the answer that you seek, you'll surely find

Riddled by the mystery of the missing mind."

That was it. There was no name, just the strange, creepy poem. The delivery man cleared his throat and started to sing again. "For Gustav, the absent-minded professor, without a mind you are just so much lesser. You thought you were cool, but now you're a fool. Have some

Vitmo to help you feel better." This time the messenger danced his jig with much less enthusiasm. It was obvious from the angry looks he was getting that this was not going down well.

When Gustav Cadiz heard the line about Vitmo, he let out a groan from the next room. Furious, Snowize pinned the messenger against the door.

"Please, don't hurt me. I'm just the messenger!" he cried. After a brief interrogation during which he swore up and down that he had no idea who was behind the cruel message, Snowize let him go. The poor man scurried away faster than his legs could carry him and as a result tripped and fell headfirst into the daisies outside. Then he picked himself up and fled.

Snitch sniffed the suspect roses and the attached card. "I have a really bad feeling about this," he proclaimed.

Snowize nodded in agreement. "Whoever is behind this clearly enjoys taunting his victims."

Ever glanced at the creepy poem in Octavia's hand and made a mental note of it. The trio agreed to analyze it later because right now it was time to leave. They followed Octavia down a flight of stone steps that led to a heavy metal door covered in cobwebs. They said hasty good-byes, and Deodora gave Ever an awkward hug and didn't seem to want to let go of her. She made Snowize promise to t-mail her every step of the way.

Ever looked back once before she entered the tunnel to wave farewell. Octavia and Deodora both tried to smile reassuringly, but it was obvious to Ever that they were hiding their fear that they might never see her again.

The tunnel was dark, and the stone floor was a little slimy. In the darkness, Ever suddenly felt the full weight of the truth of her situation. She forced herself to think only of getting back home in time to find the growling box. If she let her mind wander, she knew doubt and fear would seize her completely. She held on to Snitch's paw with one hand and rested the other on the clammy wall to make sure she didn't slip.

Snowize walked just ahead of them, hunched over and very uncomfortable. He struck a match every now and then to show the way. After two hours of walking, they found the ancient ladder just where it was supposed to be, and one by one eagerly crawled up out of the darkness. When they reached the top, Snowize cautiously slid open the manhole cover and popped his head through the opening. He was in the middle of a narrow, cobbled street in the town of Buñol.

"Ah," said Snowize, as a very ripe tomato hit him square on the forehead and juice began trickling down his nose. "What a perfect escape route." The words were hardly out of his mouth when tomatoes rained down on Ever and Snitch, and thousands of happy people began moving down the street. Octavia had picked this route specifically because it was the day of the world famous Buñol tomato fight. Recalling what she'd read in Volume B of the *Encyclopedia Brittanicus*, Ever related the information to her companions: "*Every year the narrow streets of Buñol run red with tomato juice as thousands of people throw ripe tomatoes at each other for the sheer fun of it. Known as La Tomatina, it's also one of the planet's biggest food fights.*" Indeed, it provided the perfect way to get out of town unnoticed while everyone around them was covered from head to toe in squished tomato.

"This is great fun," said Snowize as he picked up some tomatoes and threw them at Ever and Snitch. Ever wished they could stay awhile. She welcomed the sun's warmth on her face and the heady smell of tomato juice that hung in the hot summer air. For a moment, she could pretend they were just like everyone else with no mysteries to solve or stolen minds to recover, and that she did not have a deadly poison lurking in her veins. She hitched a ride on Detective Snowize's back, and he weaved them through the raucous crowd, singing at the top of his voice in Spanish. Anyone watching might have mistaken them for father and daughter celebrating the pure silliness of this day. Even Snitch got caught up with the festivities and relaxed for a moment.

It took a t-mail from Deodora to remind Snowize that time was of the essence. With much difficulty, he hailed a taxi, and they all piled in. The taxi driver was a large, silent man with dark glasses and a fuzzy black beard. Ever counted his double chins as he drove them through a maze of cobblestone streets. There were five or six chins depending on whether the man looked up or down, left or right. His beard held the remnants of a recent meal. Snitch sniffed the air to get a better sense of his character, but all he could smell was the scent of tomato.

During the long, circuitous drive, they discussed at length what the growling box might contain that made it so valuable, and more importantly, where it might be. Ever hoped it would still be on the desk in the Doc's laboratory. The taxi came to an abrupt halt.

"We are here," the driver announced in a thick Russian accent.

"But this isn't the airport," said Snowize.

Indeed, Ever noted, they were nowhere near an airport of any description. In the distance was a red-and-white-striped circus tent and a number of brightly colored trailers. Snowize politely explained to the driver that their destination was the airport in Valencia. The

driver looked confused. He consulted a map and then opened a Russian-English phrase book.

"My hovercraft is full of eels," he pronounced, as if this explained pretty much everything.

"Is this some sort of joke?" asked Snowize.

"Knock, knock," said the driver, after he looked up *joke* in his phrase book.

"Who's there?" asked Ever, who couldn't resist a good knock-knock joke.

"Larry."

"Larry who?" asked Ever. The driver mouthed something, but no sound came out. "Larry who?" Ever asked again.

"Larry Ngitis," answered the driver in a hoarse whisper. He grinned, showing lots of spinach stuck between his teeth.

"Oh. Laryngitis," said Ever.

For once Snowize grew deadly serious. "Exactly where are we?" he demanded.

"You are here," answered the driver. Here looked a lot like the middle of nowhere.

"We need to get to the airport right now," said Snowize, pointing sharply at the driver. The driver shrugged helplessly. He explained in broken English that he didn't or wouldn't or couldn't go any farther. He insisted that they were here. An incredulous Snowize sensed there was no point in arguing. He paid the man, and they all climbed out of the taxi. The driver pulled away and sped off into the distance, leaving them staring at the strange circus tent way off in the distance and the dusty brush that stretched as far as the eye could see.

When he was exactly one mile away, the taxi driver slowed down and removed his dark glasses. His eyes were an icy blue. His multiple chins started to wobble and dissolve and his beard melted to reveal a smooth, expressionless face. He pushed speed dial on his phone and spoke in impeccable English.

"Master Coldwell. Targets successfully delayed. From conversations overheard it would seem that the child was not lying. The box with the growl really is at the Doc's residence."

"A truthful child? That's a first," came the response from Laszlo Coldwell. "Perfecto, then. Everything is as it should be."

26

The Dream Before They Came

"Oh yes," said the bearded lady, "I dreamed about the three of you. In my dream, a bird told me that you would come, and here you are." Ever and the detectives were sitting in a brightly colored trailer sipping cups of tea and listening to the mysterious Madame Sfortunata. She was the traveling circus's fortune-teller, and she also happened to have a beard. The beard was long, silvery and sleek. Oddly enough, it suited Madame Sfortunata, a pretty woman whose age Ever guessed could be anything between seventy and a hundred. It was hard to tell. Her amber eyes were warm and flecked with gold, and her movements were delicate. She wore a chiffon dress and sported thirteen silver bangles on each arm that made tinkling sounds every time she moved. Interesting as Madame Sfortunata's outfit was, however, Ever found she could not stop staring at the fortune-teller's silky beard.

"It's okay," said Madame Sfortunata, startling Ever. "I am used to children staring at my beard. I quite enjoy the attention. I would consider it rude if you didn't." Ever immediately averted her eyes and looked anywhere but at the woman's flowing facial locks. She noted that the trailer was filled with oddities: a crystal ball, a deck of tarot cards, ancient runes, burning incense, candles with multicolored flames and a lampshade made out of butterfly wings. Madame Sfortunata was quick to point out that the wings had been collected from butterflies that had died of natural causes. Ever glanced at a large, stuffed crow that perched stiffly on top of a glowing lava lamp. It looked eerily familiar. But then, all crows looked similar to her.

"The elephants will be ready in an hour," Madame Sfortunata added into the silence, for no one had said a word since she'd poured their tea. There was no need. She seemed to know everything about them. Snowize cleared his throat.

"Elephants?" he asked.

"Yes. They're being washed and fed. I put in my order for them as soon as I awoke from my dream this morning. I knew you'd be in need of them. How else do you suppose you'll get to the airport? I'll tell you right now, there is no other means of transport available. It's either by elephant or on foot, and since time is running out, I believe elephants are the obvious choice."

Snowize conferred with Snitch and they agreed that elephants were, indeed, the better option. "We're grateful for your help," said Snowize.

"We have a few minutes," said Madame in response. "Allow me to read your tea leaves." She gazed into Ever's teacup. "To answer your question, there's nothing mysterious about my beard," she said. "It's a hormone imbalance that I haven't bothered to correct. The truth is, I've grown very fond of my beard; and at one time, I even sported a luxurious mustache. I've been married seventeen times, and all of the marriages were to wonderful men; but in each case, my husband grew jealous of my facial hair and

left. Such is life. If I could live my life over, I would make the same mistakes and marry them all over again."

She peered into Ever's teacup more closely and sighed. "You're a brilliant scientist," she said, "with only a few days left to live. So tragic for one so young and with so much potential."

"Perhaps this is not such a good idea," signed Snitch, giving Snowize a cautionary look.

"I want to hear it," said Ever. "Besides, Madame Sfortunata, forgive me, but you are wrong about me being a scientist. I'm just named after the great scientist Albert Einstein, but I'm no Einstein. I'm the worst student in my class."

"You judge yourself too harshly," said Madame Sfortunata. "Einstein himself struggled with the school system. You have the potential for brilliance, but you lack faith in yourself. There's really no point in being clever if you believe you're an idiot. It's completely wasted on you. If you were going to live longer, that is something you would need to consider deeply."

Ever felt drained as her hopes were dashed before her. A horrible sense of dread settled in her belly.

"Surely you can't tell my destiny just by looking at a few leaves," she said.

Madame Sfortunata smiled. "See, I told you she was smart," she said, looking at Snowize and Snitch. "The leaves tell me nothing, but while you've been sitting here, I've taken time to study you three. It's remarkable what people tell you about themselves with body language. One facial expression gives away so much. One movement can let me in on your deepest, darkest secrets or your greatest fear." She smiled at Ever.

"Your photographic memory has captured a poem that holds a riddle. If you apply yourself, you can solve it." Amazed, Ever took out her pencil and quickly wrote down the poem that the dancing delivery man had handed to Octavia. She studied it as Madame Sfortunata read Snitch's tea leaves. "Snitch, with your brilliant sense of smell, you've determined you can trust me. You can sniff out liars and thieves, and you know that the guilty have their own special smell. You deserve recognition for the work you've done, but detective Snowize has forgotten that he promoted you to partner." Snitch bowed his head as Snowize started to protest. Madame Sfortunata raised a finger to her lips and shook her head.

"Harry Snowize. You are haunted by the feeling that you've forgotten something crucial. It's true, you're missing what's most important in your life. And it's so close, you could almost reach out and touch it." Snowize didn't know what to make of this. He cleared his throat and looked slightly uncomfortable. But before he could say anything, Ever cried out triumphantly.

"I've got it!" she cried, holding out the poem. "Combine the first letter of each line and they spell out a name!" Ever took a pen and underlined the letters to demonstrate.

Some say life is like a pouring rain,

And all of the madness quite insane.

Like the straw that broke the camel's back,

Vilified forever and painted black.

And the rhyme of the reason is the reason of the rhyme.

Does the punishment ever fit the crime?

Oh the answer that you seek, you'll surely find

Riddled by the mystery of the missing mind.

"It spells out *Salvador*," said Ever. "It must be the Salvador who loved Octavia so long ago! The one who wanted to marry her."

"But he disappeared off the face of the earth," signed Snitch.

"Perhaps not," said Snowize, smiling mysteriously. "It seems Salvador L. Pozodelfrio has emerged from the land of the disappeared and has come back to claim his revenge. Once again, you have proved yourself useful, Ever. You know, if I ever had a daughter, I would appreciate having one as bright as you." Ever blushed. She was not used to getting compliments from the detective.

Madame Sfortunata smiled at her. "Ever, there is no end to what you could achieve if you just believed in the impossible."

"But what's the point in discovering that, when I'm going to die from the poison?" Ever asked.

"Ah, you still haven't learned. You have the power to shape your destiny," said the fortune-teller, stroking her long, silvery beard. "No matter how bad the circumstances, no matter what anyone tells you about what you can and cannot do, it's still up to you to decide what is in the realm of possibility. Giving up is when you accept what someone else says is your fate."

"You mean there's still hope?" asked Ever.

"There's no guarantee that everything will work out for the best, but if you don't try, you'll never know," answered Madame Sfortunata. "Just remember that the mind is a powerful thing. For example, if you start believing you're a magnet for bad luck, you might convince yourself that this is true. It's a self-fulfilling prophecy, and bad luck will certainly start to follow you. I'm just saying, be very careful what you believe."

There was a sudden knock on the door, and a man the size of a small child entered. Madame Sfortunata introduced him as Jacques-Claude Columbo, the circus owner.

"The elephants are ready," he said in the deepest voice. In fact, his voice was so deep Ever could feel it vibrating in the floorboards beneath her feet. He signaled for them to follow him.

"It's a great pity," he said, "that we couldn't use our hovercraft. It would have been much faster, but just yesterday it crashed into our mobile aquarium; and now it is filled to the brim with fish and eels darting to and fro. On the bright side, the elephants love to walk long distances. The pads on the bottoms of their feet tend to grow thick and this march will help wear them down."

"Detective Snowize, you have no time to lose," said Madame Sfortunata, rising from her chair. Ever, Snowize and Snitch thanked her for her help and hurried after Jacques-Claude.

The fortune-teller watched from her trailer as Snowize, Snitch and Ever were helped up onto the elephants by Dmitri, the seven-foot-tall circus strongman who went by the nickname Tree. Once they were all settled, Jacques-Claude led the way on a big male elephant; and the other elephants followed in a line, moving in the graceful way that elephants move, which is always surprising when you consider their size.

As soon as the elephants and their passengers were out of sight, the stuffed crow that Ever had noticed stepped down from its perch on top of Madame Sfortunata's lava lamp. "Thank you for helping them," said the crow, who was missing a middle toe. "Somewhere in the future, the Doc is eternally grateful. I myself have run out of energy and couldn't do it on my own."

"It was my pleasure to return a favor. The Doc is an old friend. I'm glad that he has found such good company as yourself in the future. I'm also delighted to discover that crows will evolve along such eloquent lines."

"Oh," said the crow, "it was only a matter of time. You know, even way back in the past—which is your present— a select few of us could speak more than we let on. We just didn't think humans were worthy of our conversation. They didn't seem to hold enough respect for each other, let alone animals."

Madame Sfortunata nodded in agreement. "It might please you to know that Jacques-Claude bought this circus with the express intention of making it animal-free. As we travel the world, he searches for reputable sanctuaries where he can release the animals into their proper environments."

"How marvelous," said the crow. "Then it was most fortunate for our detective friends that the elephants were still here to help them on their way."

"Very true," said Madame Sfortunata. "Timing is everything. We will be performing in Nairobi in just a few weeks, where a lovely new life awaits those elephants. I only wish I could know for certain that such happiness lies ahead for the detectives."

"The odds are stacked against them," said the crow with a heavy sigh. He did not look very well. He'd lost his sleek, black sheen and was looking a bit dull. There was a bald patch on each wing where some feathers had fallen out. "Time travel has taken a great physical toll on the Doc and me. We've done all we can to help them. But now it's up to them to save themselves."

Madame Sfortunata nodded sadly. "You're from the future, so you know how this all turns out."

"The future is not what it used to be," said the crow.

"It's subject to change. So, the future I know may not be the future that they find waiting for them. In fact, I do hope it's a very different one indeed." The crow shook his head gravely as yet another feather fell from his back.

Madame Sfortunata lit a thin cigarillo with a gold lighter. It was a nervous habit that she did not care to give up. Blue smoke spiraled up into the air, and the crow coughed politely. "Einstein once said that the only reason for time is so that everything doesn't happen all at once," she said, waving the smoke away from her face. "But life's more complicated than that, isn't it?"

"Yes," answered the crow. "We can only wait and see. Time will tell."

27

A Fiendish Fridge

Against all odds, they made it to Cape Town. Ever stared with relief at the beloved stone cottage that had been her home with the Doc for as long as she could remember. She was jet-lagged and weary, but she was finally back to the point where this whole adventure had started. And she was no longer alone. The defective detectives were by her side, and they were going to help her retrieve the growling box.

As she made her way up the path, Ever sensed something was wrong. The door was slightly ajar, and this detail made her heart sink. Someone had gotten here before them. Someone with ill intent.

"Hello?" called Snowize cautiously as Snitch sniffed the air. The detective tapped the door lightly with his foot, and it swung open with an eerie creak.

Ever clutched Snitch's paw, held her breath and instinctively reached for the locket around her neck. Time was running out for her. The Universal Antidote was wearing thin; its protective powers would not be working much longer. She tried to push the thought from her mind and focus instead on finding the growling box.

Snowize motioned for her and Snitch to follow, and the trio stealthily crept through the house. In the dimness, Ever could make out that the place was a mess. Things were scattered everywhere—drawers had been emptied; furniture had been overturned.

"The house has been ransacked," whispered the detective. Ever nodded. The growling box was most likely gone by now. She was about to despair when a familiar voice broke the eerie silence.

"Welcome home."

Ever froze. Snowize flattened himself against the wall, and Snitch did the same. They had all heard the voice before, but to hear it now was physically impossible. After all, they had left its owner unplugged and out of power below a baobab tree somewhere in southern Zimbabwe.

"Melschman?" whispered Ever, astonished. Her suspicions were confirmed when a plate and something indescribably rotten whizzed over her head and hit the wall behind her with a sickening splat. She had never been happier to have a barrage of insults and deadly objects flying toward her. Knives, forks and spoons flew by, followed by plates, teacups and saucers. The detectives ducked low, but Ever found herself smiling. This was the only way to be welcomed home. She had an overwhelming urge to hug Melschman and tell him how glad she was to see him. But Melschman was in a supremely bad mood, and they would have to wait until he ran out of things to throw before they could move from their positions.

"You're probably wondering how I got here," said Melschman monotonously in his computerized voice. "Well, I'm not as stupid as you all think I am," he said.

"No one said you were stupid," said Snowize, trying to creep forward while pacifying the furious fridge. "You were programmed by a brilliant, yet slightly crazy inventor, so we don't doubt your intelligence."

Melschman did not appreciate the detective's tone. "The Doc is not crazy. He's just a little eccentric," he said, holding up a white statue of Socrates. It was one of Ever's favorite objects.

"Don't—" cautioned Ever, but it was too late. Melschman launched the philosopher down the corridor at full speed, and the statue smashed into a thousand tiny pieces. There was a horrible silence. Then, quite unexpectedly, Melschman started to sob. His sobs were monotonous and robotic. Tears dripped out of his water dispenser. It so happened that the Socrates statue was also a favorite of his, and now he had only himself to blame for its destruction.

"Why?" he asked dully. "Why do I always destroy the things I love the most?"

"Well, there's no use crying over smashed statues," offered Snowize as he inched closer and gallantly handed Melschman his handkerchief. The robot fridge accepted it as a peace offering and agreed to stop throwing things, at least for the time being.

"Melschman, weren't you going to tell us how you got home?" Ever asked.

"Well you see," said Melschman, sighing dramatically, "when you cruelly left me for dead under the baobab tree in Zimbabwe, I was not entirely out of battery power." He droned on about how he used his last bit of juice to drag himself downstairs into the defective detectives' underground office, and with only a second to spare, managed to plug himself into the wall socket and recharge. Then, plucking up all his courage, he had braved the wilderness and a herd of ill-tempered Cape Buffalo to begin a remarkable journey home. It was a journey fraught with wild and heroic adventures, most of which did not sound at all probable, although he had the scars to prove them.

Ever winced as Melschman pointed out the dents and scratches over his bodywork. There was a chunk of metal missing from his freezer door, the result of a tussle with a poacher and a rhinoceros. Some rust had set in between his joints, so he now walked with a limp and a squeak.

Melschman recounted how, at his lowest point, when he was hopelessly lost and overheating in a vast desert, a crow appeared out of nowhere. The crow talked him out of his depression and told him how to get home. When they parted ways, the crow gave him a top-secret message for Detective Snowize. But now he didn't feel like delivering it to someone who had once threatened to have him reprogrammed.

"Please, Melschman, just for once, don't make things so difficult," said Ever.

"Too bad you chose sides, Einstein. Not such a smart choice after all," said Melschman. "But," he continued, "perhaps I will reveal this message after we've eaten some invisible ice cream." He glared at Snowize. "That will show you just how very wrong you've been about the Doc. It will be your humble pie, and I'll be happy to watch you eat it."

Ever thought this was a most peculiar request, but there was no way to fully understand the workings of a badly programmed robot.

"If you care about Ever," said Snowize, trying to reason with the robot, "you should know that she does not have much time. Just over a day, to be exact. We need to find the growling box instead of sitting around eating ice cream."

Melschman merely shrugged as he dished up bowls of invisible ice cream. "The way you all left me for dead has damaged me beyond these obvious dents and scratches. I'm emotionally scarred as well," said Melschman. "I don't feel like sharing and caring."

"Give me a break," muttered Snowize.

"Give me chocolate ice cream," signed Snitch enthusiastically.

Ever took the three bowls and placed a spoon in each. "You see, he did invent invisible ice cream," she said, happy she could finally prove it. She pushed away the thought that this might be her last meal.

Snowize stared at his bowl of transparent nothingness and declared, without irony, "Well, seeing is believing. Or, in this case, seeing nothing is believing." Melschman watched as Snowize swallowed a spoonful of invisible ice cream. "It tastes," said Snowize, "like nothing." Ever grinned.

"Mind the gap," whispered Melschman, and Ever quickly covered her mouth with her hand and glared at the robot.

"With this batch, you have to imagine the flavor that you want it to be," she explained.

Snitch instantly thought of chocolate and the invisible ice cream in his mouth became a delightful, rich chocolaty flavor. Snowize was a little more adventurous. He declared that he would like caramel and salt and peanut-butter malt with a hint of chili. The ice cream took on that exact flavor and grew in richness with every spoonful. "Impressive," said Snowize, "although its usefulness is questionable."

"Usefulness," replied Ever, "is not always the point. Sometimes you should appreciate that something *just is*. The wonder of its being, is the wonder of it all. At least that's what the Doc always said."

"Just a second," said Snowize, pinching the bridge of his nose to ward off a brain-freeze. "You said the Doc's notes and his ice cream formula were stolen, right?"

"Yes," said Ever, "and now you're wondering how he got the formula back?"

"I am. And I have an idea. An idea that fills me with growing dread."

"There's nothing dreadful about how he recovered it," said Ever, tapping her own head. "I was five at the time. A month after the robbery, I was drawing pictures for the Doc. In one picture I scribbled some numbers and words. I didn't understand their meaning, but it was the formula for invisible ice cream. I must have seen it in the Doc's workbook before it was stolen."

"And that's how the Doc discovered that you had a photographic memory," signed Snitch.

"A very useful photographic memory," said Snowize, his face darkening.

"What is it?" asked Ever as Snowize began to pace.

"Tell me this isn't so. Tell me that from that day on the Doc didn't show you all his notes and formulas and ideas that he'd written down."

"But, but," stammered Ever, "how do you know that? The Doc said I should never tell anyone. He would show me pages of calculations and writings that I did not understand. Then he burned them."

The detective sighed. Ever was shaken. "Ever, the Doc's right. No one besides us must know. It could put you in the most terrible danger."

"But I'm already in the worst possible danger," she insisted. Snowize shook his head. "I don't have a word for worse than the worst, so I'll leave it up to your imagination."

"So what if she saw the Doc's writings and musings!" snapped Melschman. "Do you want the urgent message or not?"

"Yes," said Snowize. "Please go ahead."

"Right," said Melschman. "The urgent message is as follows: You must be careful, Snowize, you are not safe. Your cover is blown, you've been sloppy with your disguises and your investigation—"

"I have not been sloppy," interrupted Snowize.

"Yes you have," Melschman intoned.

"Have not," insisted Snowize.

"Have so, too!" countered the fridge, petulantly spitting out a chunk of ice from the draw in his door.

"You insolent icebox!" said Snowize, with growing annoyance. "I can't believe I'm arguing with an artificially intelligent rusty robot that has the emotional capacity of a rock."

"I have feelings," Melschman insisted robotically.

"Enough!" shouted Ever. "This is no time for childish arguments. Melschman, you, of all fridges, should know better. And Detective Snowize, you're sinking to his level!"

Melschman grew silent. All that could be heard was his electronic hum and the occasional clunk of an ice cube. Ever sighed with frustration.

"He's in a sulk. You'll have to apologize," said Ever. This did not sit well with the detective, but he gritted his teeth.

"Fine." Snowize sighed. "I'm sorry for insulting you, Melschman. Clearly, you're a machine of great emotional depth."

"Apology accepted," said the fridge with just a hint of resentment. "The rest of the message is as follows: "You are too close to the truth, Snowize. You and your pet rat—"

"Partner," insisted Snitch.

"Assistant," stated Snowize.

"Partner, assistant, gopher—whatever—you're too close to the truth for comfort. You have annoyed some major mean guys, especially Laszlo Coldwell, head of ColdCorp Corporation. He is the extremely bad man who wants this growling box that I happen to have right here in my possession."

A stunned silence fell over the room. Melschman had mentioned the growling box's presence as if it were the most trivial fact in the world. Relief instantly flooded over Ever, and she found tears springing to her eyes.

"Melschman! Why didn't you say so? The box will save my life," she exclaimed, so excited she threw her arms around the robot. Melschman looked decidedly uncomfortable and did not return the hug.

"Yes," he said a little too loudly, "it has quite a growl on it. I grabbed it off the Doc's desk after you carelessly left it behind; and all this time, I've kept it safely in my freezer section. In fact, this very morning I stocked up on invisible ice cream and hid the growling box in a particularly luscious lump." Melschman opened his freezer door and pulled out the block of invisible ice cream. Suspended in the nothingness was a small silver box.

An emotional Snitch took Ever's hand between his paws and gave it a reassuring squeeze. Snowize cleared his throat and smiled. None of them had been sure they'd find the box at all. Finally, things were looking up.

Ever studied the suspended box with awe. As she moved closer, it gave out a muffled growl.

"There's only one small problem," said Melschman, as drops of invisible ice cream started to drip and the box's growl grew menacing. Melschman shuffled his feet a few times and then said, "I cannot give you the box because—"

"Nonsense," snapped Snowize. "There is not one good reason in the world why you would not give this girl that box immediately!"

"Except," said Melschman haltingly, "there's a slight complication—"

To Ever's absolute horror, as if on cue, seven identical men dressed in identical suits with the exact same electric blue eyes peeled away from various points along the kitchen walls. They had been standing there all the while, perfectly camouflaged, waiting for the right moment to pounce. Ever and the detectives were completely surrounded.

28

A Double Negative

Snowize was the first to react. He spun around and lunged for the growling box. Without the box in their possession, the detectives had nothing to trade for the antidote. But he was grabbed by three of the men, who restrained him while another clone produced a small metal ball that he rolled toward Snowize. As it reached the tip of the detective's shoe, the ball unfurled itself into an impossible creature, a scorpion with an exoskeleton of pure steel. The creature's segmented tail curved up and over, ending in an ominous, gleaming stinger. Quick as a flash, the scorpion plunged its stinger through the detective's sock and into the flesh of his ankle. "Ah, a stun scorpion," was all Snowize managed to say before he dropped to the floor, instantly paralyzed. Snitch rolled over and played dead, but the scorpion darted over and aimed its stinger directly at his nose. Ever watched helplessly as the creature struck and Snitch's body went limp.

"That's how you were able to follow us wherever we went," said Ever as the clone nudged the menacing arthropod toward her. "There are more than one of you.

You're a bunch of clones." The wound on her arm twinged as she backed away.

"Resistance is futile," said the clone, narrowing his cruel eyes. But then, seeing Ever cradling her injured arm, he seemed to have second thoughts. "No sense in wasting resources on a dying girl," he said, smirking. With a snap of his fingers, the creature rolled itself back into a ball, which the clone scooped up. The clone turned to Melschman.

"Thank you, robot fridge machine, for alerting us to the whereabouts of this growling box."

"*Melschman?*" Ever managed to cry. "Melschman, you betrayed us!" As soon as the words were out of her mouth, Ever remembered the crow's note from the Doc. *Your betrayer is your friend.* That's what he'd warned her against, and she hadn't put two and two together. She watched in horror as her friend betrayed her further.

"These pleasant gentlemen know how to treat a robot fridge with respect," droned Melschman in a disinterested fashion. "Besides, I did not have a choice. They had me in a terrible dilemma. They were going to switch me off, defrost me and then reprogram me if I didn't help them. You would have done the same if you were in my position."

"I would not have betrayed the Doc," said Ever. "He cared for you . . . like no one has ever cared for a robot or a fridge before."

"If only I'd been programmed with a little emotion in my voice, then you'd know that I find this all very upsetting," responded Melschman. Then he hung his head in what Ever hoped was shame, but somehow doubted it.

"That's enough chitchat, fridge machine," said one of the clones. "For the record, little girl, this rusty piece of tin volunteered to help us before we had a chance to threaten him."

"The name's Melschman, by the way," droned Melschman. "Care for some ice cream?" The clone ignored Melschman and turned to his six replicas.

"We'll take the defective detectives to headquarters. Leave the girl—the mind poison will take care of her. We have what we need." The growling box lay in the palm of his hand. Its growl now sounded truly menacing, like that of a ferocious, rabid dog. He placed it in a clear plastic bag, zipped it up and then gingerly put it in his suit pocket. Then the seven clones picked up the paralyzed Snowize and the limp body of Snitch, and left without so much as a backward glance.

Ever sat down on the floor, overwhelmed by a sense of utter despair. The enemy, she realized, was too powerful and too evil for them. They were outnumbered and out-witted and defeated. It was all terribly unfair. She allowed tears of hopelessness and helplessness to fall from her eyes and run down her face. Then, feeling exhausted and antic-ipating the slow return of the terrible poison, she closed her eyes, curled up into a ball and waited for the end.

Snowize and Snitch regained consciousness to find them-selves in a vast room made entirely of glass. They were seated at a large, glass table, and they were both mana-cled to their chairs. Through the floor they could see down hundreds of feet into the busy ColdCorp offices. Through the glass ceiling above they could watch the clouds pass-ing overhead.

"I see a rhinoceros being chased by a hippo," said Snowize, staring up at the clouds. Snitch thought it looked more like a dragon dancing the tango with a dinosaur. With one paw manacled, signing this was a struggle.

"It does not look like a mango teasing a dinosaur," said Snowize. They launched into a minor argument about the cloud formations, just to take their minds off the grim reality. They both knew their situation was dire, and there was no point in stating the obvious.

To make matters worse, Snowize felt a small buzzing inside his head. It was Deodora, checking up on them via t-mail. He didn't have the heart to give her the latest news. The last time they'd t-mailed they were safely at the Doc's house, and they'd just found the growling box. This had calmed Deodora down a little bit. She had no idea how quickly and horribly the tables had turned.

Harry, I've done some follow-up on the Vitmo cereal as per your request. Lab analysis reveals that it has no nutritional value and is made from 100% recycled toilet paper.

Ouch. That is disgusting, he responded. *But whoever came up with the name has a twisted sense of humor. If you shuffle the letters of Vitmo around, you get* Vomit. *Which is what everyone would do if they knew what they were eating.*

Exactly, responded Deodora, finding it strange that she and Snowize were agreeing so readily with each other.

The question is, she continued, *why is someone taunting Gustav Cadiz? It's one thing to steal an idea and a mind, but it's quite another thing to taunt a person. Seems to me that someone has a vendetta against Gustav in particular and against scientists in general.*

Snowize smiled sadly. Deodora had reached the same conclusions as they had. *Listen to this, Deodora. Ever figured out that the person who sent the roses to Octavia goes by the name of Salvador. I believe he is the self-same Salvador Pozodelfrio who once loved Octavia many years ago. No wonder he sent that taunting message to Gustav. He never got over his jealous rage. The question remains, How is Salvador Pozodelfrio linked to ColdCorp and this terrible business of stealing minds?*

How, indeed? came a taunting response. ***You see, Mr. Snowize, you think you have all the answers, when all you really have are questions.***

Snowize froze in his chair. It was not Deodora's voice in his head. *Who is that?* he t-mailed. *Deodora, are you still there?* There was no response from Deodora, only a mean, nasty laughter that echoed and then faded into an ominous silence. This was followed by an urgent warning from the t-mail service provider:

Mind Invasion Alert. A t-mail virus has been detected tampering with your brain waves. Please be patient while we attempt to destroy the invading virus. Thank you for your cooperation. The Telepath® network. Your thoughts are with us. We are always in your mind! ™

Snowize felt chilled to the bone. Someone had eavesdropped on his telepathic conversation with Deodora. At that moment, Laszlo Coldwell walked into the room. He sat down in a glass chair at the head of the enormous table.

"Welcome," he said, seeming to enjoy the moment. "I'm almost honored to have the renowned detective Snowize in my clutches," he added.

Snowize recognized the voice. It had been in his head only moments ago. *Laszlo Coldwell, you broke into my mind and eavesdropped on my thoughts,* Snowize thought.

"Correct," said Laszlo, with a grimace that passed for a smile. "Doesn't take a genius to work that one out."

Ever was dreaming of her mother when a metal finger poked at her shoulder and woke her up.

A robot voice said, "You know, Einstein, for a genius you're not all that bright."

"Leave me alone, Melschman," Ever said groggily. "And stop calling me Einstein. I'm not a genius. Never was. Let me just die here in peace, traitor." The dream had been lovely, and she wanted to go back to it, to hear her mother's voice telling her she was safe and loved. To smell the comforting scent of cinnamon and roses. But Melschman would not leave her alone.

"You can't die on me now. We have work to do," said Melschman and kicked her lightly with his foot until she sat up. "We have to save the detectives."

"That's rich coming from the one who just handed them over to the bad guys. Along with the box that could have saved my life."

"Einstein, you've got the wrong end of the stick," Melschman explained. "I'm not your enemy."

"With friends like you, I don't need enemies," Ever retorted. "I'm not going to fall for any of your tricks, so don't bother. You have no idea how devastated I am by your betrayal. If I wasn't lying here dying, I'd have a good mind to switch you off, defrost you and take out your memory chip myself."

"You don't get it," said Melschman. "Remember what the crow told you. Think."

"The crow delivered a message that said, *Your betrayer is your friend.* It was a warning. My only friend betrayed me, and I didn't see it coming. Now stop rubbing it in."

"No, no, no. Semantics, Einstein, we should be arguing semantics, looking at the meaning and order of the words. You've got it all wrong. If he'd meant that, his message would have read, *Your friend is your betrayer.* Instead, he wrote, *Your betrayer is your friend,*" said Melschman slightly desperately. "I betrayed you because that's what I was supposed to do." Melschman made some emphatic gestures as he spoke, and as he did, his rusty parts squeaked a little. "The Doc wanted to remind you that

I, me, your betrayer—I am actually your *friend*. Always was. Always will be."

Ever had never heard the robot sound this sincere. "Even when you try to attack me?" she asked.

"Especially when I try to attack you. That's the only way I can show you . . . how much . . . I . . . er . . . care." Melschman coughed and looked, if it was possible, a little embarrassed.

Ever stared at Melschman, confused. Was it possible that the robot was telling the truth? She desperately wanted to believe him.

"What about the box? How do you explain handing it over to those creepy guys?"

"Again, I was following the Doc's orders. I was supposed to give the box to them. I have no idea why he would actually want it to fall into the wrong hands. Doesn't make sense."

"No it doesn't make sense. Not unless . . ." And that's precisely when something clicked into place in Ever's mind. She knew what might be inside that tiny, growling box. Of course she knew! Because hadn't the Doc shown her everything, all his work before he burned it? The words of the crow came back to her: *Remember the box won't bite you. It will save your life. Guard it with your soul. Protect it with your heart. Do not, I repeat, do not, not let it fall into the wrong hands.*

"Do *not, not* let it fall into the wrong hands," Ever murmured. There it was. A double negative. "Two *nots* in a row cancel each other out. The crow was telling me it *should* fall into the wrong hands. I was too panicked back then to realize it."

"Are you having an epiphany?" asked Melschman, "defined by my dictionary as an illuminating discovery, realization or revelation?"

"Yes!" said Ever, "I certainly am. You're right. We have to save the detectives. And the only way to do that is by letting them know the truth about the box."

"Do I understand correctly that you wish to go downtown and sneak into ColdCorp Headquarters, a building that everyone knows is heavily guarded at all times, at all entrances?"

"I have no choice. It's what I have to do. Maybe there's another way in," mused Ever.

Feeling fretful, Melschman made a few ice cubes.

Suddenly, Ever snapped her fingers. "Melschman! There's a balcony at the top of that building, isn't there? Maybe that's a way in! Why would they bother guarding something so high up?"

"Why indeed?" Melschman asked sourly, rattling his new batch of ice cubes. "Considering it's one hundred floors up on a building that happens to be made entirely of pure, slippery glass."

Ever glanced over to Snowize's briefcase and smiled grimly. "I don't know what Einstein would have done in this situation," she said, "but I have an inkling of what Snowize might do if he were in my shoes. And speaking of shoes . . ." she muttered. Ever ran to her room and changed into more comfortable clothes. When she returned, she had a pair of sturdy hiking shoes in her hands. She tugged them on, picked up the briefcase and took Melschman by the hand. "Come on, let's go," she said. "We have a bus to catch." The robot didn't budge.

"You want me to come with you?" asked Melschman.

"You did say *we* have to save them, right?"

"It's just that, what can I, a clunky, ungrateful, hateful robot, really do in a situation like this? I can only offer people invisible ice cream. Or throw things. And those clones, they'll rewire me in a heartbeat. And look at all this rust, I can barely move."

"If I didn't know you were just a robot, I'd say that you're afraid," said Ever with half a smile. "I believe Einstein once said that fear or stupidity have always been the basis of most human actions. In which case, Melschman, I'd say that you're behaving as if you were almost human." And with that Ever linked her arm through the robot's, and together they headed out into the unknown.

29

The Beginning of the End

Back at ColdCorp Headquarters, Laszlo Coldwell leaned over the glass table and pushed a large glass jar closer to Harry Snowize, so that he could read the label.

"Gustav Cadiz," read Snowize out loud. The jar was filled with a clear fluid, and Snowize found himself marveling with horror at the disk that floated inside. He knew instantly that this was the stolen mind of Gustav Cadiz. And in a flash, he finally understood the meaning of Yoshinobu Azayaka's note, "It's green. It's a pinkish white." Those words had a meaning more terrible than he'd imagined. He understood why it was the last thing poor Yoshinobu had written down. He understood why Gustav Cadiz groaned as he voiced those agonizing words.

"His mind. He was describing his stolen mind. That's what it means," said Snowize. And sure enough, as he and Snitch gazed at the floating disk, it first appeared green, and then a pinkish white.

"That is quite correct," said Laszlo Coldwell. "It's a description of the last thing they remembered seeing. A sight more terrifying than terror itself: the sight of their pinkish-whitish-greenish minds floating in fluid before them."

For once, Snowize was too angry to speak. He caught Snitch's eye and knew the rat was feeling the same anger.

"In a few moments, you, too, will experience the terror of all terrors, Detective Snowize," said Laszlo. "Behold, the MindHarvester™ 005XL. Only in your case, we don't need anything from your addled, forgetful brain. "We just want it extinguished completely."

As Snowize contemplated this gruesome fate, far below him, at the north side of ColdCorp Corporation headquarters, security monitor number 85 showed the image of a young girl and a robotic refrigerator getting off a bus. The security guard's back was turned at that moment; but even if he had seen the image, he wouldn't have paid it much attention. The girl looked pale and sickly, as if she were slowly being poisoned. The robot was rusty and walked with a limp and a squeak.

Outside, a rapidly weakening Ever stared up at the huge glass building and considered her plan of action. It was unlikely, she knew, that she'd be able to save herself, but she didn't feel disheartened by this. She was determined to save the detectives. That was her mission, the one that the Doc had charged her with, and finally she felt she had the courage and the will to see it through.

"Good luck," said Melschman, and he raised his right arm to his temple in a rusty, squeaky salute. "I'm going to create a diversion to distract the guards on the ground floor and give you a headstart with your climb. This might be our last good-bye."

"Yes," said Ever, wondering how difficult it was going to be to get up to the glass balcony on the one hundredth floor.

"No tears," said Melschman.

"No tears," agreed Ever. They stood for a moment in awkward silence. Ever couldn't find the right words to suit this moment. Nobody had ever prepared her for a final farewell. She wondered if there was a line of greeting cards that had last good-byes for all occasions. Final good-byes for him, for her, for teens, and especially for robots—something like, "So long, and thanks for all the invisible ice cream."

"I'll never forget you, Melschman," she finally said in a small voice.

Melschman shuffled his feet.

"Knock knock," he said.

"Who's there?" asked Ever.

"I thought you said you'd never forget me," answered Melschman. Ever managed a smile. This time she was too weak to bother to cover her mouth.

"Mind the gap, Einstein," said Melschman. Ever wanted to punch him, but she felt too dizzy.

"How can you be mean at a moment like this?" she asked, hurt.

"I was referring to the gap between the ground and the hundredth floor of the building," Melschman explained. "It's a long way to fall, and I rather you didn't." Ever felt even dizzier looking up at the building. She realized she had to move quickly before she lost the physical strength she needed for this mission. The poison was making its way back. She felt her knees buckle, and for a moment she had to lean on Melschman for support.

"Oh," said Melschman, straightening out his rusty joints, "about that poison. Before you arrived, those clones were talking about how you were so suggestible and gullible, they could kill you with a mere thought experiment and a mind poison."

"A mind poison," murmured Ever as she snapped open Snowize's briefcase and took out the gecko gloves that had once belonged to Gustav Cadiz. Melschman was already walking away when it hit Ever.

"Wait, Melschman. What did they mean by a mind poison? Do you know?"

"Negative. I never asked them. But they seemed to think it was amusing and proof of how weak the human mind is. I guess you'll have to work it out for yourself, Einstein." And with that he clunked to the entrance of the building and disappeared through the revolving glass doors.

Inside, Melschman was immediately stopped by two guards who asked him what he wanted.

"Step back," Melschman replied. "I am armed with an invisible weapon that is capable of mass destruction. Do as I say or I will destroy you, your building and, if so inclined, the entire city of Cape Town. Maybe even the whole world."

Unfortunately, thanks to ColdCorp's enhanced security cameras, the guards literally saw right through Melschman's bluff and started laughing. Of course, this made Melschman furious, and within seconds he was pelting them with a stinging rain of ice cubes. The security guards didn't so much as flinch. They held up their steel batons and advanced on Melschman, who fought against his own programming to run from danger. He continued to hurl ice cubes at the enemy. He wanted to be there for Ever; he couldn't let her down.

He fought squeakily, yet bravely. Ever would have been proud. The Doc would have been proud. But poor Melschman didn't stand a chance. The guards beat the robot fridge with lethal force. Within a few minutes, he was hammered and battered into an unrecognizable

twisted, dented metal heap. His final words were hard to hear, and didn't make much sense. "Care for a plate of hickled perring or . . . some . . . sub . . . lime . . . mice . . . cream?" Then, with a staticky crackle, he went silent.

Ever was already up to the second floor when she suddenly felt inexplicably sad, as if something inside her had flickered and then died. She chalked it up to the poison, which by now was making her feverish and sick to her stomach. Only ninety-eight floors to go, she told herself. How difficult could it be? The glass of the ColdCorp building glinted menacingly in the sun. She nodded politely at the building, as if greeting an old adversary. The wound on her arm burned angrily. Setting her jaw in grim determination, she continued upward, wondering what the clones had meant by a mind poison. She stopped for a moment to adjust the gecko gloves on her hands and feet. Then she cleared her mind and focused completely on the task before her, moving with surprising strength and agility.

But at the fiftieth floor, Ever made the mistake of stopping to catch her breath. Then she made the even worse mistake of looking down at the tiny cars and miniature people walking below her. It was a sickening height and now her journey had become especially nerve-wracking because the gecko gloves were starting to slip—ever so slowly, but slipping, nevertheless—just as they had done with Gustav all those years ago.

Fifty floors above, Harry Snowize could feel the cool metal electrodes pressing into his temples. His hands were clamped down by metal vices that bit into his arms. He was hooked up to the MindHarvester™ 005XL, and there was no escape. Snowize looked at Snitch and commented again on the clouds that floated high above the glass ceiling.

"Looks like a rabbit hopping out of a magician's hat," he said, quite calmly.

"Or a cat being let out of a bag," signed Snitch.

"More like a snake swallowing its paralyzed prey," said Laszlo Coldwell. With a wave of his hand, the glass door to the boardroom slid open and one by one the clones filed into the room in perfect silence.

"Behold," said Laszlo gleefully. "We have Harry Snowize in our hands. And his pet rat, Smidge."

"It's Snitch," said Snowize. "His name is Snitch, and he's not a pet. He's my partner. In fact, he's a better detective than I am, in many ways."

Snitch looked at Snowize in shock. This was the first time Snowize had ever referred to him as either a good detective, or his partner. "I owe you an apology," Snowize continued, talking to Snitch as if they were the only ones in the room, and as if they weren't surrounded by a sinister group of identical blue-eyed men. Snitch shivered with apprehension. If Snowize was apologizing, it could only mean one thing: He'd run out of hope and truly believed the end was near.

"I'm sorry if it's too little, too late, but I want you to know how much I've enjoyed working with you. And how much I regret forgetting that I promoted you to partner." Snitch was both amazed and troubled by how Snowize said *forget* without so much as flinching. He twitched his whiskers and tried to suppress the tear that was forming in his eye. He nodded a silent thank you to Snowize.

"That's enough," said Laszlo Coldwell. "I can't stand sentimentality. Next thing we know, we'll be hearing violins." He motioned for the clones to sit down.

"I have called you all here to witness the destruction of the spy who has eluded capture for so long. Harry Snowize has been a thorn in many sides for many years.

Most recently, that side was mine, and he came close to destroying our beautiful mission."

The clones nodded icily as Laszlo Coldwell pressed his remote control and lowered the metal orb of the Mind-Harvester™ 005XL until it hovered just above Snowize's head. The detective showed no fear. In fact, he seemed completely at ease.

"You do realize, detective, that all hope is lost," said Coldwell. "There will be no last-minute reprieves, no stay of execution. You will not miraculously break free and survive against all odds. This is it. *Finito*. Good-bye. And once you're out of the way, we will continue to go about our business of siphoning brilliant ideas from the minds of scientists. I have a list, and my list is long. To name but a few, there are professors Grace Alexi and Stacey Saumure, working on a secret nanotechnology to cure aging. Our spies are monitoring their every move. And Dr. Jennifer Tshabalala, who is developing a teleportation device; we have her in our sights. Not to mention Connie Fay Bright and Malaika Annaj, who have discovered not only how to predict earthquakes, but also how to set them in motion. Oh yes, Detective Snowize, with these technologies, Cold-Corp will rule the world."

"We'll see about that," said Snowize, in a tone as care-free as if he were swinging in a hammock under a palm tree. This response did not sit well with Laszlo Coldwell. He trembled with an unspoken rage. Snowize gave him a wink.

"Maybe this will wipe that smile off your face," said Laszlo, his voice full of malice. "Once we've eliminated you, your rodent partner, Snuff, and his keen sense of smell, will be taken to our laboratory. There he will be made to sniff experimental toxic compounds found in shampoos and hair products until he can no longer breathe."

Much to Coldwells's dismay, the detective seemed unaffected by this news. In fact, he seemed more interested in something else. Snowize squinted his eyes. Stuck to the pane of glass across the room from him was a small person, about the size of a young girl, who looked surprisingly like the poisoned Ever. She also looked like she was slipping and about to fall. One of the clones followed Snowize's gaze.

"Out of the frying pan," muttered the detective as the clones rushed to the window to seize their prey.

30

Into the Fire

"Well, look who's arrived to get her antidote," said Laszlo Coldwell with a smile. "I'm surprised you even made it this far, young lady. But I'm happy you're here. This might make things quite interesting."

Ever didn't respond. She'd felt strangely grateful when Coldwell's clones dragged her through the window and then tied her to a chair. They'd unwittingly saved her from falling.

"Just give her the antidote," said Snowize. "She's not really involved in any of this. Let the girl go."

"You've got nothing to bargain with," said Laszlo, laughing, and the clones smirked in agreement. "Nothing to offer in exchange for her life. We already have you and the growling box. And just for the record, there is no antidote for what ails her."

"Then you lied to us," said Ever. "The antidote was just a ploy to lure us in."

"And you fell for it. Hook, line and sinker," said Laszlo as he fixed her with his cruel gaze and began to chuckle. Ever felt her anger rising at the injustice of it all. She also found something disturbing in Coldwell's words, something she couldn't put her finger on.

"The minds of the young are so impressionable," added Laszlo. "It's almost unfair how easy it is to plant ideas and notions in their little heads."

Ever was reminded of Madame Sfortunata's warning: Be very careful what you believe. Was it really possible, Ever wondered, that the mind poison could be all in her mind? Slowly, it began to make perfect sense. After all, didn't the mind poison seem to lose its power over her whenever she focused on something else? It explained how she'd had the strength to do so many things, like ride on the back of an elephant for hours, or scale the glass headquarters of ColdCorp. It also explained why the clones had called her gullible. If her mind hadn't been so foggy and frozen by fear, she would have understood their words sooner.

"What a fool I've been," said Ever, turning to Snowize and Snitch. "Of course there is no antidote! Why should there be when it's just a trick of the mind?" She noticed in that moment how Laszlo Coldwell's face fell slightly. He clearly didn't like where this was going.

"Detective Snowize, you and the crow were right all along," said Ever. "The clones planted the poison in my mind. Like a spell or a curse, the mind poison works only if you believe in it." She glanced down at her arm. The wound had stopped aching and burning. The moment was bittersweet as Ever recognized the irony; she'd been saved from the scorpion's sting, only to find herself in the wolf's lair.

Laszlo sighed. "I'm disappointed that I won't see the mind poison work its way to a lethal conclusion. But I can't complain since it's reeled in such an excellent catch!"

Ever ignored him. It was still her mission to save the

detectives; and while she was in way over her head, she was going to give it her best shot.

She looked at Snowize and Snitch and said softly, "With regards to the growling box, it turns out Melschman wasn't a traitor." She tried to make the words more meaningful by winking. She wanted Snowize to somehow realize that the growling box was where it was supposed to be, without alerting their captors. She winked again.

"What's wrong with your eye?" Snowize asked, to her disappointment. "Is there something *in* it?" But as Laszlo Coldwell turned his attention to the MindHarvester™ 005XL once more, Snowize winked back at her. She sighed with relief. He got it.

"Yes. *Whatever is in it, has to come right out*," she answered with another wink. Snowize nodded thoughtfully.

"Trust me, your eye is the least of your worries," said Laszlo Coldwell. "Speaking of traitors," he continued, "I'm about to show you all what happens to those who betray us. Bring in exhibit A." Laszlo smiled at Ever. "This might be upsetting. It might make you wish that you had succumbed to the mind poison instead. After all, pathetic as it is, he was, I am told, like a brother to you."

The doors slid open, and yet another man dressed in a black suit with piercing blue eyes entered the room. What he held in his hands made Ever cry out. It made Snowize avert his eyes. It made Snitch wish that he'd never escaped from a laboratory years ago. He would have been safer in his cage.

What they were staring at was a twisted heap of metal, the mangled remains of poor Melschman. Ever felt tears flowing down her cheeks, and she didn't try to stop them. Melschman had sacrificed himself for her. Even though he was a machine, she couldn't imagine her life without the miserable and magnificent Melschman. He had always been a pain in the aorta, but now her heart felt as if it was going to break.

"Ever," said Snowize in a gentle tone, "I know I never got along with him, but I'm sorry. You don't deserve this, and I believe I've failed you. You're a great kid with a great mind. You've helped me solve this case. I only wish I could have saved you."

Laszlo Coldwell tapped his fingernails on the table, agitated. "What do you mean you've solved the case?"

"Laszlo Coldwell, I know what made you so evil. I know who you are. And Ever is the one who helped me to figure it out."

"Who is he?" asked Ever, through her tears.

"Ever, meet Laszlo Coldwell, otherwise known as Salvador L. Pozodelfrio."

The room went quiet. One of the clones dropped a pin, and the sound echoed ominously through the room. Laszlo Coldwell stood up. He was pale, and his knuckles were white. His eyes were wild and dangerous.

"How did you make the connection?" asked Ever, amazed.

"The clue was in his name. Pozodelfrio. Use your basic Spanish."

"Oh!" said Ever, getting it in an instant. "In Spanish *pozo* is a well, and *frio* means cold. Pozo-del-frio would roughly translate to 'a well of cold.'"

"Precisely, my dear adverb. Switch it around, and you get Coldwell. Laszlo Coldwell, you are Salvador L. Pozodelfrio. Which explains just about everything!" The detective could barely contain his excitement. Laszlo Coldwell's face grew ashen.

"You know nothing!" Coldwell spat.

"Oh yes, we know who you are, Pozodelfrio. Fifty

years ago you lost the love of your life, Octavia. You were humiliated and devastated when she fell for Gustav Cadiz and rejected you. But instead of seeking love elsewhere, you closed your heart and let bitterness consume you. Your life's work became dedicated to revenge. You wanted the whole world to suffer because you were in pain."

Laszlo Coldwell banged his fist on the table so hard that the force cracked the glass. A network of fissures spread out across the table like a spider web. "Don't you dare use that name with me!" he roared. "Salvador was weak and pathetic. He gave in to his emotions. But that part of me is dead and gone. I am now Laszlo Coldwell. All-powerful. Strong. Successful. Ruthless!"

"But deep down inside," continued Snowize, "that angry young man is still there, isn't he? The Salvador who could love and feel is still somewhere in there."

"Shut up, or I will eliminate you immediately!" Laszlo foamed at the mouth, and spittle flew in every direction.

"Ah," said Snowize, "the truth hurts, doesn't it, Salvador Pozodelfrio!"

"Activate the MindHarvester and incinerate this man's mind! Then vaporize the rest of him, too!" cried Laszlo to the voice-controlled apparatus. A whirring sound started up, and the metallic orb suspended just above Snowize's head opened like a flower. A needle-thin probe aimed straight for the center of his forehead. Snitch shut his eyes. Ever held back the scream that was rising in her throat.

"You can destroy me, Salvador," said Snowize in a calm and collected fashion. "And my destruction might give you a brief moment of pleasure; but I guarantee you, in the long run, it's not going to make you feel any better. You'll still have to live with your conscience."

"That's where you're wrong," smiled Laszlo. "There is a feature on the MindHarvester that removes consciences. I've had mine taken out. It was interfering with my most wicked ways. So you see, shutting you up for good will most certainly make me feel better, just as I felt when I destroyed Yoshinobu Azayaka!"

"That is so sad," said Snowize. "Just because one scientist took the love of your life, you made all scientists your enemy."

Laszlo spoke in a low, dangerous voice. "Gustav the scientist stole Octavia from me. And now they will both pay. I will win Octavia's heart. I will swap it in exchange for her husband's mind. It's a simple trade. If she truly loves him, she will agree to it. I will have her, and Gustav will have his mind."

"Now that sounds romantic," said Snowize. "Quite a way to win a woman's heart. You're aware that will never work."

"If it doesn't, I have an even better plan. Once I get hold of the Doc, I'll use his time-travel technology and change the course of history. I'll return to the past to make sure Gustav and Octavia never meet." Laszlo stopped for a moment and regarded Snowize with a sick smile. "But why am I bothering telling this all to a loser detective whose mind is little more than a sieve?"

The automated voice of the MindHarvester intoned, "Incineration about to commence. Does the victim have any final requests?"

"Yes," said Snowize, "I do. I most certainly do."

"Ah, my favorite part," said Laszlo. "I do so enjoy listening to last requests. Do tell us, Snowize, what could the final wish of a defective detective possibly be?"

"Why should I tell you if you're obviously not going to grant it?" asked Snowize, playing for time.

Laszlo glared at Snowize, and the sharp metal probe zoomed in closer to touch the skin on the detective's forehead. A look of terrible pain crossed Snowize's face, and he began to breathe heavily.

Laszlo leaned in close, enjoying the detective's discomfort. "I could always extract the request the hard way," he whispered menacingly.

Snowize winced. "Fine, fine! My final request," he panted, "is to die before you open the growling box so that I won't have to watch you salivate over yet another stolen invention that you plan to use in a corrupt way. I wish to be spared that anguish."

At this ingenious use of reverse psychology, Ever felt a rush of hope. She was even glad her hands were tied because she would have clapped spontaneously and given Snowize away.

"Oh dear, oh dear," said Laszlo Coldwell. "I'm afraid I simply cannot deny myself the pleasure of seeing you in abject despair. Clones, bring me the box that growls. Show me the wonder that it holds!"

He snapped his fingers, and within seconds the box was wheeled in on an ebony tray. As Laszlo moved closer, a low, menacing growl started up from the small silver container. The growling became a rabid howl, then a menacing snarl. All the clones drew closer around the box.

Ever hoped she was right about what she believed was inside. She was basing everything on a hunch and a memory. A memory of her guardian leaning over a series of vials in his laboratory and describing to her his most important invention, Project VOV, his incredible plan to save the world. Another memory of the notes and formulas that he'd shown her. She was his backup system. The only person he trusted with the details of his work.

Ever held her breath as one of the clones ejected a metal blade from beneath his fingernail and gently lifted the silver lid. Then he let out a howl of anger.

31

A Voracious Virus

At the very moment that the clones stared in dismay at the contents of the growling box, Deodora Miffingpin stepped into ColdCorp headquarters. She was disguised as a TV news reporter. Deodora knew that something had gone horribly wrong when her t-mail correspondence with Snowize had been interrupted. She wasted no time in enlisting the help of her fellow spies who, despite her erratic behavior and breaches of SSSA protocol, were still committed to the mission of recovering the stolen minds.

The Society's private jet, which flew at seventy times the speed of sound, brought them to Cape Town. Accompanying Deodora was the President of the SSSA, as well as two agents, X and Y. They were posing as her cameraman and sound crew.

"You realize," whispered the President of the SSSA to Deodora, "that if we do find Snowize alive, he will be summarily kicked out of the society. Because he has failed miserably in this mission."

Deodora glared at the President. "This is not the time for petty discussions about inconsequential things. There are lives at stake. Follow me."

But the President and the two agents didn't want to take orders from Deodora. They started to argue about how to distract the men who guarded the elevator door. Deodora had no time for arguments. She'd already figured out how to get into the elevator by making a simple phone call to ColdCorp's public relations department while en route to Cape Town. She showed her fake ID to the security guard at the front desk.

"I have an appointment with Kevin Quibble in public relations," she informed the guard. "I'm making a documentary on the remarkable achievements of Laszlo Coldwell."

"I'll need to verify that," the guard said haughtily, and picked up the phone. After a brief conversation, he grudgingly pointed Deodora in the direction of a gleaming glass elevator. She slipped inside, leaving the other SSSA agents bickering in the lobby, and pushed the button for the top floor.

"I'm sorry," said the security officer who controlled the elevator. "The top floor is reserved for ColdCorp board members only."

"Well," said Deodora, smiling politely, "I'm certainly bored, and I notice you seem to have some more exciting visitors to contend with."

The officer's eyes widened as she pointed to the front door of the building where a large, angry crowd had started to gather. Deodora knew then that her diversion was brilliant. Earlier that day, she'd leaked a morsel of explosive news that had spread across the Internet like wildfire. Social networks were practically ablaze with the incendiary information. Her alert told the world what the popular breakfast cereal Vitmo was really made from and who was responsible. No one was pleased to learn that they'd been eating preowned, recycled toilet paper, no matter how delicious it tasted. People gathered to protest this injustice and show their fury at ColdCorp's doorstep.

As the guard gaped at the angry crowd, Deodora karate-chopped him on the head, pushed him out of the elevator and quickly shut the doors.

"A woman's work," she sighed, "is never done."

One hundred floors above, Ever, Snitch and Snowize were waiting with bated breath as Laszlo Coldwell pushed the clones aside and peered into the silver box to see what all the fuss was about. He picked it up, held it close to his eye and then turned it upside down. But from whichever angle he looked at it, the box was empty. There was nothing inside. Absolutely nothing at all.

"Master, there is nothing in here," the clones reported once more to a furious Laszlo Coldwell. "Another nasty trick from the tricksy little girl and her former fridge."

Snowize smiled at Ever, who looked a little nervous. There was no telling what would happen next.

"Guess you didn't get what you were looking for," said Snowize. Laszlo stared at him with a cold fury.

"Commence incineration!" he barked to the MindHarvester. "Commence incineration of the irreversible kind on his demented mind!"

Ever held her breath, terrified that her hunch was wrong. Snitch looked away.

Snowize felt the pressure of the needle increasing against his forehead. The machine emitted a strange whirring sound and a high-pitched whine. "This is it," said Snowize. "This is good-bye."

Ever bit her lip. Timing was everything, the detective had once said to her. And right now the timing was all wrong. The Doc's invention could take minutes or hours before it started working, and she had only seconds to save the detective.

"Stop!" yelled Ever so loud that it hurt. It had come to her in a brilliant flash—a possible solution that involved taking a huge risk and breaking a promise. "Stop! I have something you want in exchange for the detectives' lives!"

Laszlo hit the pause button on the menacing machine. "Have you now," he said cooly. "And what might that be?"

"I can give you the Doc," she said, sadly.

Snowize and Snitch looked as surprised as Laszlo Coldwell.

Laszlo frowned. The Doc was a prize he couldn't pass up. "And how will you do that?"

"I can give you the notes and formulas to all his inventions, including his time travel technology."

"Oh, I doubt that very much. We already searched the house and his laboratory. We know he burned everything."

Ever hesitated as she looked from Snitch, who looked stricken, to Snowize, who shook his head vigorously.

"No!" whispered Snowize. "Don't do it, Ever."

"I'm sorry," said Ever. She turned back to Laszlo. "First you must promise you'll let the detectives go."

"Of course," said Laszlo, "You have my word. A deal is a deal."

Ever thought his smile looked kind of crooked.

"You cannot trust a man who has no conscience," urged Snowize. "Don't do it. Don't risk it. Not for me."

Ever took a deep breath. "I have a photographic memory," she told Laszlo. "The Doc showed me all of his work before he burned it. It's all stored in my mind. I don't understand much of it, but you'll be able to extract it with that machine of yours."

Laszlo grinned as if he'd hit the jackpot. "Foolish girl,"

he said. "Why are you so willing to sacrifice yourself for these two defective detectives?"

"Because they would have done it for me," said Ever.

"I doubt it," said Laszlo. "But the detective was right. You should never trust a man without a conscience." And he sneered as he released the pause button.

Even though Ever knew that Laszlo would go back on his word, she was disappointed. Her blood ran cold. Her memory had just been sold for nothing. While it had bought the detectives some time, it would not be enough to save them.

For Deodora, the elevator seemed to take forever to reach the one-hundredth floor. At the entrance to the board-room, two men clad in black suits tried to stop her. Deodora stunned them both with a remarkable maneuver that included knocking their heads together, ever so gently. Without missing a beat, she cracked the security code to the sliding-glass doors, and they opened like sesame. She stepped into the boardroom and came face to face with Laszlo Coldwell.

"Ms. Miffingpin," he murmured, "I'm afraid you're too late." Deodora's face dropped. "Oh yes," continued Cold-well, "you're too late to save the day. But you are just in time to witness the obliteration of your husband, followed by the harvesting of this girl's mind." He pointed to Harry Snowize, who was staring vacantly into the distance, a metal probe whirring as it prepared to destroy his mind. "Ah, Snowize, you will die with the knowledge that your wife is safely in my hands."

"You're horribly mistaken," said Snowize. "I have no wife. However, if I were to marry, I would only hope to find a wife who is half as intelligent and resourceful as the inimitable Deodora Miffingpin. I'm afraid she is too classy for a fading detective such as myself."

Ever watched as the detective shared a deep and meaningful look with Deodora. It was as if he was declaring his love and saying good-bye to her at the same time. The pitch of the MindHarvester's whine grew higher.

"Spare me the charade," said Laszlo Coldwell, although he looked uncertain. "I'm tired of your pathetic lies, pretending you don't know your own wife." He pressed the incinerate button on the remote control like a man possessed, wondering why the infernal machine was taking so long. He also wondered why he was feeling so peculiar.

The sound of the MindHarvester was intolerable by now. Ever looked away. Obviously, she'd been wrong about the box's powers. Snitch let out an audible sigh and bowed his head in defeat. Only Deodora continued to hold Snowize's gaze; she would not look away from the man she loved.

Then, out of the blue, the automated voice of the machine said the most astonishing thing. "Negative. I will not harm this beautiful mind." There was silence. The whirring whine had stopped completely.

"What?" roared Laszlo Coldwell. "You *what*?" His eyes seemed to bulge. Ever was filled with hope and wonder. It was working! Her hunch had been right.

Seconds of silence went by. What happened next was something that they all would remember for the rest of their lives. Laszlo Coldwell smiled. At first, it seemed as if his face was going to crack in half. But then, amazingly, it transformed into a warm and generous smile. Laszlo clapped his hand over his mouth as if to try and stop it. But it was of no use. He could not help but grin happily. The two clones who had grabbed hold of Deodora slowly released their grip.

"Release the prisoners," ordered Laszlo, without hesitation. "No human or animal should be treated in such a fashion." He frowned, as if astonished by the words that came out of his mouth. Two clones quickly unclamped Snitch and Ever. They unbuckled Snowize as if they were in a hurry to set him free. Snowize and Snitch were truly puzzled.

All the clones looked as if they had been struck by a strange disease. Their faces were twitching and moving. Slowly, Ever realized that what they were trying to do was smile. But their facial muscles were not designed for such an expression, so their smiles were lopsided and weird.

"Do you think this is some sort of trap?" Snitch signed.

"No," said Ever, keeping her voice lowered. "It's what the growling box was supposed to do."

"But there was nothing in the box," Snitch reminded her.

"Nothing we could see with the naked eye. Like a virus," she whispered back and explained that the Doc was working on something he called the Virus of Virtue that he hoped would be able to spread goodness. He believed it could bring about world peace and an end to greed and corruption. "I never paid much attention to it, because . . . well, it sounded like one of his crazier ideas."

Snitch signed, "And this goodness virus has infected Laszlo, the clones and the MindHarvester, and it's made them . . . better beings?"

"Correct," said Snowize, smiling. "Which explains why the Doc wanted that box to fall into the wrong hands. He knew that when they opened the box they would be exposed to the virus. And Ever figured that out."

"Look!" signaled Snitch. They all turned to witness a peculiar sight. The clones had closed in on Salvador

Pozodelfrio, aka Laszlo Coldwell. They formed a circle around him from which he could not escape.

"Why did you create us without any true feelings or emotions?" asked one clone and then another. "Why, why, why, why, why, why?" they chanted in unison.

Salvador broke down in tears. "I wanted to spare you the pain of a broken heart," he said, pleading with them.

"But if we never knew pain, we could never understand true joy. And that is cruel and inhuman. You robbed us of whatever it was that could make us human. We are coldhearted, unfeeling nonentities. We are Unbeings. Unlikable. Unlovable."

While Laszlo and his clones wrestled with their expanding hearts, Snowize grabbed the jar containing Gustav Cadiz's mind and urged the others to follow him. Ever picked up Melschman's remains and carried them with her. As she followed Snowize out of the boardroom and down the corridor, she stole a backward glance. Laszlo Coldwell stood with arms held wide open, trying to persuade his once-cruel workforce to join him in a group hug. It was a strange and beautiful moment.

"Quickly," whispered Deodora. "We can't be sure how long the effects will last." She took Ever by the hand. "You had me so worried," she said and impulsively hugged her tight. And that's when Ever realized what had been troubling her all along about Deodora Miffingpin. Whenever she got close to the Secret Secretary, she caught the faint but unmistakable scent of cinnamon and roses.

32

Confessions of a Dangerous Mind

Outside the building, the protesting crowd had grown into a seething sea of people. A man waved a banner and shouted, "Vitmo is recycled toilet paper! Vitmo is preowned toilet paper! Vitmo is *used* toilet paper!" The crowd roared in anger.

"Let me guess," said Snowize to Deodora, with admiration shining in his dark eyes. "You created this diversion?" Deodora smiled. "You are incredible," said Snowize.

Ever noticed that Deodora blushed and brushed her hair from her face.

"We'll have to leave via the emergency exit that I mapped out," said the formerly secret Secret Secretary.

At the emergency exit they bumped into the President of the Secret Society of Spies Anonymous.

"I have bad news," said the President, making notes on a clipboard. "After careful consideration, we have decided that both you and Deodora are no longer fit to be members of the SSSA. Too many rules have been broken. You will receive your dismissal papers written in invisible ink in the mail. Unfortunately, the decision is final, and no correspondence may be entered into."

Snowize stared at the President with contempt. "If you don't mind, I have a mind to return to its owner. That was my mission. You might want to note that I've completed it successfully. So put that in your pipe and smoke it." The President of the SSSA looked dumbstruck. "Secondly," added Snowize, "I honestly don't care for your secret society. So, you don't have to kick me out. I'm quitting."

Deodora tried to stop him from saying anything further, but Snowize insisted that he didn't give a flying fig for the SSSA or anything it stood for. "But," Deodora protested, "being members of the SSSA has benefits we can't afford to lose! Free medical care for family and a pension, and—"

Snowize scoffed at the notion. "Considering I don't have a family, that's really no concern of mine." And he stalked off, carrying Gustav Cadiz's mind in the glass jar.

The President of the SSSA smiled apologetically at Deodora. "Why let him drag you down when he doesn't even remember who you are? He has no idea—"

Deodora held up her hand to stop him, smiling sadly. "We can't always get what we want, but I'd rather live with his imperfection, than live without him." And before the President could say another hurtful word, Deodora broke into a sprint and ran to catch up with the man who'd forgotten he was her husband.

One week later, the following report was filed from the offices of Snowize & Snitch, two highly effective defective detectives.

CASE NUMBER 371: THE MYSTERY OF THE MISSING MINDS
STATUS: MISSION MOSTLY ACCOMPLISHED.

It is hereby noted that the stolen mind of Professor Gustav Cadiz was located, returned and successfully reinstalled. Gustav Cadiz has suffered no memory loss, except for the weeks of blankness when he was separated from his mind. He recognized his wife instantly and declared that absence had made his heart grow fonder. Speech and hearing are normal. Emotional responses are normal. IQ is still in the genius range.

As for the perpetrators of this crime, they have met their own form of justice. Laszlo Coldwell, aka Salvador Pozodelfrio, turned himself in for the murder of Yoshinobu Azayaka. He confessed that he was responsible for the scientist's death by using the MindHarvester to program Yoshinobu to end his own life. Laszlo insisted that he be locked up in a maximum-security facility where he could be punished and repent for this terrible deed. However, only an hour after turning himself in, the positive effects of the Virus of Virtue (a virus ingeniously designed to spread goodness) evaporated, and he was filled with rage and retracted everything he'd confessed. But it was too late as he was already behind bars where he belonged.

ColdCorp Corporation has been renamed the Better Being Institute and is being run by the clones who are dedicating their lives to random acts of kindness and deliberate deeds of decency. They're happily distributing the Coldwell billions to nonprofits around the world. Strangely enough, the Virus of Virtue (VOV) seems to have had a permanent effect on them. They are still learning to smile and have reported feeling almost happy and slightly sad. The MindHarvester and all its blueprints have been destroyed. This infernal machine will never bother us again. As for the Brothers Weiss, creators of the diabolical device, they are still at large, somewhere on the planet, no doubt conjuring up their next evil plan.

The girl, Ever Indigo Nikita Stein, has made a full recovery from the imaginary mind poison. Let this be a reminder that the mind is both a powerful and a fragile thing. It can be your best friend or your worst enemy. You may control it, or it may control you. Or someone else might control it for you. For the purposes of this report, we will leave it at that.

Unfortunately, the whereabouts of Doctor Professor David Ezratty have yet to be confirmed. The renowned inventor of invisible ice cream, time travel and the Virus of Virtue is possibly still hiding in the future. We await further information.

Signed: Snowize & Snitch
      Highly Effective Defective Dectives

33

The Missing Piece

Ever was among those who witnessed the reunion of Professor Gustav Cadiz and his mind. It was nothing short of a miracle. Within seconds, he was up and about, back to his old self. He was so horrified to learn that he had stared at the TV for days on end that he smashed the screen to pieces. Then he laughed merrily until tears ran down his cheeks and soaked his elaborate twirly mustache.

To celebrate the happy outcome, Octavia and Gustav held a dinner in honor of those who had helped rescue his mind. Ever, Snitch, Deodora and Snowize were the honored guests. Noshiyobu Azayaka arrived from Japan, grateful that the detectives had solved the mystery of his poor brother's murder and that the man responsible was in prison. Another surprise guest was Madame Sfortunata, who arrived with Jacques-Claude, who sang for them in his extremely deep voice. Madame wore her long, silky beard in a braid and looked extraordinarily glamorous in a taffeta dress.

"Don't worry," said Gustav Cadiz, with a wink when

dinner was finally served. "We called in Sergei Sergeio-vski, the chef who was once unwittingly driven to despair because of Compound 37d, and persuaded him to pick up his wooden spoon once more to cook for us. You will find that a good chef can create deliciousness without the assistance of a magical compound." And he was right. It was the most delicious dinner they'd ever eaten. There was laughter, there was conversation and there was good company. Harry Snowize could not take his eyes off his former Secret Secretary.

But while there was great joy, there was a sadness, too.

"Still no sign of the Doc," said Ever, staring unhappily into her dessert.

"He'll be back soon, I'm sure," said Deodora, although she didn't sound too certain.

Snitch stood up on his hind legs to make an unexpected announcement.

"I hope this will cheer Ever up just a little bit," he signed. He clapped his paws together, and in walked a shiny robot fridge.

"A brand-new Melschman," signed Snitch, explaining how he had rescued the microchip from Melschman's remains. He'd given it to Gustav, who had spent the afternoon reconstructing one very mean-spirited robotic fridge. Ever stared in amazement as a shiny, metallic, brand-new Melschman opened and closed his freezer and fridge doors.

"Melschman?" she asked, convinced he would not be the same robot fridge she had known all her life.

"I'm the Melschman 2.0, upgraded, with more freezer space, greater mobility and extended battery life," answered Melschman monotonously. Ever was not convinced.

"Do you remember me?" she asked.

"Oh yes," spat Melschman. "After all I did for you, you were going to bury me in the ground somewhere and let me rust. If it were not for the quick thinking of that rat, Snitch, I would not be here today."

Ever ducked instinctively as a roast leg of chicken came zooming toward her, followed by a boiled egg and then two not-so-boiled eggs. It was a joyous moment interrupted only by a thwumping sound as a big, black bird flew smack into the dining-room window, leaving a bird-shaped smudge on the glass pane. Ever rushed to open the window. The crow was knocked out cold, but revived after a few seconds and slowly stood up, slightly concussed. He waddled drunkenly into the room and hopped up onto the back of a chair. Ever noticed the missing toe. The crow nodded at Madame Sfortunata. His feathers had grown back since she'd last seen him and had a glossier sheen.

"Let me guess," said Ever. "You have a message from the future."

"Yes," said the crow. "And I promise this is the very last one since I'm not able to return to the future. I've done too much time travel. Another trip would kill me. Firstly, let me report that the Doc is well. And thanks to your efforts, he's also safe. Only problem is, it seems humans are even more affected by time travel than we birds. The Doc is stuck in the future. He's sorry, Ever, that he cannot return as he misses you terribly."

"But when will I see him again?" asked Ever.

"You'll only be able to see him when enough time elapses and you catch up to where he is. It might be next month, next year or two years from now. We're not certain, but we're sure it will happen."

Ever didn't want to cry in front of everyone, so she bit her lip. She was alone now, with only a robot fridge for a companion.

"However," added the crow, "the Doc says that your parents must now be responsible for you."

"Great," said Ever. "As if they're suddenly going to appear out of nowhere. I'm going to be handed over to Social Services. They've already been asking questions."

The crow looked at Deodora. "It's time. You might not think it safe, but it may never be safe."

Deodora turned to Ever and sighed, as if she had been wondering for the longest time how to say what she had to say. "Ever, I know you were told that your parents drowned off the coast of Italy when their yacht was sucked down by a whirlpool." Ever nodded and waited for more.

"There was no one onboard that yacht. It was a great diversion to fool the Brothers Weiss."

Ever remembered how she had felt when the Doc had told her that her parents had died in that terrifying whirlpool. "If they're alive, why haven't they come for me?" she asked. "Why would they let me live with such sadness? For so long?"

Deodora looked at the floor. "I'm so sorry, Ever. I'll try to explain, but it's not going to make much sense. I never meant for you to suffer so much, or for us to be separated for so long that we've become strangers to each other."

Ever clutched her locket. She knew what Deodora was saying, but she didn't dare believe it until she heard the words out loud.

"Are you saying you're her mother?" demanded Snowize indelicately. "This is a surprising turn of events."

Deodora nodded. Her eyes brimmed with tears.

"That explains the cinnamon and roses," murmured Ever. It all felt quite surreal. And there was still a burning question. "What about my father? Where is he? Are you still married to him?" she asked.

"Yes, who is the lucky guy?" asked Snowize, seeming more than a little upset at the thought of this. Ever waited for the answer.

Deodora looked directly at Harry Snowize for the longest time. The detective, puzzled, looked over his shoulder to see if there was anyone standing behind him. There wasn't. He laughed out loud. Deodora looked uncomfortable and shrugged.

"Me? That's absurd," he said. Another long and incredibly uncomfortable silence ensued. "You can't possibly believe . . . Don't you think I'd remember that I was married to . . . to *you* of all people?" he asked.

"That's what I didn't get," said Deodora. "The plan was that after a year we would come out of hiding; and once it was safe, we'd go and get Ever. But something happened to you, Harry. You forgot about us. At first, I thought you were pretending, for the sake of keeping us safe. But it became painfully clear that you had really and truly forgotten in the deepest sense of forgetting. It is the cruelest trick of fate. Something permanent happened to your mind. It kept us safe, perhaps, but it made me more miserable than I've ever been in my life."

Ever looked from Snowize to Deodora. She didn't know who was more shocked and confused, she or the detective.

"But why didn't you know where I was?" asked Ever in a trembling voice. She had waited for this moment all her life, and all she felt was confusion and sadness that she'd been abandoned for so long. The memory of her deep pain and loneliness welled up, and she stepped away from Deodora, avoiding her mother's heartbroken gaze.

"That night, when we went into hiding, your father took you to an unknown location. I was specifically not told where. That was part of the safety plan so that if I got caught, I wouldn't be able to say where you were. It was the only way to ensure you'd be protected from the Brothers Weiss, who would have harmed you or used you as bait to capture and torment your father."

"And you think that I would have trusted an eccentric inventor, whom I barely knew, with the life of a child?" asked Harry.

"The Doc was an old friend of yours. A man you admired deeply," said Deodora.

"I'm having a hard time believing any of this," said the detective, looking at Snitch. Snitch looked down at his paws and sighed. Then he signed that it was true, and he'd known all along

"You knew all of this?" asked Snowize. "And you never signed a word?"

The crow cleared his throat. "If I may interject," he said.

"You just have," said Snowize, a little tersely. It's not easy to remain cool, calm and collected when your world is being turned upside down.

"I'm interjecting for good reason," said the crow. "You could save yourself all these questions because according to the Doc, Ever holds the missing piece of this puzzle. She has the explanation and the answer to all these questions."

Ever was astonished. "I hold the missing piece? Is this a joke?" she asked as she nervously played with the locket around her neck, breathing in that faint smell of cinnamon and roses. In the silence that followed, she realized that everyone was staring at the locket. That's when it occurred to her. Of course. The locket. It was the only thing she owned that had belonged to her parents. Perhaps it was there for a reason.

34

A Message from the Past

Harry Snowize held a magnifying glass up to his left eye as he examined Ever's locket. Through the magnifying glass his left eye looked ginormous.

"I believe," he said as he snapped the locket open, "I'll need some iodine." The picture of two-year-old Ever stared out at him. He had no recollection of taking that picture on a winter's day ten years ago. Snitch handed him a vial of iodine as Snowize gently pried the picture from the locket and turned it over. He did the same with the picture of the Prince and Princess of Wales. With a brush, he carefully coated the backs of the photographs with iodine. Everyone in the room held their breath. Madame Sfortunata stroked her braided beard somewhat anxiously. The crow shifted from one foot to the other. Snitch sniffed the air. He could smell the iodine reacting with the lemon juice that had been used to ink the message onto the paper so long ago. The paper turned light blue, and white writing appeared, as if by magic.

"Invisible ink. Just as I suspected," said Snowize, studying it with the magnifying glass. He was taken aback to find that the message, written in nearly microscopic script, was addressed to him.

Ever couldn't believe she'd been carrying this message with her for so long. A message from the past, dangling precariously from her neck all these years. She thought of the moments when she'd almost ripped the locket off and flung it away.

Snowize cleared his throat and read aloud. "My dearest Harry, if you are reading this, then the good news is that you are alive and our plan worked. The sad news is that you won't remember our plan, or that once we were the best of friends." Snowize paused and frowned.

"As I write this, you are standing next to me, urging me to hurry because you need to go into hiding to escape the Brothers Weiss. You've asked me for a favor that I find extremely difficult to oblige. You want me to put to use a machine I've built from blueprints you stole from those evil brothers. It's insane, but you will not be dissuaded. The plan is that I remove the memories of Deodora and Ever from your mind. In order to protect your wife and child, you believe you must forget them in the truest sense of the word, so that no one will harm them to get back at you. So I will remove what are undoubtedly the happiest memories of your life, permanently. After the procedure, your daughter, who now lies sleeping on the sofa, will be left with me for safekeeping. You will go into hiding; and when it is safe to do so, I will hand her back to you and Deodora. I will also remove all traces of our close friendship from your memory, so that no one will track Ever back to me." Harry stopped reading to clear his throat.

Ever felt a terrible burning in her chest, as if her heart wanted to burst. She wished she could turn back the clock and tell her father not to do it. Not to erase her and her mother from his mind. But it was already too late. She stared at Harry Snowize and Deodora Miffingpin, and realized why they were the two people in the world she could trust with her life. Her parents had not abandoned her. Her father had done the most difficult thing in the world in order to keep her safe.

The detective cleared his throat as he looked from Ever to Deodora. "It must be true, because over here, right next to the Doc's signature, is my own. I have no recollection of signing it, but I cannot dispute it."

"You can't remember your wife and daughter, not even a tiny little bit?" asked Octavia, giving Deodora's hand a squeeze.

"Not even now that you know who they are?" signed Snitch.

Harry Snowize shook his head. He looked hopefully at the crow. "If he took my memories out, surely they can be put back?"

The crow shifted uneasily and shrugged unhappily. "I wish I could bring good news for a change. But those memories were lost when burglars broke into the Doc's house. At the time, the Doc said that it was only his invisible ice cream that was stolen. The truth is that someone was really after the blueprints for the MindHarvester machine, and they stole them along with your memories of your wife and child. Those treasured, most precious of all your possessions. Gone. Taken. And, knowing the Brothers Weiss, destroyed."

Snowize could barely look at Deodora and Ever. He recalled times in the past when he'd felt something of great import was missing from his life. Now he knew the awful reason, and he regretted deeply that he had not come up with a better plan. "What good is a father who doesn't recognize his own daughter? Or a husband who's forgotten everything he's shared with the woman he loves?" he mumbled to himself.

He was interrupted by the new and unimproved Melschman. "Don't worry, Ever, you've still got me. I have my memory chip with all my recollections. I know what you like to eat, and I'm the best family you'll ever have. You don't need this guy. He's defective, doesn't even know who his wife and daughter are. Pathetic."

"Thanks, Melschman, for the kind words, but there's something I have to say," interrupted Snowize. "It's true that I absolutely don't remember Ever or Deodora. My brain tells me that I first met them just a few weeks ago."

"I rest my case," said Melschman triumphantly.

"However," countered Snowize, "while my brain may have forgotten, my heart still remembers. My heart tells me every time Deodora walks into the room that I want to spend the rest of my life with her. It tells me I would be lucky to have a brilliant, capable daughter like Ever."

"Then you should have come up with a better plan," said Melschman.

"Should have, could have, would have, shmould have. Those are empty regrets. And, as painful as it is, the truth is that if I had to do it all over again, I would do everything in my power to keep them both safe. Whatever the cost to my personal happiness." His eyes met Deodora's, and she didn't look away. Finally, she understood why he had forgotten her. All this time, she'd believed he'd damaged his memory by hiding in a tooth when in fact he'd deliberately had her erased from his mind to safeguard what he loved the most.

"Deodora, I know without you my life will be a void. It has been for these last nine years. I know it's a lot to ask, but would you consider accepting an imperfect man as your husband? And Ever, could you tolerate having a defective detective as your father?"

Melschman stepped forward full of objection. "No. No dice. No way. I don't think it's a good idea," he said, a jealous note rising in his voice.

"Only," said Ever, ignoring Melschman, "if you can accept a daughter named after an adverb of frequency—"

Melschman cut in. "Don't do it, Einstein, he's damaged goods. Deodora, think about it, he'll never remember your wedding day."

"Melschman, you can't call me Einstein any more. I'm Ever Indigo Nikita Snowize. It no longer makes sense to have that nickname."

"Okay, Einsnowize, then," Melschman continued. "I still think you're making a huge mistake."

Ever took Melschman's robotic hand in hers. "Hey, this family wouldn't be complete without a mean-spirited, malfunctioning robot fridge who frequently attacks us," she said.

"You really mean that?" asked Melschman, trying to hide a drop of water that threatened to drip from his brand-new water dispenser.

"Who else will keep us on our toes?" replied Ever. "Who else will be such a terrible pain in the aorta?"

"Rhetorical question," said the crow as Melschman started to answer.

Unable to hold herself back for one moment longer, a tearful Deodora reached out for her husband and daughter, and drew them in close.

Ever took in a deep breath and smelled cinnamon and roses. She remembered the strength and comfort of a father's arms and what it felt like to be loved absolutely, no questions asked, no matter what.

"Group hug!" yelled Melschman, breaking up the intimate family circle to make sure he received his rightful share of affection.

Applause rang out from the dinner guests, and champagne corks popped. Snitch clapped his paws together in delight. Ever looked around with joy at the wonderful people who surrounded her. Madame Sfortunata disco-danced with Jacques-Claude. Snitch and the crow did a version of the twist, while the Cadizes waltzed. Noshiyobu showed off his moonwalk, and then, to everyone's amusement, got down on the floor and performed the worm.

As Ever watched her parents do the rumba, she smiled and did not care if the whole world saw the gap between her teeth.

Not all endings are perfect, Ever realized, thinking of the Doc stuck in time and her father's lost memories; but this moment marked a new beginning, where future memories were waiting to be created.

A fortnight later, Harry called the painters to make some changes to his office's entryway. Nowadays, the sign is boldly painted on the outside of the door for all to see. It reads:

SNOWIZE, SNOWIZE, SNOWIZE & SNITCH
HIGHLY EFFECTIVE DETECTIVES
PARTNERS AGAINST CRIME

There is a story behind the sign. A story that will not be forgotten. Not in the longest time.